This book is lovingly dedicated to:

My Mom

My siblings:
Brenda and Mike, Brian and Sue, JoAnne and Bruce

My wife, Carol

The kids:
Joanne and Jim, Chad and Lynn, Jason and Daniela, Becca and Zach

The grandkids:
Mitchell, Sophie, Ashley, Isaac, April, Emmalee, Tomas and Olive

And everyone else who has shared this journey
aboard Spaceship Earth with me…..it's been a great ride…..

FOREWORD

To dream or not to dream; that is the real question….
For those who dream are forgotten today,
but remembered tomorrow;
While those who do not dream are remembered today,
but forgotten tomorrow…

Feeling pretty fortunate to have the chance to get another book out. When I published the Memories for Sale collection, I thought it would constitute the sum total of my publishing efforts. I would say that Memories for Sale was a critical success, based on the many, many wonderful things both said and written about it. In fact, a number of people said it was "one of the best books" they'd read and, indeed, there have been a ton of really kind comments about it. However, based on the fact that I was only able to sell about 450 copies over the last four years, the book was obviously not a "popular" success. Even the four tiny royalty cheques weren't proof the book was popular.

Memories for Sale was a totally fictional work, the short stories and Gawd Book containing figments of my real life, but seriously fictionalized. This book, My Lefthanded, Backwards, Upsidedown Life and Assorted Short Stories, differs from that because it contains a significant portion of a memoir I've written about my growing up and coming of age years in my hometown of Hanover, Ontario, Canada. I grew up and came of age during the 1950's and 1960's and both of those decades saw massive changes in small town Ontario, as I'm sure was the case in small towns everywhere – at least in this part of the world. My memoir reflects that. When my life began, it was sort of like a combination of Andy of Mayberry and Leave It To Beaver, and, when

I got older, it was more like Happy Days. Sorry to use the TV metaphors but most folks of my vintage will totally get it.

I almost called the memoir, Me and Glen, because, as was the case in Memories for Sale, my good friend, Glen Pupich, figures prominently throughout. He was the one guy who did the most to open up my world when I was young - in many, many ways. To me, he was a towering figure in our local counter culture in ways I'm not sure even he understood. I will love him always and hold him close to my heart.

My Lefthanded, Backwards, Upsidedown Life is intended to be a mostly humorous look at my growing up years. Because although I suffered many difficulties during my adolescent years, caused by sometimes serious bouts of mental illness, I have almost nothing but fond memories of the "old days".…..back when we were famous…or we thought we were. It is my hope that the people who take the time to read this work will understand how much incredible hope there was back then. My generation of young people really and seriously thought we could change the world – and for the better. We have indeed changed the world – in a huge number of ways – but it would be hard to argue we have made things better. Most of the problems faced by humanity in the here and now were well known in the old days. But rather than solve them to make the world a better place for our children and grand-children, we seem to have failed on a truly grand scale.

I have included a number of short stories in this book. They are what I do best so I thought I'd better sneak a few in. I call my short stories emotional thoughtscapes because it is my hope that they create vivid emotional images in the mind of the reader. I tend to write short stories about ordinary people dealing with what some people might think are ordinary situations. But the real drama in life often comes from dealing with the real stuff of life. And so my characters deal with poverty, aging, illness and coming of age, while all the time struggling to somehow figure life out – to somehow know why they are here.

TABLE OF CONTENTS...

Assorted Short Stories

MY LEFTHANDED, BACKWARDS, UPSIDEDOWN LIFE

I am born....and so on...and so on...and so on.....

I was born on a stormy winter's night two days after Christmas in 1952… sort of at the end of the baby boomer cohort. My mother, whose own mother had died giving birth to her, had for some reason, not considered that her newborn child might be a boy. And she and my father were so uncertain how to handle the situation of having a manchild that I laid in a bassinette for the first few days of my life with no name and a couple of frightened parents. Finally, my great grandmother came to check me out – she was aghast that I had not received a name and that my parents seemed to be unable to really get me started on my journey through life. She gave them $10 to name me after her father, Johanne Friedrich Adler, so I became John Frederick Gardiner. My parents used the money to buy me something called a bunting bag to keep me warm during the winter and I was off and running.

In those early days, my mom and dad and I lived in the back of my mother's stepmother's house in a small apartment. I don't remember much about it, but there is one thing that stands out in my mind. When I was maybe two or three, my Dad caught a mouse that had been foolish enough to come into our house. I followed him as he took it around to the back of the house. Once there, he took a piece of 2x4 and gave that little bugger a terrific whack, causing its tiny eyes to bulge clear out of its head. It was a lifelong lesson for me about what happens to things that get caught in traps. Watch out for those traps in life.

Another thing that stands out from those early days was going over to my aunts to watch a very early television set. Most people, including my parents, didn't yet own their own TV, so we would gather at Aunt Vi's on Sunday evening to watch whatever the lineup was back in those days. Ed Sullivan and Bonanza would come later. But we wouldn't get our own TV until I was much older. Then, when we did finally get a TV, for years we only got one station; the local CBC affiliate. But we watched it in awe and couldn't believe the technology. When I was a little kid, I was always convinced that there must be little people inside the television box....even today, I have trouble even beginning to understand the simplest pieces of technology...televisions were 'way beyond my scope back in those days.

Life was a tough go for my parents in those early days. My Dad didn't make much money and worked two jobs.....he worked at Peppler's Furniture during the week and then at a nearby creamery making butter and ice cream on the weekends. The neat thing about this was that although my Dad didn't make a lot of money, we seemed to have an endless supply of butter and ice cream – which was pretty cool for a little person. I mean who could complain about endless ice cream.

When I was four years old, my Dad built a tiny house on a lake that was several miles from town. And in those days, it was like living in the wilderness. We had no phone, a hand pump in the kitchen for water and heating was provided by one small oil space heater that sat in the middle of the house...meaning there was zero heat in the bedrooms – even in the dead of winter. We had an outhouse for a washroom, except in the really cold weather when my Dad set up something called a chemical toilet in the house's one empty room. I don't remember much about having to use an outhouse – can't say that it scarred me for life – but I must have used it. I also don't remember using old Eaton's catalogues for toilet paper, although I've heard lots of those stories from the old-timers over the years.

I remember sitting with my Dad in the little lake house and watching hockey on the tiny, blurry TV that had been purchased. It was, of course, not just hockey we were watching.....it was the Toronto Maple Leafs and they were somewhat sacred back in those days. I learned watching hockey with my Dad on that tiny TV, and I learned to love the Leafs, and that was something that stayed with me through much of my adult life. Even when I was a teenager and was out partying all night, my Dad would leave me a synopsis of the game and the score on the kitchen table before he went to bed on Saturday night. I regret now that I didn't stay in and watch more Leafs' games with my Dad in those days. I guess I took it for granted and didn't really understand how important it was. Now that I've had my own kids and had them find their own lives, I know how disappointed my father must have been not to have me stay home to watch the games with him. It's a grim reality in life that most people don't recognize the important stuff until it's too late. And another grim reality of life is that there's no going back and there's no turning back. Life is linear – you go from one end to the other and there are no places to get off along the way – and there's no way you can slow it down. Life runs by its own clock – you're just along for the ride.

I started school when I lived at the lake.....I started when I was four years old because my birthday was in December. And while many people joke about having to walk a mile to school through snow drifts waist high back in the old days.....that's pretty much what I did on some winter mornings those first couple of years. In fact, because we lived down a road with no winter service, which meant that the snow plow didn't come down, my Dad and the few other men who lived along our road would sometimes get up really early in the morning after a snow storm and shovel out the road up to the bigger road.

We had a bunch of adventures at the lake. I learned to swim and skate really well because our front yard was filled with a swimming pool in summer and a skating rink in winter.....by the time I was six or seven, I could both swim and skate really well. And my parents got to know a guy who had a cottage at the lake, so was only there in summer. And he had a pretty big motor boat and he and his family and friends were big water skiers – there was even a ski jump out in the middle of the lake. Now Mr. Sternel – that was his name – had a small, black dog and in due course he built a special water ski with a small wire basket on the front…and he would ski around the lake and the dog would sit in the wire basket and have a ride. This was a great delight to the other cottagers who would sit out on their boathouses and cheer the man and his little dog.

But Mr. Sternel wasn't done performing circus tricks for the cottagers yet. And, as it turned out, my circus career was just about to begin. And, so, Mr. Sternel would get me up his shoulders and the little dog on the front of his special ski and away we would go – around the lake the three of us would go while everybody cheered and clapped. It was the start of a long life in performance. I didn't know that then, but it was the way it was going to be and it was the way it was…..

There were some other kids whose parents had decided to rough it on the lake all year long in those days. So, there were playmates for me and we hung out around the lake and in the lake and on the lake and we had no end to good times from what I remember. One remarkable thing that happened while I lived at the lake involved my friend, George…..We were out horsing around in the farmer's fields one day and George had a sudden urge to poop. So, rather than go home, he just went over behind a tree, dropped his drawers and let her go…..After he'd finished, he called me over to admire his pile of poop – that's the kind of thing kids used to do. And the remarkable things about his poop is that it had ended up looking exactly like a Dairy Queen soft ice cream cone, all swirly and such. We stood and admired it for a couple of minutes amazed that something like that could happen. It's a strange but true reality that I've never seen anything like this again in my life. And George is dead now. And that's that.

One of my sisters was born in 1956 – while we lived at the lake. She was my first sibling and I don't have many memories of her from those early days. My first real memory was when she was three or four and thought it would be fun to lick the big oil tank that stood on the back porch. Now, one of the early lessons you learn in life is you keep your tongue away from cold metal things in the winter. Unfortunately, my sister found that out the hard way. Mom really didn't know how to solve the problem so my sister stayed with her tongue stuck to the oil tank until my Dad got home from work. He knew the old hot water trick, so he boiled the kettle and poured that water down over my sister's tongue and the oil tank finally released its relentless hold on her.

Now, Mr. Sternel of waterskiing fame had a daughter and even though I was just a wee lad, I knew this girl was incredibly beautiful. She and her friends laid around the dock in tiny bikinis that even made an eight-year-old weak in the knees. One time, the Sternels had a big tent out behind their cottage. And the older girls invited George and me and a couple of other youngsters in for our first nudie show. It was pretty exciting, even though I'm sure I had no idea why back in that time. Images of those girls have stayed with me to this day. I'm not sure I'd want to say I was traumatized, but things from that day have certainly stuck with me for a really long time. When I got older, I remember seeing Mr. Sternel's daughter somewhere and she was indeed a Greek goddess….that was for sure.

Some time when I lived at the lake, one of my Mom's friends, Lucy, came to visit with her husband, Nick. Now, I later heard stories about Nick that weren't too pleasant, but when he came to visit us at the lake, I thought he was a pretty neat guy and that's because he came to visit in an amphicar….I don't know much about amphicars, but they were a real item back in the 1950's……I've seen a couple since at car shows but they're pretty rare, likely only made for a year or two. Anyway, Nick and my Dad and I climbed into this little red, convertible amphicar and Nick drove it straight down the bank and into the lake….I remember this thing riding really low in the water, so you were sort of sitting down in the water and not really riding on top like in most boats. We toured around the lake for a while, marvelling at modern technology, then drove up the bank and out of the lake. I was kind of dazzled by that when I was a kid.

One day, I was walking single file down the hall at James A. McGee Public School with the rest of my kindergarten classmates when I got pulled out of line by this pretty old guy. He asked me my name, then said, "Your grandfather plays in the town band. You should learn to play an instrument and join the junior band. Come to my office after school and I'll get you started." And that was my introduction to formal music training and Mr. Esser, who was the school janitor and also ran the junior town band. And because he worked at the school, he had plenty of recruits for the music program. I, of course, went down to his office in the boiler room after school. Imagine that happening in today's world. A four or five-year old kid going into the boiler room with a strange old guy.….

Anyway, Mr. Esser presented me with a song flute, gave me a quick lesson and said he'd phone my parents. And just like that one of the most important things in my life happened and I'm sure I had no idea. From song flute, I graduated to clarinet and joined the junior town band.….I was generally third clarinet, but I worked my way up to second after a while. I found that Mr. Esser and his band was affectionately referred to as "Professor Esser and His Musical Racketeers"…and I was now part of that crowd. I played with the junior town band for quite a few years and because of a shortage of woodwind players, I graduated to the senior town band when I was eight. I used to march in fall fair parades with all the older guys – they had to make me a special uniform and hat because I was so small – and I had real trouble keeping up during the marching. We got three dollars each for playing a parade – that was big money back in those days.

There was a big music festival in Owen Sound every spring – I think it was run by the Kiwanis and they have festivals all over the place. Anyway, Mr. Esser would enter a whole bunch of his band in the different categories like clarinet solo and trumpet duet and we'd go to Owen Sound and compete against other kids from the area. Us guys from Hanover were thought of as the country hicks because we didn't have uniforms or super new instruments. In Hanover, the junior band players wore their Sunday best and you didn't get a uniform until you reached the senior band. So we looked okay but not quite as sharp as the Owen Sound bands, both of which represented high schools in the city. In fact, we took home a lot of hardware from the music festival in Owen Sound and we generally won the band trophy as well. We might have looked like country hicks, but it seems we knew how to make music.

I made my first visit to Toronto while I was playing in the senior town band because each year the band performed as part of Band Day at the Canadian National Exhibition. It was a really big thing for me and because I was so young my Dad was allowed to come along to keep an eye on me. I still remember playing in the giant band shell at the CNE and newscaster Lloyd Robertson was the MC of the show – I remember thinking that he looked taller on television. The one year I went, we won a really giant trophy and were the best band of the day. It was a huge thing in my life back then and music has stayed with me always. I haven't played the clarinet for a while but have fond memories of when I did. Mr. Esser lived to be over 100 years old and only died a couple of years ago. He was a great guy and taught a whole lot of kids a whole lot of music back in the day.

We moved to town from the lake when I was eight because Dad had allergies and living in the country made his life a misery. I remember he started sleeping with a handkerchief tied around his nose and mouth to keep out the bad stuff and I thought he looked exactly like a bandit most of the time. We moved to the house at 436 6th Avenue and my parents lived there for 50 years. It will always be my home for as long as I live even though I've lived other places longer at this point in my life. I'll always remember the funny little linen or towel cupboard in the bathroom and the tiny trap door in the downstairs closet – somewhere you could hide a special treasure knowing it would never be found.

I liked living in town. Our new neighbourhood was full of kids and it was a really fun time. Most of the guys who lived in the neighbourhood were a year or two older than me and that made life interesting for me. I sort of learned things a little sooner than most kids my age and was always just a bit ahead of myself. One of my earliest memories of living in town were the carnivals we used to hold.....even though I was a junior partner, the carnivals were always held in our backyard. My friends and I would think up all these games of chance – ring toss, guess the number of marbles in the jar – we'd put up posters all over town and we'd pack the backyard on carnival day.... of course, we were really doing this to bilk the other town kids out of their money. Then, we'd take the money and go over to Norm's Snack Bar and buy ice cream and pop and other stuff that was bad for us. We'd even have a side show at the carnival. Remember one year, we took a giant empty vinegar jug and filled it with water. Then, Frank Fry, who later became a CBC newscaster but is dead now, stood in the window of our old garage and pretended to drink the whole thing down. The kids who were watching oohed and awed and thought this was the most incredible thing they'd ever seen. I'm not sure this would work that well today. Kids somehow seem smarter.

It's like somehow people weren't quite as smart back in the old days. I remember watching the gas jockeys at the Fina Station across the road from our house, and they'd often gas up cars with a cigarette hanging out of the corner of their mouths – or they'd set it on top of the gas pump while they gassed up the car and cleaned your windshield. This is a strange but true story. I'm sure people must have kept blowing up all the time because it's not really all that smart to have fire around gas....but it took a couple of generations for us to figure it out....we're slow learners most of the time.....

Now when I first moved into town, I wasn't wise to the ways of the world and early on I learned a lesson for life. I fell in with a bad crowd, about five or six of us, and we'd have to walk up the main street in town to get to school.....we walked really early, earlier than was necessary and I thought this was odd. One morning, though, as we walked up the street past the town's businesses, we stopped in front of Geddes' Drug Store....one of our number, perhaps who might be called the ringleader of this group of merry pranksters, pulled a popsicle stick out of his pocket and knelt down in front of the store's front door, and much to my surprise, he went to fishing around under the door with the popsicle stick. Even more to my surprise was the result. Coins started to appear from under the door and it was then that I figured out that people were buying newspapers from the stack near the door before the store opened – so they'd slide the money for the paper under the door so old Mr. Geddes could gather it up when he came in and opened the store. It was a good plan until some ten-year-old nefarious youngster caught on to what was happening.

And so it went. Every morning we pulled the same scam. And after the ringleader guy had fished out the money, we headed on up the street to Sandlos' Grocery to buy candy which the leader doled out as he saw fit. Now I must say that I recognized the illegality of the scheme right from the first morning and I never got much candy because I was clearly not a main member of the gang, but sort of a junior member or something like that. Still, I knew it was wrong right from the start and I'd earned my bars in Sunday School and I should have turned around and hightailed it out of there. But I didn't. I kept in on the scheme and ate my candy so was surely an accomplice.

When you're a kid, you really don't give adults much credit for being very smart. But, surprisingly, most of them are sort of smart. So it didn't take all that long for old Mr. Geddes to figure out what was happening early in the morning outside his store. One morning, after several successful bits of thievery, just as our ringleader was fishing with the popsicle stick under the door, the door burst open and old Mr. Geddes reached out and grabbed him by the collar and the jig was – as they say – up. And a few of the gang were apprehended right on the spot. I was standing out on the sidewalk and I just walked away and off up the street. Nobody grabbed me or followed after, so I just kept on walking and headed to school….no candy that morning.

It was, of course, quickly all over the school about the Popsicle Stick Gang…..the ringleader and a couple of his cohorts were in the principal's office no doubt being brutally tortured for more information on the gang. I was sure it was only a matter of time before I, too, would be called to the office to pay for my crime. It was, without a doubt, the single longest day of my entire educational experience – even taking into consideration the occasional all-nighter I pulled at university. I sat and sweated all day long, sure I would at some point get the call. As if to further terrify me, a couple of other gang members were called down over the course of the morning. Somehow, though, I escaped retribution. I was spared. But I got new friends. I knew I wasn't suited for a life of crime. So, I got new friends.

Of course, there was this one other time. I was browsing through the toy section in Merscoe's Department Store, and, for some reason unknown to me even to this day, I shoplifted. I pinched a very tiny Matchbox car. It was no big deal. I just stuck it in my pocket and waltzed out of the store. Problem was that in those days, when money was scarce, you couldn't just bring home a new toy without some reasonable explanation about where it had come from. I was so frightened that my parents would somehow discover the new toy, that I hid it in a drainpipe in an alley on the way home…..I only had courage enough to stop by for a quick glimpse of the car a couple of times on the way home from school….Even a stupid little kid like me seemed to understand that crime didn't seem to pay….no more of that crap.

Money was always a problem for kids back in the old days….most of our parents were working stiffs and most of our Dads toiled in the furniture factories for fairly low pay. So, there wasn't a lot of money for the kids other than what the kids could figure out how to scrape up on their own. I was immensely lucky when I was a kid because my Dad managed to get me a job as a Toronto Star paper boy. I earned 2 ½ cents for every paper I delivered, and the Star wasn't the most popular paper in town, so I had a modest route of about 25 dailies. Saturdays were a whole lot busier because the Star had a great magazine called the Star Weekly and lots of people liked it because of the TV Guide and comics and the extended sports coverage. So I had over 50 Saturday Onlys and it was a busy time.

Then, the newspaper had a big contest to increase circulation. They took all of the newspaper boys and partnered us up with an older high school kid. And the high school kid took us around and tried to sell subscriptions. And the team of high school kid and newspaper boy that got the most new sub-scriptions, won fabulous prizes, like the newspaper boy could win an English racing bike and I think the high school kid got some money for college or whatever. Anyway, my particular high school kid was what you would call a real go-getter. He was supposed to stick to the area where my route was already located, but instead he saw the whole town as his oyster…and he set out to win the contest.

And I must say that he did. When the contest ended, I had over 60 dailies and about 155 Saturday papers. It was like – wow – what could I say. I won an English racing bike and the high school kid won the money. And then they forgot about me. And I had to deliver and collect for 155 Saturday papers every weekend. In the good weather, I used my bike and newspaper carrier and with about four trips out from home could do it by maybe eight at night. In the winter, when I was hauling the toboggan, it would take me until ten or eleven at night to get the job done….holy crap, did I work like a dog for a while. I darned near killed myself for 2 ½ cents a paper. But, man, was I rich.

And I must admit that the newspaper boy story leads directly to the donut story and another valuable lesson I learned in life as a boy. Even at 2 ½ cents per paper, the money started to pile up. Before I knew it, my Dad was telling me that I'd built up about $300 in the Guarantee Trust. And I was well on my way to gathering up my first million and I was barely ten-years-old. One winter's night, though, it was particularly stormy and snowy and I was out collecting for the paper and I'd missed my supper and I ended up walking past Schultz's Bakery at about the time I was feeling particularly hungry and tired and worn out. And - the big front windows of the bakery were all steamed up and a woman came out the front door as I passed, and it was like out came this amazing aroma with her and it stopped me in my tracks.

Now, technically, I had no actual money even though the change purse I was carrying was full of the stuff. That's because the money in the change purse sort of belonged to the Toronto Star and only a small cut of it was mine. My money was in the Guarantee Trust. All the same, I was drawn in through the front door of Schultz's and was soon standing in front of a huge rack of honey dipped donuts and a vast array of other baked delicacies. A lady in a white apron approached on the other side of the counter and asked me what I'd like. I was nervous and blurted out the first thing that came to mind… .."Honey dipped donuts"……when she asked how many I wanted, I imme-diately replied "a dozen", because that's how many donuts people always got. And soon, I was back outside in the cold and stormy winter, but I was holding a whole box of donuts that were all mine…..Not like back at home where these donuts would be spread around among six people – these were mine.

So, as I walked the rest of my route, I gorged myself on the donuts. I ate the whole dozen and totally and completely enjoyed myself while doing it. They were likely the best donuts I've eaten to this day – and I've eaten a lot of donuts over the years. And when I finished, I got rid of the evidence – the empty box – and made my way home. And I had learned my lesson. Saving was fun but spending was even more fun. And once I got into the spirit of it, there was no stopping me. I started buying things at a feverish pace and soon I was pretty well broke. And I've stayed broke pretty well right to this day but have somehow been able to avoid living in the street or under a bridge….and that's mostly because people have been kind to me and because of my loveable and charming personality.

When I was in Grade 4, I had two traumatic things happen to me. The first was when my teacher, Mrs. Dankert, tried to switch me from being a left-handed person into a right-handed person. She was convinced that life would go better for me if I was right-handed, and this caused me no end to grief and my Dad finally went over to the school and had a chat with her. And that was that. I'm a lefty. The other thing was likely more traumatic and it involved our music teacher, Mrs. Holland. Now, when you went into Grade 4, you automatically became part of the junior school choir and that meant that you had to sing in the choir at the same Kiwanis Music Festival I played the clarinet in. But while my clarinet career went okay, my singing career was another story.

When you first entered the choir, Mrs. Holland wanted to know a little about how you could sing so she knew where to place you – which section you would be part of. So, she had us march down to the auditorium one at a time and she auditioned us for the choir. And after your audition, you were classified by the type of bird you sang like. There were canaries and bluebirds and robins and all manner of birds. But if you were really bad, and perhaps you didn't sing like a robin or a bluebird, you could be classified as a blackbird. And if you were classified as a blackbird, you didn't actually get to sing at all – instead, you mouthed the words….and that was my fate. I was named a blackbird and have been a blackbird ever since. It's funny how these days parents are all concerned about the self esteem of their children. When I was a youngster, adults seemed to do everything they could to humiliate and degrade children. It was part of growing up in life. They said it built character. I'm not so sure. Not at all.

My life as a Boy Scout……

Like most young boys my age back in that other time, my parents signed me up for Wolf Cubs, which was sort of the junior partner of Boy Scouts and was part of that organization. I remember going to a meeting room over the Hanover Legion where we held our little gatherings. And I learned how to "Dib, Dib, Dib" and "Dob, Dob, Dob" and it was an okay time. I had just moved to town, I think, so I was meeting new friends and, as I said earlier, every young boy in town was in Cubs or Scouts….

Cub Camp was likely the most interesting part of my scouting experience. The first year I went, I was terrified out of my shorts, never having done anything like it before in my life. I got there all right and things were going okay, until we went to the beach on Lake Huron – a place called Inverhuron.

We horsed around in the water a bit so we took off our shoes and our big high scouting socks and got in our bare feet so as not to get the shoes and socks wet. When the horsing around came to an end, and it was time to head back to camp, away I went, following along with the other Cubs. I went only a short distance, though, and I realized that I had foolishly forgotten to retrieve my shoes and socks. So, I broke off from the rest of the kids, and headed back toward the beach on my own.

I found my shoes and socks okay and got them on my feet, then started after the rest of the troop. Only I couldn't find them for love nor money. I looked and looked and looked and tried several different paths. In the end, though, I was hopelessly lost – had no idea where the rest of the troop was – or where the camp was. Yikes! So, I stood there a moment, collecting my thoughts, then decided I'd better try for civilization. I headed for the main road, feeling that was my best chance to find someone who might be able to help me find my way back to the camp.....

So, there I was, nine or ten-years-old, and lost in the wilderness for the first time in my life. I got walking along the road away from the beach, feeling pretty uncertain and frightened. As I walked, a huge, black car glided up beside me and stopped. The back window went down, and an old woman looked out at me. "Where are you headed, young fellow?" she asked. I explained my dilemma to her, that I was lost and trying to find my way back to Cub Camp. "Well, you poor dear…you climb right in here beside me and we'll get you back where you belong." Now think about this happening in today's world. Yea, right….So, I climbed into the huge car, which was actually a limousine with a guy in a uniform sitting in the front and driving the old lady around.

She said something to the driver and away we drove. She asked me a few questions like where I was from and what grade I was in in school, but I wasn't really in the car for that long because I guess the Cub Camp was fairly close by. So, this big limousine rolls into the camp and everyone in the camp comes running, wondering what extremely important person is arriving in such a huge, glamorous car. And, of course, I climb out, feeling fairly sheepish about the whole thing, but thinking back on it, I'm realizing it was a pretty strange experience that could have turned out differently. These days, everybody would have panicked. Back in those days, it was just the sort of thing that happened and nobody gave it a second thought.

I went back to Cub Camp for the second year the next year, but my stay that year didn't last too long. My first night there, I developed a brain-crushing ear ache and my Dad had to drive all the way there in the middle of the night to pick me up and take me home. I didn't die from it and it was more embarrassing than anything else. The next year, I graduated to actual Scouts and that also didn't last too long. All they wanted you to do in Scouts back in those days was tie knots – or at least that's what it seemed to me. And I'm not good at stuff like knots and the like, so I gradually dropped out and ended my Scouting career.

Minor sports.....

My experience with minor sports was fairly limited when I was a kid. My Dad gave me a chance to play stuff, but it just didn't stick. I tried baseball one year and I think I was in about Grade 4, because that's the year my Dad took me to Canadian Tire to buy me a brand-new baseball glove for passing. I still have the glove and it's one of my prized possessions from when I was a kid.....I only played a couple of innings of organized baseball, though. I went out to a couple of practices and things were going okay, then we played our first game and I came up for my first at bat. Opposing pitcher went into his wind-up, he let the ball fly – he missed the strike zone and I forgot to duck and took one right to the side of the head – remember, no batting helmets back in the old days....we were tough back in those days....tough and stupid.

Anyway, I quit baseball on the spot – that was the end of my career. I couldn't see much point playing anything where you could actually get hurt. So, I pulled myself out of the game, walked over to my Dad, and told him I was retiring. I continued to play a lot of sandlot baseball and had great fun doing that over the years, but never played another inning of organized ball.

I also played organized hockey, but, again, it was a brief foray. I'm pretty sure I played the year I was 10 and I'm pretty sure it was Peewee division. I'm pretty sure I was a fairly good hockey player when I was a kid. I'd grown up at the lake and spent all winter long skating, so I was pretty good at it and could go forwards and backwards with ease – something a lot of kids my age couldn't always manage…..I was made a defenseman on the team and things looked good for my hockey playing future.

Our coach was quite a young guy and he was really enthusiastic and wanted to do a good job with the team. Somewhere he heard about a special program that was being offered by Jello where if you collected up enough boxtops, you could get actual hockey sweaters for the whole team. Wow! Now, remember, this was back in the days when minor hockey wasn't a Cadillac operation. There were no team uniforms – not even sweaters – for the players. Instead, we wore our own jerseys, brought from home, and what that meant was that nearly every player in Hanover Minor Hockey had either a Toronto Maple Leaf sweater or a Montreal Canadiens sweater because those were the two teams everybody in our community cheered for back in the old days. We were all Toronto Maple Leaf or Montreal Canadien fans with the very odd kid cheering on Boston or Chicago. Everybody wearing the same sweaters worked okay in practice, but when we played games, we had to wear these T-shirt-type things over our sweaters, so that teams could sort of have on at least the same colour.

So, our coach got us matching sweaters – green and white – and we became the Shamrocks – a name we weren't really all that pleased about because it didn't sound all that tough…..and the season was underway and we played pretty well and only lost a couple of games all year – both times to a team called the Flyers, who had this one kid who was a really excellent player. Unlike today's minor hockey, when we held our practices and played our games, there was almost no one in the arena. The place was virtually empty because we had ice time at about 7:00 a.m. on Saturday morning. The only time my Dad had a chance to watch me play was at the end of the year when there was a Family Night. Parents just didn't tag along after their kids in those days. In fact, I had trouble doing up my skates tight enough at that age, and my Dad always worked on Saturdays, so I well remember my Mother helping me lace up my skates in our kitchen, so I could skate off up the road to play hockey at the Coliseum.

Anyway, we were pretty excited about Family Night when all of our parents would be coming to see us play. Our team, the Shamrocks, had finished the season in second place in the four-team house league division. That meant that we were playing in what was being billed as the championship game for the Peewees. And, of course, the Flyers had finished first in our division and they were the other team in the big game. So, we played them and battled hard all the way through the game, and the arena was packed to the rafters and it was pretty exciting stuff. Our nemesis, the dreaded Flyers, scored an early goal on us, and try as we might we couldn't get it back, but the really important thing was that we held them to that one goal – our goalie was outstanding and so were me and the other guys of defense. I can still remember one play when our team got caught up ice, and I was the lone defender back on a three on one. Somehow, I got my stick on the puck on one of their passes and managed to steer it into the corner and thwart their rush. I could almost hear my Dad cheer on that one.

It was sort of a fun year, I guess, but for some reason, I had no urge to go back the next year and I never played organized hockey again. In fact, I've never felt like much of a team player, which I'm not sure is a good thing, but it was the way I was nevertheless….I had one more experience in the world of team sports, but that was later, after I made it to high school….and that was fairly memorable as well. But that's another story…….

I Meet Glen…..the beginning of fear and loathing

Likely the single most important thing that happened to me while I was at James A. McGee Public School happened on my first day of school in Grade 7. I was in a split class that year – Grade 7 and 8…..there were two rows of Grade 7's and three rows of Grade 8's and it was a curious mix of students although I sort of got it when I got older. The Grade 7's in Mr. Ewing's room were, in theory, the brightest of the Grade 7's in the school, while the Grade 8's were the worst students in the school. Most of them were 15-years-old and were waiting to turn 16 so they could quit and go work in the furniture factory or Swift's……they had zero interest in school or anything that happened there. However, little did I know that there was a surprise waiting for me in that group of supposed juvenile delinquents.

I sat in the very back desk on the inside row of the Grade 7's, and sitting beside me, in the back desk on the inside row of the Grade 8's was a new kid. His name was Glen and we became fast friends right from the start. And over the next several years, he opened up my world and likely had more to do with who I became than any other person in my life. To my small-town sensibilities, he was a wonder. It was 1964 and the times were indeed changing. Glen's parents had purchased the Queen's Hotel in Hanover, so he had suddenly been transplanted from the metropolis of Toronto into the backwaters of Ontario. He was not initially happy about this, and his parents continued to own a hotel in the city for a while, so he beat a path there at every opportunity when he first moved to town.

And that made things very interesting in the small town where I'd spent my growing up years. Because Toronto was exploding with the hippie drug subculture and Glen dove right into it. I can remember walking to school with him one day the first year I knew him and he was wearing Union Jack bell bottoms and one of those frilly Paul Revere shirts....it was unbelievable and the teachers and Mr. Miller, the principal, didn't have a clue what to do. So, they sort of seemed to go with the flow that first year and Glen sort of dressed the way he wanted. However, it quickly became apparent that Glen's eccentric behaviour was going to challenge the norm in Hanover and it did just that for the next several years. And I went along for the ride. And I learned about life and love and everything else there was to learn about.

Eventually, before the end of that first year, Glen and I had settled on black. So, we dressed totally in black for a while there, and we washed the Brylcreem out of our hair and combed our hair down over our foreheads and let it sit on the top of our glasses. It was a pain in the ass, because it was constantly in our eyes, but it earned us our first trip to Mr. Miller's office for what was called "questionable behaviour". Our parents were called, and, apparently, there was a dreadful fear that our very souls were in serious jeopardy. Anyway, I was scared out of my wits, but Glen handled our defence, and our parents promised that the Brylcreem would be restored to our hair by the next day. And we complied, and so made our way back to Mr. Ewing's room. But from that day forward, we were marked men – known troublemakers. It was my first black mark.

Glen Searches for God

Glen's parents weren't religious from what I knew. Unlike me and pretty well all of my compatriots back in those days, Glen didn't have to go to church every Sunday. And the rest of us were enormously envious of him. But when it came time for confirmation classes, the stuff you have to learn to join the church as an adult, and something most kids in town had to endure around that age, Glen somehow got enrolled by his parents. So, the two of us attended our confirmation classes together at Trinity United Church under the spiritual guidance of Reverend Edgar Cowan.....who I remember was extremely bald and had a very deep voice and also had several daughters. We waded right into our Bible lessons and were soon on our way to becoming men of the church.

One day, Reverend Cowan had given us a break from our studies and we were just sort of hanging out waiting for things to resume. Suddenly, one of our classmates who'd gone outside for a breath of air came running back in exclaiming that there was a kid up on the roof of the church.....we all ran like maniacs out of the church with our eyes skyward and, sure enough, there was indeed a kid 'way up there on the very steep roof of Trinity United Church – and his eyes were also looking skyward, his gaze on the heavens. And it was, of course, Glen up on the roof.

Reverend Cowan was beside himself. He called out to Glen and finally got his attention – got him to look back down toward the earth. The good reverend shouted up at Glen and asked him what in the world he was doing up on the roof of the church. And Glen hollered back down that he was trying to get closer to God – that he thought he'd be closer to God if he climbed up as high as he could. He'd been going for the steeple but got a bit nervous and stopped partway up. So there was considerable coaxing to get my new friend back off the roof of the church. But a few adults who gathered were finally able to talk him down. He got in big trouble for that one – but it didn't really bother Glen. Stuff like that didn't even faze him.

I spent Grade 8 in another split class and with the same group of kids I'd been with in Grade 7.....except, of course, my friend Glen had graduated and was off into high school....so I was left alone to represent the counter culture at James A. McGee and I'm not sure I was really up to the challenge. I sort of let myself get wimped back into my old self while I was at school and had to be happy being a bohemian while I was with Glen. And that was often. Glen, you see, lived in a room over the Queen's Hotel – actually, two rooms with the wall between taken out.....there was a sink for washing up at both sides of the room and it had two doors...it was both Room 15 and Room 17 at once. And my newfound friend had a private entrance to the outside world, unlike all the rest of us whose parents could track our every movement in and out of our homes. So, I slept over often at Glen's and we haunted the nooks and crannies and the streets and alleys of Hanover long after others our age were in bed.

So there I was in Grade 8 with a bunch of brainiacs, mostly smart girls, and a couple of other guys and it was a mostly boring year. Except for the fact that our classroom adjoined the principal's office and, indeed, Mr. Miller was our teacher for half the day. The other half he did principally stuff in his office. And one of the things principals did back in that other time was beat and torture students. And because there was only a thin wooden door between Mr. Miller's office and our classroom, we often heard punishment being dispensed. One Grade 8 female student was particularly incorrigible and was constantly being beaten in the principal's office. We'd hear her shrieking and screaming and wailing so loudly we'd have to interrupt our class and sit quietly listening.

And that's about all I remember about Grade 8, except for the end of it. There was, of course, a graduation ceremony planned for the end of the year. But that wasn't the half of it – because – and to my complete horror – there was also a dance planned for after the graduation ceremony. The prospect of attending a dance terrified me to the very bottom of my soul. I can't say I wasn't keen on girls in those days. After all, I'd been walking a certain young lady home from school since Grade 7 and had, I think, a terrible crush on her. But I wasn't psychologically equipped to deal with it back then. So I walked her home and thought of her as sort of just another friend.

But she'd be at the dance…..and all the other girls. And I might have to actually dance and I had no clue how to dance or what was involved in dancing. One night, about two weeks before the big event, I confessed my fear to Glen. He looked thoughtful for a couple of minutes, then confidently boasted that he could teach me to dance – all the latest moves – we'd work on it together over the next couple of weeks and by the end of it I'd be a regular Mr. Bojangles…..

Glen had a huge collection of records back in those days and a pretty good record player and that was because his Dad got him to work in the office at the Queen's and paid him $10 a week to do it. In those days, there were no motels and there were lots of travelling salesmen and so they stayed in the old downtown hotels – like the Queen's. Glen worked in the office checking in travellers and directing them to the dining room and even carrying up the odd overnight bag. So Glen was rich. Ten bucks was a huge amount of money in 1965. So Glen was rich and could afford to buy all the latest record releases and have a pretty good record player. And we often sat around his room and he spun platters and we grooved to all the great new music that was happening.

The next two weeks were interesting. Most nights after school, we spent dancing away in Glen's room, me hoping desperately that no one would ever suspect what we were doing. I wondered how the other guys in my class were wrestling with the dancing problem and was pretty sure they weren't dancing with their best friend. One of the redeeming qualities of modern dance steps in 1965 was that there was no physical contact. Our parents thought it was a crazy way to dance, but when Glen was teaching me I was glad for this small mercy. I was amazed at my friend's dancing repertoire – he seemed to know all the popular dances of the day….the Swim, the Monkey, the Fruge, the Mashed Potato….and I did my best to learn, but was so embarrassed even in Glen's room that I was pretty sure I wouldn't be able to do this in public.

I was pretty nervous as the big night approached. I had a brief thought that I could still pull off a colossal collapse and fail Grade 8. That way I'd be spared the utter humiliation of having to dance with a real actual girl. It was a stupid thought but I almost could have tried it. Of course, when the actual event arrived, it was fairly anti-climactic. Absolutely none of the guys danced with any of the girls, so the girls ended up dancing by themselves and the guys stood around the punch bowl and looked and felt awkward in their Sunday-go-to-meeting clothes.

The year I graduated Grade 8 and because I was a favourite of Mr. Esser in the town band program, he hired me to help with some janitorial chores around the school for part of the summer. I don't remember too much about the experience, except riding my bike down quiet small-town streets at a very early time in the morning to get to work. And my last day was spent travelling to all the classrooms to pick dead flies off the window sills – just the perfect way to end a summer of janitorial work. I must also add that I earned 50 cents per hour at the job – I worked 40 hours and received $20 for my efforts. Small change today. Even for collecting dead flies.

As the summer was winding to a close that year, I was, of course, filled with fear and apprehension at my entrance into Hanover District High School – good old HDHS. But it wasn't so much the actual school part that had me worried. No, it was something entirely different than scholarly exercises that had me worried. It was Grade 9 Initiation Day.

Grade 9 Initiation Day was the ultimate day of humiliation for all young people back in the old days. It's something that would not be allowed in today's world where we worry about damaging young people's self-esteem. In my early days, there was no concern about stuff like that. So, all Grade 9 students – no exceptions – were made to take part in Initiation Day. Where you were forced to dress in a ridiculous costume – in my case, it was a baby outfit, complete with diaper, baby bonnet and the like. Imagine being a self-conscious teenager, still uncertain about your place in life, and here you are forced to dress like a baby and then to perform a host of stupid and embarrassing tasks at the whim of the senior students. It was a hard time in a young person's life back in that other time. It was a hard time for me, for sure.

Glen had already been through initiation once because he was a year ahead of me. Still, sort of as punishment for failing, if you were still in Grade 9, you were fair game for initiation. So, Glen was going to have to do it all over. He told me to stick to him like glue because he'd already been through it and knew the ropes. This, of course, was a huge mistake on my part because my best friend was what you would call a "marked man" at HDHS. Glen had spent his first year in high school – while I was continuing to languish at James A. McGee – being a bit of a character, which was what Glen was. He had been suspended for growing his hair long a couple of times – suspended for wearing jeans when dress pants were the rule – he was generally a pain in the ass of the administration and loved to provoke the senior students and was constantly pulling pranks involving them.

So it was sort of a bad thing to be sticking to Glen like glue and it took me a while that day to figure it out. And I paid for it dearly. But I'd figured it out by the time of the big parade – that's right, folks – not content that the Grade 9's were totally and absolutely humiliated in front of their peers at the school, the poor, unfortunate wretches were forced to parade through the downtown while the whole community came out to watch and laugh. Oh, yea, this was bad. The senior students could pull you out of the parade at any moment to give you a dose of personal humiliation if you were really unlucky. This was another long day in my life. Very long, indeed. Although it was pretty funny at the Kangeroo Court set up at the end of the day to deal with Grade 9's who'd been a problem for the senior students. And, of course, Glen was front and centre during these shenanigans.....It was fun to watch him drive the older kids crazy – which is what he did.

Well, back in the old days, I was pretty much terrified of girls. I knew I liked what they had to offer, but was pretty uninterested in actually seeking them out. Didn't like to put them in the awkward position of having to crush my dreams and didn't like to be put in the position of having my dreams crushed. Problem was that I'd made new friends in high school, and these guys were obsessed with chasing girls – it was pretty much all they thought about – except possibly how to get hold of some liquor and get drunk – because that was starting to happen as well – but that's another story. Anyway, if you were intent on chasing girls, it meant that you were likely going to end up going to dances – and, if you remember, dances were not my favourite activity.

However, in order to be one of the crowd, I knew I'd have to attend dances. So, I bucked it up and went to the first few dances of the school year. Everything was going okay because I would sort of hide off to the side of the event and let my buddies have their way with the girls. In those days, most dances featured a live band, so it was always good to watch the band – mainly because things were happening in that area of my life as well – but that's another story, too. And, so, I ended up in my Sunday best at the annual Valentine's Dance. Not really too worried, but knowing I'd need to keep my guard up nonetheless……

And the dance was going okay, and I was doing my usual hiding, when something unfortunate happened. One of my newfound buddies wanted to dance with this certain girl in the worst way – but she had a friend she was with…and none of the other guys seemed to be around. So, he asked the inevitable question in a circumstance like this. Would I go with him and ask the friend to dance. I said, "No, man, I don't actually dance." He responded that it was a dance I was attending and he'd buy me a "ten-to-go" bag of French Fries after if I'd do it. So, off we headed across the dance floor. And before I knew it, I was dancing. It was a slow tune and for my generation of dancers what that meant was that all you had to do was grapple with your partner – there were no real steps but it was good if you kept your feet to yourself. I made it through the song, whereupon the girl I had asked said her thanks and headed off. I don't remember how my friend made out, but I had done my duty….and I'd danced with a real live girl and lived to tell about it.

Now the thing was that at the annual Valentine's Dance, they had a tradition at old HDHS and that was that near the end of the night, they crowned the "Queen of Hearts". And the way they did this was by putting all the girls' names in a big empty thing, then drawing out one of them. And, of course, they pulled the name of the girl I'd danced with. So, she headed off up to the stage to receive her honours. And when she got there, something truly horrible happened. They asked her who she had last danced with – and, you guessed it, it was me. And, suddenly, I was on stage and I was the "King of Hearts".…….Wow.….They slapped a cardboard crown on my head and shoved a sceptre into my hands and I was all set. Truly one of the most traumatic things that has ever happened to me. I did survive, but it was a close call. It taught me that I'd need to do a better job of hiding as I journeyed through life. Hide well, my friends, because there are bad things in life and they're just waiting out there to get you.

Spring of 1967 was a heady time to be a young person coming of age. It was the beginning of the Summer of Love, the country was celebrating its Centennial and also gearing up for Expo '67......young people were breaking out all over and it was exciting even watching it on TV...watching the hippies trying to change the world on the nightly news. And we were wannabe hippies ourselves. Growing our hair long. Buying bell bottoms at Kornblum's in Owen Sound. Smoking banana peels and taking aspirin and Coke....but... and it's a big "but"....it was also time for army cadets at Hanover High....All Grade 9 and 10 boys at the school were forced to take training as army cadets in the spring of the year. That meant seemingly endless hours of marching the streets around the school, trying desperately to learn how to be soldiers – because in those days, the Second World War was fresh in everybody's mind.....the war had hardly ended when the Sixties came along....I don't think we really appreciated that as we were growing up....

Anyway, cadets was another trying time to be a young guy. They gave us these incredibly old, woollen, terribly scratchy Canadian army uniforms that even came with things called "puttees".....now you've got to be old to remember puttees....they were these cloth things that soldiers used to wind around the bottom of their pants so they wouldn't flap about while they were busy attacking things and stuff like that. So, we had to learn to wrap puttees..... and we were divided up into squads of maybe 20 guys each, and we all had commanders and the commander guys were the high school kids who wanted to be real soldiers when they graduated – and they were usually 'way more serious about the soldiering stuff than the rest of us were....

I think there were maybe five or six or seven or eight squads of kids, and all of the squads except one were given real rifles to train with. But there was this one squad where the kids were not – shall I say – all that receptive to learning the soldiery stuff....they were sort of not real good at following orders and being well behaved. And that was the squad that contained both me and my best friend, Glen, and a most interesting collection of juvenile delinquents, hoodlums and petty criminals. And we were "F" squad and while the rest of the troops got real rifles to drill with and carry around, we got fake wooden ones that would have made good toys when we were about eight. I'll never be completely sure what I was doing in "F" squad. I was basically a good kid. I had great marks and usually managed to avoid trouble and being in the spotlight. But it was common knowledge who my best friend was and Glen, as I've mentioned, had already gained quite a reputation at old Hanover High.

So cadets was one adventure after another. Of course, our commander guy was the hardest ass of all the commander guys and there was a constant and huge struggle of wills between him and the squad. So that stuff like this really happened. One day we were marching through the parking lot at the high school and getting our left/rights pretty good and our commander guy got talking to another commander guy and wasn't really paying attention to us. Now, he had pounded into our brains repeatedly and relentlessly over our training so far that we absolutely had to follow orders. Only do what we were told. Cadets don't think – they only do. So, we're marching along, more or less on our own, and we leave the school parking lot and proceed across 7th Street and straight through Ruth Peppler's big hedge and right up her front porch and into her front door where we just sort of marched over top of each other until we all lay in a big clump. Got in major crap for that one. Pretty much destroyed the hedge. But followed orders pretty well on that one occasion.

And cadets ended each year with a big Inspection Day, when some real soldiers came from a real army base and inspected our little army – checked out our marching and waving of guns and that sort of thing and made sure we had our puttees properly wrapped. And, of course, this day was hell. It was usually really hot and the uniforms itched and drove you nuts and they were hotter than hades to wear and, of course, in order to properly humiliate us, we were again forced to march through town so the whole community could come out and be impressed that their sons were now ready to be cannon fodder in the next great war. I got real lucky with cadets, though. It stopped being compulsory in Grade 10 after my Grade 9 year. So, my soldiering days were over at the end of Grade 9. And it's a good thing. Heaven knows what type of trouble I could have gotten into if I'd had to do any real soldiering.

Music changed totally for me around this time. I traded in my clarinet and the Kiwanis Music Festival for the bass guitar and Teen Town dances. I had a respectable career as a clarinettist....won a whole bunch of awards at the Kiwanis Festival…travelled to the CNE and helped win the really big trophy….marched in a huge number of fall fair and Christmas parades…. played plenty of concerts in the town hall….had quite a run. But by the mid Sixties, pretty well every boy in town wanted to be the next Beatles – and you couldn't do that playing the clarinet. My friend, Glen, figures prominently in this story as well. Remember Glen's job in the office at the Queen's and the money he earned. He used some of it to buy a Silvertone guitar and amp through the Simpson's catalogue…..and he set out to be a rock star.

He didn't stick with it though, and, finally, the Silvertone guitar ended up sitting in the corner of his room, the top three strings broken off, covered in spilled pop, and, generally, looking pretty beat up. So he bought a used set of drums. A gorgeous set of old Ludwigs with a huge bass drum and he started banging away on those. And he got sort of okay at it, playing along with records, but soon that wasn't enough and he wanted someone to "jam" with. At which point, I started to pick up the Silvertone and the accompanying five watt amp, and trying to play along with him. The guitar, as mentioned, was missing the top three strings, so I sort of started plunking away on bass lines. And before long, we were struggling through some fundamental rock stuff like "Get Off My Cloud" and other favourites. And we started to invite other guys down – guys who'd taken a guitar lesson or two – and might even be able to sing – and before we knew it, we had a primitive band going.

Problem was you couldn't really play real bass guitar on a six string guitar with the bottom three strings on. I needed a for real bass guitar, but I had no money. This was the start of Grade 9 and as luck would have it, the school held a fundraiser that involved all of us students selling magazine subscriptions and the more you sold, the more your name was entered into the big draw for great prizes and cool stuff. I sold exactly one subscription – and that was to my parents – so I only had one entry in the big draw. My chances were slim to say the least. However, the fates conspired to blow a fair breeze in my direction for one of the few times in my life, and I not only won a prize in the big draw – I won the grand prize.

Which was a newly invented piece of technology that allowed you to take pictures, then have the photo roll out the front of the camera instantly – you then had to smear a couple of different chemical concoctions onto the picture, and, in theory, it would develop right before your eyes. It was considered amazing back in the day. And I was thrilled to have it. But that was before I found out that the thing wasn't as easy to operate as it seemed, and you had to continually buy more chemicals and film if you wanted to keep taking pictures. I was already broke. I needed the camera like I needed a whole in the head. What to do?

A few days after I won it, I was over at the Queen's hanging out in the office with Glen, and I'd brought the camera along. Glen's Dad noticed it sitting there on one of his trips into the office and started asking me question about it. He ended up buying it off me for $15 and that went immediately into the bass guitar fund. Still, I felt I needed about 50 bucks to get an adequate guitar, and that was a ton of money in the old days. My Dad, who was struggling with six mouths to feed, couldn't help me out. Somehow, my Aunt Vi caught wind of my dilemma, and she had a bit of money back then because her first husband had been killed in a bad accident right after the war and she got a big insurance payout. So, she lent me $35 and I had my guitar money.

Back in that other time, likely my Dad's favourite TV show was Circle 8 Ranch – a music show that featured good, old-time country stuff. And, of course, the show had a sort of house band and the fiddle player was a really, big man called "Wee" Rossy Mann. And he had a music store in the tiny village of Bluevale, down near Wingham and Dad suggested we go there to search out a guitar for me. So, away we went, and I ended up buying a Kent bass guitar and the thing came with no case, so I carried it around in a garbage bag for years, and it seemed to never go out of tune. It was a good, old guitar and it served me well over the years. I suspect you'll hear more about the Kent bass guitar in the pages ahead.

Anyway, the five watt Silvertone amp also wasn't going to cut it – things were getting louder and louder. So, somehow, I came up with another 60 dollars and, after locating what I thought would work for me in the Toronto Star want ads, my Dad and I travelled to Toronto to buy a Vox guitar amp that I used for a little while. Again, not the ideal set-up for a bass player, but it was the best I could afford at the time and it worked okay. And we started to practice and practice and practice, until, finally, we reached a point where we thought we should go public.

Glen likely wasn't the best drummer I ever played with – but having him in the band gave us a place to practice in the Queen's Hotel banquet room where the town's Rotary Club held weekly meetings and there were lots of other events as well. And when it came time for us to hold a public event, the banquet room was a perfect spot. So, we picked a night, produced a primitive poster and spread word of the "dance" far and wide. We charged a bit of an admission, sold pop and chips and had to have our parents attend as chaperones if we wanted any girls to attend. That's what it was like back in those days.

And we gave our first public performance as rock musicians and we played our hearts out……Little Red Riding Hood, Hanky Panky, Wild Thing, Gloria, Tobacco Road were a few of the tunes. We didn't have a huge turnout but a few kids came and we did okay. I remember we did a huge psychedelic thing in Tobacco Road and Glen kicked his drums over and the rest of us writhed around on the stage while a home-made strobe light flashed and made us look like we were moving in slow motion. It was very theatrical even back in those days. Even then, we had some slight notion that we were entertainers as well as musicians. It wasn't much, but it was a start……

I really can't leave this part of my life without writing about the "chicken" thing. And this is how the "chicken" thing went. Hanover high was a pretty rural school and Hanover was located in the midst of farming country so there were lots of farm kids at the school. And I guess the way the thinking went was that the town kids should know a little about farming, so all Grade 9 town kids were forced to take a course called "Agriculture"…..I'm not sure how they divided everybody up making sure that only town kids were in the class, but they managed it somehow.

One of the projects you were automatically involved in when you were in Agriculture class involved chickens. In fact, we learned the answer to the eternal question, "What came first, the chicken or the egg?" We found out that it was definitely the egg because that's what we were introduced to one day in class. Everybody got some eggs, and out we went to the little barn behind the school and we put those eggs in things called incubators and we kept those little eggs warm for a while, and, finally, out came these cute, fuzzy little baby chickens. Then, for the rest of the semester, we fed and cared for the little chickens until they became big chickens and they became sort of like our children. I was leery about the whole thing when it started, but finally got into the spirit of it and really tried to take good care of the chickens I was assigned to.

Well, one thing led to another, and the end of the semester approached, and, finally it was almost upon us. One day in Agriculture class, Mr. Whitehead, our teacher, asked for everyone to pay attention. We were supposed to wear old clothes to class on Friday because it was "Kill Day". This caused a sudden silence to descend in the room. "Kill Day"......I want you to think about this.... What could we possibly be "killing" on "Kill Day"? Aaaaaaaaahhhhhhhhhh! The chickens! I actually remember getting faint for a minute, but you didn't want to show weakness when you were a Grade 9 boy back in those days, so the next thing, I was sitting quietly while most of the rest of the boys were rejoicing at the prospect of "Kill Day" while the girls were shrieking hysterically and sobbing. It was a bad scene. I would have felt like I was a character in an Andy Warhol movie but I didn't know who he was back then.

I can't actually regale you with tales about "Kill Day" because it was the first time in my entire educational career that I was truant. Yup, I skipped school for the very first time in order to avoid "Kill Day" and I'm sure I was glad I did. Don't really remember getting into any particular trouble for skipping, either. I'm sure they must have allowed compassionate leaves for scenes like that – even in that other somewhat more cruder time.

Like every other male kid in Hanover back in those days, I thought of myself as a mighty hunter. Almost as soon as you could walk when I was a kid, you wanted a BB or pellet gun so you could carry on what is really man's oldest profession – killing things. And it's a fact that when I was in my pre-teen and early teen years, I used to head to the railway tracks like all the other kids to shoot frogs and small birds and any other unfortunate thing we could bring our sights to bear on. And there was this kind of natural progression you followed. First, you had a BB gun, then a pellet gun, then, when you were old enough to get a hunting licence, you got a .22 – and that could kill real stuff – actual animals.

And I followed along on the progression, exactly as expected, except my Dad was not a hunter or a gun guy and he really didn't want me having any sort of weapon. He grudgingly let me get a BB gun and a pellet gun, but he drew the line at a .22. And I was pretty disappointed about the whole thing. Glen was an actual hunter, because his Dad was a hunter and had actual guns. So, Glen made the move up to the .22 right on schedule and I'd go out hunting with him, but I usually didn't have a gun. He started using his Dad's .410 Over and Under finally and our main prey was rabbits….and it seemed okay to me because Glen would shoot a couple and his mother would cook them up into a great feast – I guess, because I couldn't bring myself to actually eat them.

One day, Glen suggested that if he was going to use the .410, I could use his .22. I was a little uncertain, but I let him talk me into it. We headed out on a cold winter's morning to get dinner. We were walking along the edge of a cedar bush, on the side of bit of a hill, when, suddenly, Glen froze causing me to do the same. We stood, statuesque, our breath blowing out in front of us and hanging silently in frozen clouds. Glen gestured to the edge of the bush and I looked to see what he'd spotted. At first, I couldn't see anything, but as I studied the scene more closely, I finally saw what had brought him up short – a pair of fluffy white ears extending up over a small snow drift just inside the tree line. At this point, I expected Glen to get the rabbit in the sights of the .410 and take it out. Instead, he whispered to me, "You get him with the .22," he said. "It's an easy shot."

I had never killed anything that I regarded as a "real" thing in my life and I didn't really want to now. But it was one of those situations where your manhood is sort of on the line. If you back down and refuse to shoot, you're somehow not a real man – that's what you're worried about. So, I bucked it up and took aim just below the rabbit's ears and fired through the small snowdrift where I thought I could do the most damage. I've never heard any animal in my life – before or since – let out a cry like that rabbit did. It curdled my blood. And yet I had not killed it. It was only wounded and took off through the bush dragging its bloodied body through the snow, leaving a bright, red trail behind it. Glen always tried to be a "good" hunter, and we both knew we couldn't leave the wounded rabbit to suffer needlessly. So, we tracked it through the bush and finally caught up to it and put it out of its misery. That's the last thing I ever killed, except the odd insect. That experience ended me as a mighty hunter and I am ashamed even to this day that I killed that poor rabbit.

So, it was 1967. It was the Summer of Love and Glen and I were trying really hard to be hippies in our own small-town way. We had sort of long hair – we wore the clothes – we listened to the music – we tried to be rebellious. But there was something missing from our little slice of the hippie drug subculture. And it was the drugs. There was no trace of any type of illegal recreational substance in our little town. We tried smoking dried out banana peels and did the Coke and aspirin thing and I must admit the banana peels left me with quite a headache. And we were drinking a bit in those days, so there was that. But what we wanted more than anything in those days was to smoke some pot – some actual marijuana. But there didn't seem to be any to be had.

Then, one day at the beginning of our Summer of Love, Glen and I were sitting on the front porch of my house where we could look across the Fina Station parking lot and over to Norm's Restaurant and good, old highway 4 ran there between Norm's and the Fina Station. And, at that moment, unless it was a mirage, there was a hitchhiker standing out in front of Norm's trying to flag a ride. And this hitchhiker looked for all the world like a for real hippie. She had the fringed vest and headband and bell bottom jeans and a pack was sitting at her feet, showing that she was travelling. Before you could say, "there goes a hippie", Glen and I were heading across the Fina parking lot to greet the girl and see where she might be headed.

Her name was Patti Bell and she was a real for sure hippie and she was out exploring the highways and byways of Canada, right now heading clear across the country to Vancouver where she lived. Glen chatted her up for a while and soon we'd talked her into coming over to the Queen's for a bite to eat in the hotel dining room – which we did. Glen then invited her up to hang out in his room – which she accepted – and I went along for the ride. It was already late afternoon and I suspected she'd stay over. So, we headed upstairs at the Queen's to Room 15 and were soon listening to the latest tunes of the day.....Stones, Beatles, Doors....good stuff. It was a blissful scene for sure – we were hanging out with a real hippie.

And it was at this point that Patti Bell did something wondrous. She asked us if we'd like to smoke some pot. Our dream came true. And she produced a bag of actual marijuana and some rolling papers that looked like the American flag. Before long, we were puffing away like mad fools. And it's true that it seems to take smoking a few joints to get off the first couple of times you smoke pot. It wasn't long, though, and we were all laughing like the drug-crazed maniacs we were and absolutely everything seemed uproariously funny – absolutely everything. I don't remember the specifics of the night, but do remember it as one of the most fun nights of my life.

We all crashed over, finally burned out and falling into a deep, pleasant sleep. Next morning, the three of us again headed for the Queen's dining room, where Glen's Mom cooked us up a great breakfast, then we walked Patti back over to the front of Norm's Restaurant, where she hitchhiked off into our memories and I've never seen or heard of her since. However, before she left, she gave Glen the name and phone number of a friend in Toronto where pot could be gotten. And our world was changed forever by that chance encounter. It's funny how that sort of thing happens in life. Funny, indeed.

Glen was down to Toronto before the week was out and he started to bring pot back to Hanover and our Summer of Love officially got underway. And it was so cool that first summer because the police had no idea what marijuana was and the War on Drugs was well off in the future. So, we could smoke pot right on the main street of Hanover and nobody seemed to figure it out. It spread through the youth culture of the town so fast that within a year, our police chief was reporting that there were 40 known heroin addicts in town and things were out of control – which was totally untrue – I'm not sure there was even one actual heroin addict in town, but you know how the police like to overstate everything so they can get more resources all the time. Well, that's what was going on then and it's still going on now. Of course, as each generation of young people since then has reverted to more and more dangerous drugs, it's become a sign of the utter hopelessness and despair at the present and the future. There is no hope today.....back then, there was nothing but hope......

I must admit – and at the risk of being labelled a complete derelict – that the drinking started around this time as well. As might be expected, I did my very first drinking with Glen – I mean, he lived in a hotel, right? But most of my drinking escapades involved a couple of new "town" friends I'd met at school and several "country" friends I'd also met at Hanover High. Now, the "country" friends lived, for the most part, in a village called Neustadt and Neustadt was what we used to call a "police village" and what that meant was that there were no police. It was covered by the OPP who passed through from time to time but there were no actual police assigned to the town. So, it was a very good place to drink when we were young guys because there wasn't much chance of getting caught – although some folks managed it nevertheless.

And it became a regular habit for us town kids to get on the school bus to Neustadt with our country friends on Friday after school to go drinking for the weekend. We'd hitchhike our sorry asses home to Hanover on Sunday afternoon feeling more than a little wasted at school the next morning. Mind you, we didn't spend much actual time in Neustadt – we were usually out somewhere in the woods, far off the beaten path, where there was even less chance of being discovered. We usually built a big bonfire out in the bush, got drunk and danced around it like wildmen in primitive times used to do. I don't remember a lot about those days – for obvious reasons – but there are a few things I do remember. I remember riding around with a guy called "J.P.", in his pick-up truck – four of us in the front and seven or eight in the back and all drunk and the guys in back rolling around in the cowshit and screaming and yelling as we crashed around the backroads.

And I remember a place called Diemerton (sp.) where there was nothing but a restaurant that seemed to be open all night and a church – which may have come in handy given the disposition of most of the patrons of the restaurant. The first time I was in Diemerton, it was in J.P.'s truck and it was about three in the morning and we went barging through the front door, and I remember there was this huge, kind of dirty and dank looking aquarium right behind the counter as you walked in. Only this aquarium wasn't filled with beautiful, graceful tropical fishies. Instead, there were several carp, each likely over a foot in length, swaying in total unison in the mirky water – and staring right into your soul – at least that's the way it felt

Anyway, I also remember being out in the bush one night and we were all three sheets to the wind as was usual, and finally everybody was pretty much passed out except me and one of the boys from Neustadt. He suggested that we walk the railway tracks to his place and catch some sleep in an actual bed. It sounded good to me, so off we went. This particular buddy lived with his mother and father and his grandmother and, if I remember right, his grandmother used to pay him some money if he got his sorry ass out of bed and got to church on Sunday morning. So, he woke bright and early the next morning and me with him, and when I pulled the sheet that was covering me away, the bottom of the bed was soaked in blood. Seems I'd broken one of my toes the night before walking along the railway tracks in sandals. Hadn't noticed it the night before but it hurt like hell for a week. And I learned another valuable lesson in life. Don't wear sandals when you go drinking in the bush with the Neustadt guys. Man, that was dumb.

The Basketball Diaries.....

I've already covered my brief hockey career and my even briefer baseball career, so I might as well fill you in my only other venture into organized sports – other than bowling. And that was my time with the Hanover District High School Midget Basketball Team......Now, basketball has never really been my thing – it was kind of an exotic sport in Hanover back in the 1960's....I mean, why would you play basketball in the winter if you could play hockey – and everybody played hockey and usually only the real jock guys in high school shot hoops. But when I first went into Hanover High, I was resolved to try to get with the program and I'd been told I'd get more out of high school if I put a little effort into it. So, I joined the midget boys' basketball team.....

We practiced for a couple of weeks before the season started and everything looked good. Most of us were just beginners to the game, other than a tiny bit in public school, but we had a couple of jock-type guys on the team and it was assumed they'd carry us to victory after victory, while the rest of us would play a strong supporting role. I actually got sort of good at the game in practice and could hit free throws pretty well and could run drill after drill with some degree of success.

We had a couple of exhibition games before the regular season and the first was against Durham High School. We battled the Durham team tough up to halftime – the game was tied. And that's as close as we got to a win all season – tied at halftime of our first exhibition game. It turned out that our team really sucked – like big time. It turned out our jock-type guys were just mere mortals and couldn't possibly hope to compensate for the rest of the team. And so we lost game after game. And what happened was that the jock-type guys couldn't stand the humiliation, so they started to quietly drop off the team – and that meant the team got weaker and weaker as the season progressed. Like at the beginning of the season, I was an extra guy on the team, but by halfway through the season, I was a starter. And I discovered that I was a really bad basketball player, mainly because of my self-consciousness, and I couldn't hit a basket under pressure in a real game for all the tea in China – whatever that means.

And so our defeats started to get more and more lopsided. Like at the beginning of the season, we were losing sort of like 42-28, but by mid-season we were losing by scores of 64-12, and as the end of the season approached, most opposing teams were trying to score over 100 points against us, while trying to hold us to less than 10. And, of course, they would announce the scores of all the school teams over the PA at morning announcements. And it got so the whole school waited for the score of our latest game, so they could all cheer wildly for us. Those of us who had stuck with the team became sort of celebrities around the school – like it was an honour to be part of what was possibly the worst midget basketball team in Canadian sports history

Anyway, there were a couple more life lessons contained in this experience. First, don't be part of a team under any circumstances, because if the team sucks, it'll look like you suck as well. If you do suck, hang in there and sometimes it sort of pays off. You get a type of fame if you're really pitifully bad at something. I mean, people laugh at you, but at least they notice you – which in some cases is better than not getting noticed at all. Still, I was glad for the Neustadt drinking trips while this was going on…..drinking is 'way more fun than playing losing basketball and pretty well any other sport as well. Words well written.

My First Great Love

My first serious encounter with the opposite sex also happened around this time. I was at a dance in Walkerton and the first time I saw her, my heart melted. She was, to me, the most gorgeous creature I'd ever seen. So I did something really out of character. I asked her to dance, while at the same time, Glen and a couple of my other buddies zoned in on her friends. Her name was Kathy and she was from a small town called Teeswater. I spent the rest of the night with her – at least until the dance was over and her ride was leaving for home – because that's the way it worked in those days....when you said you spent the night with someone, it wasn't the actual night, it was only until the girl went home and you got a kiss good night if you were lucky.

I was totally and completely smitten with this girl....I could not get her off my mind in the days and weeks that followed. However, the fact she lived in Teeswater, which was likely 40 minutes from Hanover by car, was a huge obstacle in those days. We were too young to drive and long-distance telephone calling was hugely expensive and only usually done in extreme circumstances. So, it was pretty tough maintaining a long-distance relationship. Still, there was hitchhiking and we did lots of that in that other time. We hitchhiked all over the place, even to Kitchener and Toronto, so Teeswater wasn't that bad. And I went every chance I got and the girl seemed most receptive and it was a happy time in my life.

One way I used to get to see her was by catching a ride with my cousin's boyfriend when he drove her from Hanover back to nursing school in Wingham on Sunday nights. He had to pass right through Teeswater to get her back, so I would catch a ride to see my sweetheart. It was weird snuggling on her couch watching TV while her parents stayed in the kitchen making sure everything was good with their daughter. I remember my ride didn't come until later than usual one night, and her Dad appeared in his red long johns to make sure things were okay.....

Likely the greatest adventure I had with her was our appearance on the CKNX after school dance show called "Uptight". These types of dance shows were popular back in the Sixties and they were sort of spin offs of shows like American Bandstand and Soul Train that were big news on TV. And so CKNX had a local version of its own and the various high schools in the area were invited to come on different weeks, and, as might be expected, Hanover's turn came. Now, CKNX was located in Wingham and if you remember, Wingham is close to Teeswater. I wouldn't normally even consider going on a dance show because I don't actually do much dancing unless under extreme duress or hopelessly in love – and this time it was the latter. But there was an obvious chance to get together with the girl of my dreams if things could be worked out.

Well, the long and the short of it was that my friends from school and I snuck the Teeswater girls onto the show and this likely wouldn't have been a problem, except for my own moral depravity. I latched onto my Teeswater sweetheart like you did in those days to slow dance and that's what we did - we slow-danced through the entire show and it was one of the most truly delicious times in my life. I can still remember to this day how she seemed to fit exactly into the contours of my body and I remember thinking that I never wanted the time to end – one of those special times which I'm sure we all have. And, finally, the show ended and we parted company, she to her home and me to mine. All seemed amazingly excellent with the world. Until the morning after the show aired, and I got a call to Principal R.A. Crawford's office where I was indeed accused of moral depravity and setting a poor moral example for a student from Hanover High. It was good with me, though. Very good, indeed.

Now, I don't know if the TV show had anything to do with it or not, but it was shortly after this that she dumped me. She didn't really tell me she was dumping me the traditional way – she showed up at one of the dances in Walkerton on the arm of a football jock – big guy – school jacket. I got a final chance to talk to her sometime later and she told me I just wasn't right for her. I had long hair, played in a band, drank, smoked, did drugs. She wasn't interested in any of that stuff…it sort of frightened her. I didn't even try to discuss the matter with her….if she didn't like any of that stuff, we were clearly on different wavelengths…sort of different planets. That stuff was me. So, it ended. She went on to become a dentist and she married a guy who became a neurosurgeon. If she'd stayed with me, I'm not sure she'd have had the same type of life. I hope she's happy and I'm thankful to her for sharing even a small moment of her life with me.….

Getting a Big Amp

Time for a quick story about the way things were back in that other time. I had to constantly upgrade my amp as the bands became more and more serious and louder and louder. Finally, I had sort of run out of options with the amp I had and needed something bigger. Glen suggested that I should go to Toronto to the pawn shops on Church Street to see what was available. It was before driver's licences for both of us, so the big dilemma was how to get to Toronto and then back to Hanover without access to a set of wheels.

"Let's hitchhike," Glen suggested – so we did. Set off bright and early one morning and hitched our way to the big city. We were, however, very disappointed in the selection of bass amps available and had pretty well given up the search. I had eighty bucks to spend and there were no decent amps in that exact price range. So there we were, sitting on the curb looking dejected and bummed out. Suddenly, we heard a sort of scraping sound and turned to see this hippie-type guy dragging a fairly good-sized amplifier up the sidewalk. As it turned out, he was taking a bass guitar amplifier to one of the Church Street pawn shops to try to get enough money to cover his rent. He'd been hoping to get – you guessed it – eighty bucks at the pawn shop, so we did a deal on the spot. It was a Sykes bass amp – a brand name that nobody today has even heard of – and I didn't even know if it worked, but I bought it just the same.

And then Glen and I were standing in the middle of Toronto with a reasonably big, piggyback bass guitar amplifier and wondering how to get it back to Hanover……and, of course, we were going to have to hitchhike; something we'd never tried with a package quite this big. Nevertheless, we carried that thing as far as we could walk toward the edge of the city – and, remember, the city wasn't quite as large then as it is now. Then, we hitched our way home and actually got rides while transporting the big Sykes amp.

The Sykes did okay for me for a while, but, finally, it wasn't quite cutting it either. So, my Dad and I headed for Owen Sound to Harry's House of Music. And Harry's was where you wanted to go if you were a young musician back in those days. It was the type of music store that almost every town and city had – Harry was the proprietor and you couldn't buy, sell or trade anything without doing a "deal". When my Dad and I walked up the street to Harry's, and as soon as we were within sight of it, I caught a glimpse of this giant humungous amplifier that took up pretty well the whole window of the store. And in we went. The amp in the window was a 1969 Traynor Bassmaster and I bought it that day, borrowing some of the money off my Dad. That amp went to pretty well every gig I played from that day until Christmas 2014, when I finally bought a new one. The old Traynor still working fine but me not so much. At this point in my musical career, smaller and lighter matters almost as much as sound quality. And that's the truth.

The Band's First Big Gig

It was funny how it worked back in those early band days. Almost every young guy in Hanover seemed to be trying to learn how to play guitar or drums or anything that might launch him along the path toward rock 'n' roll stardom. And it was kind of a cruel process because it was sort of like the survival of the musical fittest. You'd get a band together with your friends – like Glen and I did – then you'd keep shifting positions until you had what you thought was the right mix of players to have the best band possible. And, so, Glen sort of fell by the wayside because as hard as he might try, he could not master any instrument well enough to keep moving up in bands. And when the final band came together somewhere around Grade 11, he moved into the technical side of things and became our band's sound and light guy for the next couple of years. And I'll tell you something – we had the best sound and best light show around.

The band that finally rose to the surface was called "Strange Brew", after the name of a tune on a Cream album – Cream being one of our favourite bands at the time. We were a four-piece.....drums, bass, guitar and vocals, and our ace in the hole was our singer who was a new kid in town who'd just moved in when his Dad got a job teaching at Hanover High. I became fast friends with the new kid and he was a great guy who could sing 'way better than anyone else in the area.

And, so, we'd started to develop our first real set list – covering artists like Hendrix, Cream, the Rolling Stones, the Ugly Ducklings, the Beatles and lots of other cool stuff. We played at a couple of house parties as we were rounding into shape and the stuff was actually sounding like music. My cousin was part of the Red Lutheran Church youth group in town, and they were just getting a coffee house going in the bottom of the Hanover Town Hall. Well, somehow, we ended up playing the first time they held the coffee house – which I think was called the Purple Onion. And it was going to be our first real gig and I think we were paid $60 for it.

So, we loaded our gear into the town hall basement while the volunteers were busy setting up. Glen had gone all out building us a spectacular light show, complete with two big light columns and a homemade strobe for the big psychedelic number, Tobacco Road. We all got a case of nerves when, just as we were about to start, in walked a bunch of guys from the band, Father Finley's Wake, the older guys in town who'd already been out gigging for a couple of years. This would truly be a test for our fledgling band, and all I can remember is that we played our hearts out and set the stage for the next couple of years for the band. Even the guys in Finley's Wake came up and congratulated us after the gig. The only real hitch had been that Glen's home-made strobe light kept bouncing all over the stage, so he ended up having to sit on it to keep it in one position. Other than that, everything went pretty well.....

Strange Brew played many times over the next couple of years and earned a solid fan base among the young people of the area. We played high schools, Teen Towns, CYO dances and lots of other events. Back in those days – before the era of the disc jockey – everybody who wanted to hold a dance hired a band, so there was lots of work. We also made really good money and became sort of rich kids in school – although we squandered every penny of it on music gear and our debauched lifestyles. The two biggest gigs we played were the Teeswater Old Boys' Reunion and the prom at Fergus High School. For the Fergus gig, we rode in a lunch truck that was windowless for the whole trip there and back, but it was a hoot just the same. At the Teeswater gig, I was, of course, trying to play really well in case my former paramour was in the crowd. Never did find out if she was, but played well just the same.

Then, our singer moved away, our drummer moved into country music where there was more money and our guitar player switched to playing drums and joined a lounge act. It was enormous fun while it lasted, but it was also hard for me to do. I'd started to have trouble with my "nerves" as I'd moved into my teenage years. I was ill almost every night before the band played – the rest of the guys would be setting up the gear, and I'd be in the bathroom being ill. We'd have to leave early for gigs because I'd be sick on the way. The problem with my "nerves" was a most unfortunate development and one that would haunt me for the rest of my life.

Roller Skating......

Roller skating was a really big deal when I was a young guy. Pretty well every young person I knew in those days headed for the roller rink several times a week in the spring, summer and fall of the year. The rink would be packed and it seemed to be great fun going round and round and round and round…... most of the action taking place in the stands where love was often found and lost – where you had a chance to meet lots of girls, besides just the ones you went to school with. Because the Hanover roller rink – which was actually the Coliseum and local hockey arena – drew kids from all over the area – but especially Walkerton.

The first year I roller skated, the kids in town were still using the old, outdoor roller rink that was downtown. It was on the cement pad that was what was left of the old Hanover Arena – it was right on the Main Street, and you went down a set of stairs to get to it. It had been the town's first real arena, but the roof had been condemned, so the owner, Deli Schleigel, tore it off and converted the cement pad into an outdoor roller rink.

I'm not really sure about the actual dates of a lot of things back in those days because I was just a kid and it was a really long time ago. But I think the

Hanover Coliseum opened for business in 1962 and that's where I did nearly all of my roller skating. Made lots of great friendships at the roller rink.... even tried to pick up a few girls myself. You would try to get someone to skate with you for the "red lights" at the end of the night. For the last couple songs of the night, they'd play slow stuff and light the place in red, and you had to have a partner to skate. It was pretty romantic stuff for our young hearts.

And, of course, after they finished roller skating, most people headed for Norm's Snack Bar for a Coke and French fries – which Norm's was famous for back in those old days. Norm's would be packed to the rafters after roller skating, and you'd order your French fries by saying you'd have a "10 to go" or a "25 to go".....and that determined how big a bag of fries you'd have – because they were served in a paper bag that was literally dripping with grease. And you'd dump your ketchup and salt and stuff into the bag, close up the top and shake the crap out of it to mix everything together. It was a delicious mess. In later years, when it became popular, some kids would have gravy poured into this morass as well – and then it was truly a mess.

Those Daring Young Men in Their Jaunty Jalopies

The big thing that most young people looked forward to as they passed through their teenage years was turning 16 so you could get your driver's licence. I was the exception to the rule and wasn't really looking forward to driving.....and actually didn't get my licence for a couple of years after I turned 16. But Glen couldn't wait to get his licence and hit the road.....and unlike most of our other friends, he wanted no part of borrowing Dad's car on Friday and Saturday nights. He wanted his own set of wheels so bad he could taste it by the time he was about 14. And even though he had his job at the hotel, he still couldn't seem to get enough money together to buy a decent vehicle. So, he decided on another course of action.

You have to understand that back in that other time, when the guy who pumped your gas might very well be smoking a cigarette, there were no such things as "safety checks" for cars. In other words, if you could get it to run, you could drive it, pretty well regardless of what condition it was in. The only thing you'd really get bothered about was excessive noise or having a headlight or tail light out…..as long as your car was quiet and you could see where you were going after dark, you could take to the roads in it.

So, Glen started buying junkers…..but he had a plan – a strategy. He didn't just buy any old junkers – he bought three identical junkers…Fords, I think. And his plan was to take the best one and use parts from the other two to get it running. He started working on the Fords even before his fifteenth birthday, so he was at it for a while. I'm pretty sure he paid $25 each for the cars, so he had $75 invested in his plan to build a workable automobile. His Dad was less than happy to have these derelicts clogging up the hotel parking lot, but he indulged Glen, mainly, I think, because it kept his son out of his hair for a while.

And the good news was that Glen's plan sort of worked. I remember going over after supper one night in the summer and damned if he didn't have one of the Fords running, and, in fact, he was bombing around the parking lot in it. So, we cheered and celebrated and I got in and the two of us raced around the parking lot, spraying gravel on the turns and hoping not to damage any of the actual customers' cars that were parked there. And now Glen was ready to turn 16. But, remember, I said earlier that Glen's plan "sort of " worked. And here's the story behind what I meant by that.

Glen's birthday arrived in September just as it always did, but this year he was off to the driver inspection centre with his Dad to try for his licence. And it was no surprise that he got it on the first try, because his Dad had been letting him drive around the back roads for the last couple of years, and one of the things he was studying at school was auto mechanics. His academic career had been a dismal failure, and, in fact, he had spent three years in Grade 9, going from the five year Arts and Science program, to the four year Tech program, and finally to the two-year Tech program. And it wasn't because he wasn't smart enough – school just didn't suit him – he just sort of didn't fit into the thing – like a square peg in a round hole….

Anyway, Glen got his licence and I was waiting for him when he got back to the hotel with his Dad…..me and another guy from the band. And right away we headed for the back parking lot of the hotel and soon had the one good Ford up and running and we were driving fools. We headed for Walkerton and it was already dusk as we drove out of Hanover. We made it over to the town that sat just west of Hanover on Highway 4 with no problem. Then, we drove up and down the main street of Walkerton, hoping there would be a few girls out for us to impress. There weren't, so we decided we should head back for Hanover.

Now Walkerton is an interesting community because it's sort of built in a hollow and on three sides there are huge hills leading out of town. And you have to go up one of those hills to get out of Walkerton on the way back to Hanover. And a funny thing happened as we were chugging up the Walkerton Hill heading for Hanover – we got about halfway up the hill and the Ford started to die – we started to lose power. Glen cranked her hard right and we ended up in a driveway before the car quit altogether. Yikes! Now what? No problem, Glen said......he suggested me and the extremely scrawny guitar player from our band should push the car out of the driveway, across the highway, then sort of backwards up the hill a bit – that way, we'd be pointing down the hill back into Walkerton and we could roll the car down the hill, gradually building up speed, until Glen popped the clutch and it lurched back to life. Sounded like a good plan to me. What could possibly go wrong?

So, we positioned ourselves at the door posts, and Glen helped a bit, and we actually managed to get the huge, heavy car out of the driveway and partway across the road, pointing sort of down the hill into Walkerton. Glen hollered for us to scramble in and we were off down the hill.....and I'll be damned if it didn't start when Glen popped the clutch and the Ford was back in operation. We got going pretty fast coasting down the hill and there were cries to slow down. Glen then discovered that when he dropped the car below 30 miles per hour, the electrical went out and the headlights – which we now needed because it was dark – failed completely. So, there we were, roaring around Walkerton, wondering what to do next, because we couldn't slow down and that meant we couldn't stop at stop signs or traffic lights, which Walkerton only had one of, so that wasn't a big problem.

Remember me saying that Walkerton is surrounded by hills on three sides – well, if you went south out of town, it was pretty flat all the way to Mildmay, so that had to be our course of action. Down the road we went and Glen had decided we'd take a backroad called the South Line by the locals, so we waited for it to approach, then screamed around the corner onto it at 30 mph – you could almost feel the outside set of wheels lift off the road as we went around. As soon as we were on the South Line, the electrical system in the car did finally fail. So, now we had no headlights. And just to remind you that Glen had only gotten his licence that very day, so was perhaps not the most skilled driver in the region – and he was now driving a road he had little knowledge of and it was pitch black. Leave it to say that it was a harrowing ride as we deked and dodged our way along the twisty, turny road, narrowly missing a couple of bridges and doing a lot of wailing and gnashing of teeth as we went.

Finally, it looked like we might actually make it. We were getting close to Hanover…one more obstacle to overcome…..the Carlsruhe corner. That's right, folks – where the South Line ended, it met the Neustadt Road which ran from Hanover to the esteemed community of Neustadt – where John Diefenbaker was born….problem was that where the South Line met the Neustadt Road there was a 90 degree turn required from the former onto the latter……and we were there almost before we knew it – no seat belts in those days – and we hit that curve going 'way faster than we should have and Glen cranked her hard left and we flew around the corner, gravel flying, car skidding wildly as it left the gravel of the South Line and hit the pavement of the Neustadt Road……AAAaaaahhhhhhhhhh!!!!!!!!!! My brief life flashed before my eyes in that moment when we went airborne and landed again sort of pointing up the road to Hanover and Glen laying on the gas to keep her going. An honest-to-goodness miracle that there was no other traffic coming up from Neustadt or we'd have all been dead.

We drove along in absolute quiet until we reached Roland's Hill, which is just on the south end of Hanover so we'd pretty well made it home. Then, unceremoniously, the Ford died altogether, stranding us. I was never so glad to get out of a car either before or since. I had been pretty sure I was about to die. We walked back to the Queen's mostly in silence. Somehow, Glen got the car from Roland's Hill back to the hotel….and he breathed life back into the Ford and salvaged a few more parts off the other two, and, eventually, we were back out cruising around in it – trying to impress the girls – in Walkerton and other locations around the area.

And that's the way it went in those days…….

Long Hair and Greasers

By the time I hit Grade 10/11, the world really seemed to be changing – there were riots on the streets of most major American cities – the war in Viet Nam was dragging on and on – John Kennedy, Martin Luther King, Malcolm X and Bobby Kennedy all died for what they believed in and the world became a hugely poorer place because of it. In our little corner of the world, we were trying hard to be hippies, but I would never really have called us hippies – more like we were Long Hairs and not real hippies. I take the term hippie very seriously and feel it had strong ideological meaning that involved rejecting what we called the Establishment, and generally trying to work toward a new world order of peace, love and harmony. I certainly bought into all the stuff back in the Sixties, but it took me a long time in my life to finally figure out what it meant and that it ain't likely to happen.

The Long Hair tribe were folks who grew their hair – if they were a guy – and they wore bell bottom jeans, did at least soft drugs and greeted each other with a peace sign. I must admit that there was a good feeling among members of the Long Hairs there for a couple of years. And it was like if you shared a joint with someone, there seemed to be some type of bond that formed. It wasn't a tangible thing but just something you could feel….and it felt good for a while…real good.

There were sort of three groups of young people back at this point at Hanover High. There were the sort of normal kids who liked to go on "dates" and drink beer and play sports and likely go to church and worked in a real job in the summer. Then, there were the Long Hairs, who just sort of hung out, smoked dope, were into weird music, were likely not really into the church scene anymore and were fighting a weekly battle about attending this traditional form of religion, and who just sort of hung out more in the summer. The third group of kids back in those days were the "Greasers" or "Grease Balls", depending on your vernacular. The Greasers generally liked to drink heavily, fail at school and go to work at 16, drink even more heavily, race their hot cars, wear leather jackets and beat up Long Hairs or "hippies". It was the way of the world back then.

And it made life really exciting back in the old days if you were one of the Long Hairs. Because no matter where you went, you had to be on the lookout for Greasers who would really like to punch your lights out. So, we travelled in packs most of the time. Always hitchhiked in pairs, at dances visited the washroom in pairs – generally tried not to get caught by yourself in a compromising position. I managed to do pretty well at avoiding getting beat up and can proudly say I've never even been in a real fight. Still, I've been at many a dance where the normal kids were dancing, while the Long Hairs occupied one side of the hall and the Greasers the other.

And I want to draw a serious line here between Greasers and Bikers…. right from the very beginning, there was a solid bond between the bikers and the long hairs or the hippies. Back in the old days, both were outcasts from traditional society and made their own way. A hippie mantra from back in the day was "do your own thing" and the Bikers had practiced that philosophy from the time they had come into being. So, don't ever confuse Bikers and Greasers. If you were a hippie back in the old days – even a wannabe hippie – the Bikers were your friends in almost every situation.

The Actual Fear and Loathing Starts…..

Things would have been different back in the Sixties if there had only been soft drugs around. But almost before that first summer of smoking pot was over, other stuff was starting to appear. Glen helped make this happen as well. But I'll tell you something you likely won't believe. We actually thought acid and organic mescaline and stuff like that would expand our minds and take us to levels of consciousness that we couldn't normally reach. We thought we could somehow see into our minds and better understand ourselves by taking some of these mind-altering substances. It wasn't all evil and sinister back in the old days. It was more innocent for a while. But only for a very short while. Then, it was party time….

I Do Acid......

Even though I've been in some fairly strange situations in my life, I'm not by nature a very adventurous sort. So, when LSD appeared on the scene, I wasn't really too keen to get involved. Still, it was almost like a hippie rite of passage back in that other time. Young people got together and sat reverently in a circle and each took a turn doing a tab of acid and then waiting for the effects to take hold. That's when the stuff first appeared and I knew that at some point I'd likely give it a go. I held off for quite some time while most of my other friends were doing some experimenting with the stuff. Finally, though, it was like I simply had to.

A bunch of us were out at the Marl Lakes, sitting around a bonfire and it was a very happening scene. I'd scored a hit of White Clinical off Glen – actually, he just gave it to me because he thought it would be a good experience for me. I split the tab in half – I'd heard stories about kids who did too much acid and ended up in the loony bin thinking they were an orange and trying to peel themselves. Yikes! And there were the other folks who'd thought they could fly and had jumped to their deaths off high buildings, though I'd thought I was safe on that count because of the lack of high buildings in Hanover and area.

Anyway, I broke the hit in half, putting the one half into the pocket of my jean jacket and hoping that no one had seen me do it. I held the other half between my fingers and pondered what I was about to do. I was filled with a type of excited anticipation, but was also frightened beyond belief. And I knew from talking mainly to Glen about doing LSD that frame of mind was really important – the wrong vibes could send you reeling into a bad trip and that could be a nightmare.

Finally, I ate the damned thing – swallowed it down. And then waited nervously. Holy crap! This was it. Either I'd be a real hippie or I'd be an orange – one or the other.

And I'll never forget that I felt it in my gums first and from then on I knew that was the signal for the start of a descent into chaos and delirium. And, finally, I remember looking into the fire, and watching intently as tongues of flame licked and lapped up into the night sky where they vanished into nothingness. I lost all track of time and when someone else finally came within my range of consciousness, I couldn't tell if I'd been watching the fire for a couple of minutes or hours. Someone wanted to go get food and somehow I ended up in the back of a convertible, hurtling along the road back into Hanover. I can still remember watching out between the bucket seats as the car seemed to speed along at incredible velocity – I couldn't believe we got stopped at the stop signs, always thinking we were going 'way too fast. First, they'd seem like they were a really long way away, and then they'd just zoom up amazingly fast and things would be a little blurry until reality had time to catch up to you

Then, we were in the restaurant. Everybody ordered huge whacks of food…cheeseburgers, milk shakes, onion rings, fries (with gravy)…..everything we could think of for a true junk food feast – before we knew it was junk food….but before the food arrived, the table descended into chaos and everybody was laughing hysterically, throwing salt and pepper and sugar at each other, and when the food did arrive, we sat in solemn silence regarding it. Mine was slithering and squirming its way across the plate – it looked bad – real bad. And ugly – real ugly. So, we ended up paying the bill and not really eating any of the food and we headed back out onto the road.

Somehow, and I don't really remember how, I ended up in Glen's room – Room 15 at the Queen's. And all I remember about being there is that I was sitting in this big easy chair – and the room was really dark – and I had my sunglasses on – so it was really dark. And Glen's record player – this was still before big, honkin' stereos had arrived on the scene – was sitting on a book shelf directly behind me, and this was one of those record players that have an arm on them so you can make it play the same record over and over. And, somehow, someone had put this Vanilla Fudge album on the turntable – the one with You Keep Me Hangin' On – and I sat in the chair and listened to that record over and over and over, while all the time fiercely worrying that I might never get straight again – ever – and I was on the way to a future of peeling oranges in the loony bin. No one had really explained to me that LSD trips can be really long and that pretty well everyone who takes one spends at least some time worrying about whether they'll ever be straight again.

Anyway, somehow I managed to finally pull myself away from Vanilla Fudge, although it seemed I had listened to it over 100 times. And what pulled me away was a really strong urge to have a bowel movement. I know that sounds gross, but you gotta know it was part of the experience. Glen had to travel down the hallway to a communal bathroom at the Queen's and I'm still not sure how I got there, but I got there nonetheless. And I got in the stall, and barely managed to get sitting down when, suddenly, it was like my whole insides emptied out in one giant swoosh. It was so sudden and so wild that I remember wondering if I was going to go with it. Oh, what a feeling, what a rush. And, then it was over and I wobbled back to my feet and stood with my pants around my ankles. And the stall was made of plywood and the pattern on the plywood started whirling and swirling in every direction. I lurched forward and sort of fell out of the stall and onto the bathroom floor.

Anyway, I woke up from sleeping on Glen's couch the next morning and he was sawing logs in his bed. My head felt like it was full of cotton, but I didn't feel high anymore and I was more than a little thankful for that. And the whole experience sort of scared the crap out of me and that was likely a good thing, because it meant I did chemical drugs only a few other times when I was young. Each time was fairly memorable, but I knew that first time that it wasn't really for me. I treated LSD and all chemical drugs really carefully and with great respect – except for a couple of times when I let the chaos and delirium overtake me again just for a bit.

School Daze, School Daze........

By the time I was in Grade 11, I was right on the edge of my life. I was still a good student – racking up a 100 in the first semester of Grade 11 Physics – and generally on cruise control. I was playing in the band, and the band was popular in those days, and even though I was continuing to have trouble with my "nerves", I was the typical maladjusted teenager struggling to get by. I had mostly left girls alone in those days, still hurting from my relationship with the Teeswater girl, and not ready to do that again any time soon. Mostly, it was the life of Riley. I was doing a bit of working but the band kept me in money and why work if you don't have to. There were lots of parties to go to if the band wasn't playing and I usually went and became the quiet observer in the corner of the room. It's what I do – it's what I've always done.

Back in those really olden days, high school students were required to take some Bill Shakespeare every year in English. Each year, you had a different play and they had the same play for each grade for decades and decades on end. So, when we were in Grade 11, the play was Romeo and Juliet, which even cultural clods like us had some familiarity with. And one of the tactics our teacher used to teach us the story was by acting it out, so at one point while we were studying it, he divided us into three groups – the brainiac kids, the normal kids and the known troublemakers. And, for some reason, even though I'd gotten 100 in Physics, I wasn't included with the Brainiacs, or even the normal kids – I was assigned to the group of known troublemakers…..and I'm pretty sure I understood why even back then.

So, the Brainiac kids chose the balcony scene, because it was, of course, the most well-known, and had the best chance to offer the cast star status. I can't remember which scene the normal kids chose….but it was probably a fairly normal and ordinary scene because that's what normal kids always choose because that's what makes them normal. We had quite a discussion in the troublemaker group deciding which scene to choose, but finally decided on the opening scene of the play, which, if you remember, features a huge brawl between the men of the Capulet and Montague families. Well, you know, why not, eh?

Well, each group went off to do their rehearsals which involved several classes and took a couple of weeks, when we were supposed to be diligently learning our lines and working out the action and so forth. And I'm not sure what the other two groups were doing, but our group was mostly buggering off and doing as little as possible….we assigned each other to parts and everybody wanted the parts with the least lines – or, preferably, no lines at all. We had, of course, to come up with swords because that's how the really old guys fought – they hacked away at each other with sharp things and tried to really hurt each other.

Well, there was absolutely zero chance that our teacher would let us use anything even faintly resembling a real sword, because we were, after all, the known troublemakers, and you don't let known troublemakers have real sharp things. After some serious discussion, and because one of our class-mates picked up the Globe and Mail every morning mainly to read Richie York, we decided our weapons of choice had to be rolled up newspapers. And we didn't really let our teacher observe the big fight scene or in any way see any part of it. We thought we'd keep that part of the action to ourselves until the big performance day arrived.

And that day came soon enough, and we went down to the gym to present the plays in a sort of real setting, but having only our classmates as audience. And, of course, the Brainiac kids went first, and did a creditable job of the big balcony scene and we all cheered and applauded when they finished. It was good work all the way around. The normal kids did okay, too. The presentation of their play was normal and ordinary, but that's exactly what you'd expect from the normal kids. Then, it was time for us to present our theatre production. And things were going pretty well and I thought we might even get a C for our work because a few people had even managed to commit their lines to memory, and our scene featured some real serious action. The problem arose as the fight scene unfolded – we were supposed to smite each other in a gentlemanly, civilized manner with the rolled-up newspapers, but one smite led to another, and, before you could shake a rolled up Globe and Mail at it, the smiting really got out of control, and then it was a scene of flying newspaper and shouting and cursing and flailing about until the whole group of us – even the girls – crashed into a heap in the middle of the stage – all dead.

We got wild applause for our effort because I guess it was highly enter-taining to watch, and I have little doubt that it was. I'm pretty sure that was the last time I acted in public, and that's likely another good thing in my life. I don't have a clue how our teacher marked us on our performance, which didn't really resemble old Bill Shakespeare much. Still, it made an indelible impression on me – as you can tell….

I did write a short play while I was in high school as well. In it, we draped these things like chains over one of my buddies, and he sat cross-legged on the floor pretending like he was all weighted down with life's problems and all the chaos in the world. Then, another buddy – the guitar player from my band – made huge feedback sounds and all kinds of other noise on his guitar, while the first buddy gradually cast off the chains and slowly rose to his feet. It was all very symbolic, I'm sure, and was a little short on dialogue – although it was my first effort so I kind of excuse myself on account of that. I think it went okay, but it's a dim memory.

My other theatre memory was something that sort of changed my life. Somehow, as if we'd suddenly been transported to another more liberal planet, our teacher got permission to take all the Grade 11 students to see the musical Hair at the Royal Alexandria Theatre in Toronto. Now, you've got to understand that although Hair was being heralded as a piece of theatre genius in those days, it was also enormously controversial. For one thing, it had full frontal nudity. And the subject matter, about the Viet Nam war and stuff like that, was all pretty much teetering on the edge of what was allowed and what wasn't.

I usually didn't go on school trips because they always used those old yellow school buses and I was still having a problem with motion sickness. If I rode for any length of time in one of those old tin cans, it would almost certainly be a trip to Pukesville for me. But the trip to see Hair I wouldn't have missed for anything – even the chance I might get deathly ill and have to barf out a bus window. So, I jostled and bumped my way to Toronto and had one of the experiences of a lifetime. We sat in the balcony and it was deadly steep, and I remember sitting in the dark with my knees tucked up tightly in front of me. It was my first real theatre experience and it has stayed with me forever. At my age, I was of course disappointed that the full frontal nudity only happened for an instant at the end of the play, and, other than that it was pretty tame visually. Still, it was a remarkable piece of theatre and started my lifelong love of live theatre.

Grade 12 and the School Newspaper....

The first week of Grade 12 something happened that would profoundly change my life. My English teacher, Mr. Dove, who was new to the school, sized me up pretty quickly, and decided I was the man for a project he wanted to try to get off the ground –and that was a student-run school newspaper. Pretty well before I knew what was happening, I was the editor of Probe, a school newspaper that was truly an innovation in the way we set it up and ran it. I rounded up the editorial staff, which were mostly friends of mine, and we soon had things up and running. We had, of course, no idea what we were doing, absolutely none of us, including Mr. Dove, with any real newspaper experience at all.

I ran the newspaper for about two years and the publishing of it was fairly sporadic because I had trouble keeping the staff on deadline most of the time. I got part of my English mark for being editor, but everybody else was a total volunteer, and it was my job to keep them moving in the right direction. We didn't go to the school staff for any support other than Mr. Dove and we ran our own show from a money standpoint as well. At the beginning of the newspaper, everyone on staff donated five bucks to the cause, and there were about 20 people, so we had a war chest of about $100. And from that point on, Probe was self-sufficient – we sold copies for 25 cents each and even hit downtown merchants for advertising. And the way we ran the paper, Principal R. A. Crawford had little control over us.

Glen, for example, who was obviously part of the project, did a piece called "Drugs and You" for the paper, and although he started with alcohol in the first issue, he was soon writing about LSD, marijuana and methamphetamines. I wrote mostly opinion pieces and there was no real reporting went on. We had lots of poetry – Glen was a big contributor to this section of the paper – we had other poets on staff and several other writers and artists who thought they had something to say. It was all very eclectic and we even organized a student newspaper conference that was held at good old HDHS. We were quite the thing there for a couple of years, and it was the start of my real writing career, and from there would come almost 40 years in the community newspaper business – I used my experience with the school newspaper to get my first real job at a real newspaper some years later.

Even with the start of my newspaper career, there was something else that happened because of the school newspaper. The school administration agreed to let me do Probe as the written part of my English mark, but they wanted me to do something else as the comprehension part. And what they came up with would also change my life. They assigned me an independent reading course and they handed the job of teaching it to me to another brand-new teacher at the school. And he was a for-real hippie with long hair and a beard and everything else you expected of a hippie. How he got hired by Hanover High, I'll never really know, but I was glad he did. He called me down to the school office one day after classes, and when I met him, he told me to come to his office in the school's boiler room the next day. And so I did.

And the first thing he said to me when I went to his office the next day was, "Well, we can assume we're not going to find any decent books to read in this town. I'll pick you up Saturday morning and we'll go to Toronto to get some books." And he was good to his word and did indeed pick me up on Saturday morning and he took me to the bookstore in the bottom of Rochdale College and we gathered up great armloads of books.....Kurt Vonnegut, Richard Brautigam, Buckminster Fuller, John Updike, Tom Wolfe, Ken Kesey and the list went on and on. And it was the beginning of my real education from that day forward. I absorbed those books almost through osmosis – I read voraciously for all of those two years and for many years after and I learned how to be a writer from that experience and I am thankful for it now and forevermore.....

Learning My Sums.......

When I was in Grade 12, Hanover High was undergoing a major transformation and there were jack hammers and saws and all sorts of other construction equipment making quite a racket and uproar around the school. The reason for all this upheaval was that Hanover was becoming more of a regional school and was about to go from about a few hundred students to over 1,000 from the end of one year to the beginning of the next. So, there was a major expansion underway and there was dust and dirt everywhere and huge plastic sheets separated the old part of the school from the new part.

In the middle of all this, I was steadily losing interest in the scholarly pursuits – at least the ones they were trying to teach me at HDHS. I was just simply not interested in learning anything when I couldn't see any practical value. And this is where Grade 12 math entered the picture.....and chemistry and stuff like that. I mean, when was I ever going to use any of this junk? So,

I started to slide away into the oblivion of the unwashed, uneducated masses and my days at the top of the class were over. And just about the first place I went sliding was in Grade 12 math…..that's the year when all kinds of weird stuff starts to surface in the world of math. Stuff like logarithms popped up out of nowhere….and here's when I thought logarithms involved natives beating on logs in the jungle and that apparently had nothing to do with it. Instead, it was some type of high mathematical wizardry that I seemed to have absolutely no aptitude for.

Our teacher that year was Miss Stewart, and although I never saw this myself, the big rumour in school was that she kept a bottle of whiskey in the drawer of her desk for when the going got tough. She was a little, old lady to me, short, stout, gray-haired and seeming like she might have taught my father. Miss Stewart's classroom was on the second floor of the school and it was in a place in the school that would butt right up to the new addition. I don't know how it happened, but somehow my fellow students and I discovered that if we all vibrated our feet really quickly and all together – like the whole class – that we could get the whole classroom floor rocking up and down and making it seem like there was a minor earthquake happening. And we'd wait to do this until Miss Stewart was at the blackboard trying to write down some wonderful mathematical formula or some such thing and she had her back to us. Then, the signal would be given and everybody would start vibrating their feet, the floor would start to rock up and down, and Miss Stewart found she couldn't write on the blackboard worth a damned because she was rocking up and down with the floor.

The first time we did this, she stopped writing and turned abruptly around, looking at us like she suspected something sinister was happening. "Did anybody else feel that?" she asked. And one of my fellow students, who was quick off the mark, told her they were using a jack hammer close to us in the construction area. "Yes", she said, "that must be it." And sure as heck, every time we pulled this off over the next couple of months, she was convinced it was the construction that was causing it. It seems kind of a dumb thing to do when I think about it now…..but it was uproariously funny back in the old days. We laughed our asses off over that one. But I failed math miserably – the first failure of my high school career – along with Grade 12 Chemistry, which

I also bombed out of. Now, if I'd failed Grade 12 anything the year before I did, I would have had to repeat my whole Grade 12 year. As it worked out, the whole educational system changed when I was at the end of Grade 12, and something called the "credit system" came into being. And what this meant was that you no longer had to pass specific courses – you only had to amass a certain number of credits in so many years to graduate. I didn't have to take Grade 12 math or chemistry again – instead, I took courses like Grade 9 Instrumental Music – after I'd played the clarinet in the town band for over a decade…..wow…..the ultimate bird course as they used to say – and that's really what I was looking for in those days……

Celebrate – Dance to the Music…..

One of the English teachers who taught at HDHS was a very creative and innovative soul and had a love of live musical theatre. So, she got together with other creative souls in the school and they created a piece of musical theatre called, "Celebrate". The story in the play was an original piece and I'm not even sure who wrote it, but the music was current rock 'n' roll stuff that was sort of borrowed and adapted. I was lucky enough to get chosen for the stage band that would play the music. It was the first time I'd ever done anything even remotely like it and it caused me no end to nervousness.

There was a great deal of anticipation through the whole town of Hanover as the springtime dates for the play approached, and, in fact, it was a complete and total sell-out for all four performances……Thursday, Friday and Saturday nights and a Saturday matinee. We got standing ovations for every performance and it was something that made a huge impact on me. I remember after the show each night, throngs of little kids would rush the stage looking for autographs. It's one of the few times in my life I've ever been asked for my autograph. It was sort of a humbling experience, but despite my "nerves" which caused me some trouble, I was learning that I sort of liked being in the spotlight. But I'm always the bass player – never the guy in the full glare of the light, but only kind of on the edge of things…..

Dief the Chief.......

When they closed Durham High School at the end of that year and all the Durham kids were going to have to come to Hanover, the powers that be decided it wasn't right to have them going to a school called "Hanover" District High School, so a new name was needed for our educational establishment. Now it happens that this was only a few years after Canadians had elected a guy by the name of John Diefenbaker as Prime Minister....he'd won a couple of big majorities, then, gradually, as he lost favour, he ended up shunted to the sidelines of the Canadian political game. Still, for a while there, he was immensely popular. And it turned out – wonder of wonders – he had been born in the police village of Neustadt, long before we'd discovered it was a good place to get drunk. So, Hanover High was about to become John Diefenbaker Secondary School.

And, of course, a big ceremony was planned for the unveiling of the new addition to the school and for the official re-naming and Dief the Chief, as he was somewhat affectionately known, was to come to the school to cut the ribbon. As part of the big celebrations, the band from Celebrate was asked to perform some of the numbers from the show on the loading dock out behind the school. So there we were, playing our hearts out and doing a little Led Zeppelin and up walked Dief and his good wife, Olive, and the rest of the official entourage. They stood directly in front of us and listened intently as we ran through a couple of numbers. Then, Dief approached the loading dock and shook all of our hands before moving on. "You look like fine young men," he told us, but I'm pretty sure he was lying, because we were kind of an unkempt bunch at that point in high school. Long hair, beards, scruffy blue jeans and denim jackets.....Still, he was more than polite to us and I appreciated that – I truly did. Because not everybody was polite to us back in those days.

My Dad stood firmly behind me during my period of rebellion – if that's what you want to call it. He had friends tell him they'd disown any son who took to looking like a girl and played in a rock 'n' roll band when some folks still considered that music to be the devil's work. Dad told them they shouldn't judge others by appearances and should look to see what was inside. And that's the way my Dad was – he always stood firmly behind me, no matter what seemingly outlandish thing I was up to that particular week. I learned years later that the only time I ever caused my mother true grief when I was growing up was when I grew my hair long. It really upset her and she tried to get my Dad to force me to cut it. He refused and told her it was my life and my decision to make. He was a good guy, my Dad.

Working for a Living……

When I was in high school, and when I wasn't playing in a band, I still needed money, so it meant having to actually work at real work-type jobs. My cousin, the nurse, was dating a farm boy from just outside of town, and, fairly regularly, his Dad, the actual farmer, would need extra help around the farm. And, so, I went on the list as being available when extra help was needed. Understand that the farmer never seemed to really know when he'd actually need help. So, he'd phone my house at 5:00 on Saturday morning to let me know I was needed. When the phone rang at this ungodly hour, everybody in the house knew it was for me, but I could never be expected to be the one to get out of bed to answer it. I mean, I'd usually only gotten home a couple of hours earlier and I needed my sleep. No, my Dad would always be first to the phone. And, remember, in those days, there was usually only one phone per household, so it meant my Dad had to get up upstairs and make his way downstairs to the living room where our communal phone was located. Then, he'd holler up the stairs in a sort of hushed voice to tell me it was for me. I'd groggily make my way down to the phone, take the phone from Dad, and tell the farmer I'd be ready for him to pick me up by 6:00 a.m.

And I remember one Saturday morning in particular when there were five or six very tired guys in the back of the truck by the time we got back to the farm – we were a sorry lot indeed. Anyway, the farmer pulled up in front of this huge several stories high barn, and we clambered out of the truck. We stood in a tiny clump at the bottom of the big ramp that led up into the main floor of the barn. "Well, boys," started the farmer…."today you can either castrate pigs with me, or shovel chicken shit with my son – you can take your pick." Quite a choice for so early in the morning. Somehow, I got my name in for shovelling chicken shit. And, later in the day, when I was shovelling away and could hear those pigs screaming in agony and terror from two floors below, I was most glad I'd made the choice I had.

Not that I had it all that great with the chicken shit......it was four to five feet deep, and we wore surgical masks to protect us from the thick, heavy ammonia-laden dust that filled the air as we forked the stuff into wheel barrows and wheeled it out of the barn. It was the job from hell but quite a bit better than dealing with those pigs. Man, those animals sounded like they were not having a good time down there in the bowels of the barn....not a good time at all.

Another time, a buddy of mine and I got a call from Student Manpower and they had a job for us over at Swift's.....now let me explain.....Swift's was where they did a variety of horrible things to turkeys when they were on the way from farm to table. When I got the call from Manpower, I was none too keen to answer it, but I was particularly broke, so I took it anyway – my buddy was in the same boat, so he accepted as well.

They asked us to bring our winter coats and gloves and such, which we thought odd, it being the middle of a heat wave in July. Still, we complied and reported to work at the designated time. And they put us to work in this big refrigeration room where we were loading trucks with a really huge number of frozen turkeys. It was really cold and the turkeys were heavy, but it was an okay job for pretty good money. My buddy and I smiled at each other often as we moved box after box of frozen turkeys. Things were going okay until the morning of the third day. Then, our boss told us there were no more trucks to load. "I'll put you to work in the plant on the "kill line"," he said. Yikes! The dreaded kill line!

My buddy and I went into the plant with the boss guy – we followed dutifully along. I quit as soon as I had a chance to see the kill line in operation – after witnessing firsthand what they did to those poor, downtrodden, unfortunate wretches that were the turkeys. I knew I couldn't have any part in that barbarous practice. So, I handed in the white coat they'd just given me, and the rubber boots, picked up my pay in the office and walked off down the road. Later in the day, I found out my buddy lasted about two hours before he turned in his coat and boots as well. There are some people who are cut out for that kind of work, and there are others who just aren't, and he and I were clearly among the latter.

Anyway, that is just a small sampling of the way the world of work went back in that other time. There were, of course, plenty of furniture factories in Hanover, it being known as the "Furniture Capitol of Canada", but the guys I hung out with and I had sworn sacred oaths not to end up in the factory. We'd heard the stories about fine, young men who'd agreed to work in the factory short term, but then they got addicted to the regular pay cheque and the money flowing in, so they stayed for just a year – and, before they knew it, it was 45 years later and they were old guys and they'd spent their lives in the factory being nothing but an automaton like their fathers were and their fathers before them. There had to be something better and we were going to find it.

I Lose My Virginity

The Sixties are sometimes referred to as the Decade of Love but for yours truly that really wasn't the case. In fact, most of my closest friends and I seemed to have continual problems trying to find the right type of girl – and by that I mean the kind who isn't afraid to drop her drawers and provide a little of the free love we kept hearing all about. Instead, it seemed most of the girls we knew from school, and even most of the dances we attended, were basically good girls, so you knew you might be able to cop a feel, but there was very little chance you were going to get much beyond the proverbial first base – and a home run was almost impossible in those days – at least with most of the girls I was acquainted with.

One night, though, I'd hooked up with a bunch of folks I didn't normally hang with and it was late, likely two or three in the morning, and the guy driving the car we were in announced that he wanted to call it a night and head for home. I was sitting in the back seat beside a fairly attractive young lady who immediately announced that she was 'way too high to possibly consider going home. The guy driving said he had to get some sleep, the others in the car said they'd head for home as well, and that left the girl and I…..it was a warm summer's evening, so I boldly suggested we head for the big, black railway bridge and the old swimming hole that was located there. To my surprise, she agreed. "Yea, let's go down to the old railway bridge," she said.

So, we got dropped in the vicinity and started the walk down through the woods to where the railway tracks were, and again to my surprise, she slipped her fingers between mine and we were holding hands while we were walking. I remember wondering where this chance encounter might lead – she'd pretty well ignored me most of the night, and now she was saying how cool the school paper was and the bands I'd played in and so on and so forth. And the next thing I knew, we were there under the big, black railway bridge and her pants were nowhere to be seen and we were really and actually doing it…. and it seemed to last forever and forever, and she just wanted more and more and I did what I could, but finally collapsed in an exhausted heap, gasping for air, beside her. So that's what everybody got all excited about. And I guessed it had been a grand time, but I think it left both of us feeling awkward and sort of confused – it left me feeling that way for sure. I could have done it again, but I didn't that night…and it would be a while before I did again…. the way I had done it had somehow felt wrong…somehow cheap and wrong. I had trouble even looking at the girl after that…no thought of a relationship…no thought at all….

That Sporting Life…….

I've told you about my illustrious basketball career in high school and how that ended, but there were another couple of noteworthy sporting highlights while at HDHS. When I first entered high school, the place was fairly dripping with school spirit….we had a winning football team, lots of great looking cheerleaders, an all-girls bugle band and lots of spirity-type things going on at the school. But, for some reason, whether it was the times, or whether it was just my particular cohort, school spirit dwindled steadily as I passed along through secondary school, so that by the time I was in my last couple of years, there was a definite dearth of spirity-type stuff. But the school always had an annual track meet where all the jocks went out to bash each other's brains out in an assortment of track and field events, all trying to earn their way to the district track meet – mainly because it meant a full day off school with minimal supervision. Anyway, as school spirit started to wane at HDHS in the late Sixties and early Seventies, people stopped volunteering to participate in the school track meet…..I mean, you got a day off school to attend the local track meet anyway….why bother to work up a sweat while you were enjoying it.

So, the school started to come up with ways to encourage us to get involved in the track meet. And one of the first ways they did this was by holding mini track meets in all of the gym classes, the idea being that if you finished well in gym class, you were off to the school track meet. It was sort of like conscripted involvement because who knew when you might be lucky enough – or unfortunate enough – to do well in an event in gym class. The first time we did this in my gym class was for the 100-yard dash. And, so, we all lined up in our starting positions and there was Mr. Heaney, our teacher, standing with his starter's pistol. We got into the ready position…."On your marks," said Mr. Heaney…."Ready, set……" And he fired the pistol and you know what happened? Nobody moved. We were all frozen in the start position, and we were all reasoning that it wouldn't be wise to break out of the blocks too fast if your heart was set on losing. So, when Mr. Heaney fired his pistol, nobody moved…..and he was more than mildly pissed off….but such was life back in that other time.

Another year, they tried putting up sign-up sheets in the gym for each event and if you were so inclined, you could sign yourself up, and compete at will. Anyway, about five minutes before the sheets were to be gathered up, a so-called friend of mine decided to play a bit of a joke on me. He took his trusty ballpoint pen and signed me up for every single event at the track meet. And, of course, the reason he did this and the reason it was such a joke was because I was likely the most unathletic student in the whole of the school. And it was a good joke, because while my friends were enjoying their day off school to attend the track meet, I was mostly hiding out, and trying not to be seen, because they were announcing my name over the loud speaker for every single event, so my name was constantly booming out over the fairgrounds where the big meet was held. And I was none too happy, but my buddies got a great laugh out of it. I, however, sort of had the last laugh. It seemed that I was the only one who "signed up" for the senior pole vault event, and I sort of won it without even having to participate. And the result of that was a day off school to attend the district track meet in Owen Sound. I went to get the day off school, but I never did actually jump.....and that was a good thing because the only thing they used for padding in those days was a little sawdust sprinkled in the pit. You've gotta be nuts to pole vault under those conditions, and, at this point in my brief life, I simply wasn't that nuts. That came later.....

I was clearly not a great athlete while I was in high school. I remember finishing my one-mile run for the big cross country challenge during Canada's Centennial year, then pulling out my cigarettes to have a smoke at the finish line. And I remember my introduction to high school gymnastics.....I took one look at the pommel horse and the high bar and the uneven bars and all that crap, and I just sort of refused to do it. Through Grade 9 gymnastics, I sat on a bench along the wall and watched my classmates absolutely destroy themselves. Mr. Heaney told me I was going to get a zero for that part of my phys ed mark. Oh well, I told him. And you know what, by the end of Grade 12, most of the class were sitting along the wall with me – all having been injured in various ways through the years and deciding that maybe I wasn't as dumb as I looked.

No, I wasn't the greatest of athletes while in high school. It was kind of like a total waste of my time, but I toughed some stuff out nonetheless, and most of it ended up being mostly funny.

The Big Bush Parties in Elmwood......

At one point during high school, Glen's Dad bought a piece of property that sort of surrounded the village of Elmwood – a few miles up the road from Hanover. There was nothing on the property, it was mostly bush and had a stream flowing through it and it quickly became one of Glen's and my favourite places to hang out.....If you walked back into the bush and came to the stream there was a kind of natural swimming hole and a type of clearing that just seemed perfect for hanging out on hot summer days. It became in some ways a special place for Glen and me and I remember us going there to smoke some hash the morning we found out one of our close friends had ended her own life. It was a quiet place to smoke and contemplate. Glen would tell me years later that he thought he finally figured out why she did it, but it was hard for us to understand at the time.

Anyway, our special place wasn't always a quiet place to smoke and contemplate. In fact, it wasn't long before we'd hauled a generator back into the woods, and soon there were lights and speakers strung through the trees and a pretty excellent party place had been constructed. And so started the Elmwood bush parties. And I'll tell you that today's kids think they know how to throw a great bush party, but the ones in Elmwood were, I must admit, rather spectacular in their own right. Usually, there'd be 30-40 cars parked along the highway just on the north edge of the village, but not a person to be seen. Because it was pretty well impossible to approach the party spot in the dark, there being a rather large grove of hawthorn trees with three-inch thorns on them between the highway and the aforementioned party spot. That meant that if you were going there to party, you went in before dark and you didn't come back out until it was light in the morning.

Of course, all the cars parked along the side of the road attracted the attention of our good friends in blue. In fact, almost everything we did back in those days attracted the attention of the police, so it was no great surprise that they were soon tuned into the bush parties. I was at a couple of parties where the police tried to catch us doing something illegal – which, of course, most of us were.

On the first occasion, the police tried to raid the party as it was actually happening – they tried coming back through the bush and the hawthorns. Someone at the party first heard them crashing around and gave us early warning, so Glen killed the generator and the whole party got suddenly extremely quiet. And it was fun and games for the police, who didn't know exactly where we were, and were soon heard cursing and crying out as they encountered the hawthorn trees. It was a pretty amusing scene and we could see their flashlights jumping about through the bush, but they never did find us and finally ended up giving up and retreating back to the road......we continued to party on and had a good laugh at the long arm of the law that night.....

The other time I remember was when they tried an entirely new strategy. The party ended one morning at first light – about five, I think, because the sun was just starting to shed a little light on the situation. We all headed out of the bush at about the same time, and when we reached the cars, we discovered something extremely odd – every single car had exactly one flat tire – and that's no lie. So there were a huge number of very upset hippies standing on the side of the road scratching their heads. And it was about this time that a convoy of police vehicles came rolling up the road and pulled to a stop. "What's the problem?" asked one of the officers. We grumbled away about the flat tires. "I wonder how that could have happened," he said. We, of course, didn't wonder at all….we knew the boys in blue had played a part in our misfortune. And what unfolded was a most comic scene as the police offered to help us change our tires, and soon there were hippies and police wandering around the side of the road with tire irons and jacks and I saw a couple of the hippies wearing police hats and it was madness and mayhem for the next hour or so. And nobody got busted and it was actually kind of a friendly encounter.

The bush parties went on for several years and were a wonderfully wild time….eventually, Glen's Dad built a house on the property and he and Glen's mom retired out there after they sold the Queen's and retired. I remember going back out there a couple of times when we were considerably older, and Glen and I were even married and had our wives along – I could almost hear the sounds of the ghosts of the hippies, and of the police thrashing through the hawthorns, as we sat in quiet and contemplated life once more. Life seemed like forever back then, but I could already sense that some things were changing, and that we were sort of growing up.

The Great Hippie Road Hockey Games......

I really can't describe to you the sort of magic feeling that happened during the late 1960's and the early 1970's among a whole generation of young people. When you saw other kids dressed like you were, with long hair, drag-in-the-dirt bell bottoms, just a certain demeanour, you knew they were a friend – or a brother or sister. You shot them the peace sign and if it was returned, you were tight. It didn't matter where you were or who you were, if you were one of the beautiful people you were just sort of accepted. And yet you were persecuted by most others in society….the police, your teachers, most older folks, the greasers and pretty well everybody who didn't look like a hippie. So that we really did hang out together. We hitchhiked from small town to small town up around Hanover and got to know kids from all over the area. It was an extremely cool time to be a young guy like me.

We really used to like to hold group activities, big parties, dances and stuff like that. So, when somebody suggested we hold a road hockey game one Christmas, everybody was on board from the start. We decided on two teams, the Hanover Hippies and the Harriston Heads, and that they would battle for hippie road hockey supremacy, with the game being held on Boxing Day, in a quiet residential area in Hanover known as Pinewood Park. So, on the aforementioned date, just a whole army of area hippies descended on the stated location for the game, and pretty well filled the neighbourhood. We formed up our teams, and in finest road hockey tradition, we fashioned goal posts out of lumps of snow, and, before you could say "see the hippies play road hockey", the hippies were indeed playing road hockey, and the action was fierce and raged up and down the street.

The people who lived in Pinewood Park were, of course, completely amazed to see their normally quiet neighbourhood so invaded. Soon, they were all standing in the big picture windows at the front of their houses, looking out in disbelief. It was likely one of them that called Hanover's finest, because it wasn't long before the boys in blues made a couple of passes through the park…..we'd all politely step to the side of the road and wave to the officers while the police car glided through our playing area – they likely ran over our goal posts, but I'm not sure of that, so I shouldn't spread unfounded rumours.

Anyway, the game was played out before a large audience – some of the girls even became impromptu cheerleaders – and the Hanover Hippies prevailed that first year. But the really cool thing that first year was that the game was followed by a dance at the Coliseum featuring the area's favourite hippie band, Naval. So, of course, we all headed there for the victory celebrations, because, of course, there were no real losers, except perhaps the rest of society.

And we phoned the score of the game in to CKNX TV sports, and someone brought an old black and white TV, and when the sports news came on near midnight, we turned the TV up and held a microphone next to its tiny speaker, the whole dance got really quiet and we listened for our score to be announced. And it actually was…..Johnny Brent, CKNX's legendary sports-caster back in those days read it out…."And in world championship road hockey action, the Hanover Hippies have defeated the Harriston Heads by a score of 7-6….strange names for hockey teams, eh, John?" He made that last comment to CKNX's legendary newscaster of the era, John Strong.

The road hockey games continued on for several years after that and became sort of an annual hippie tradition on Boxing Day each year – usually with a dance following. Until the hippies just sort of disappeared…grew up and moved away….got jobs…..had families, got responsible….whatever happened to them back in that other time. But it was real special while it lasted and I could go on and on about the good times we had and how much we've lost as people since those glorious days of old…..

The Grade 13 Common Room……

When I entered my first year of Grade 13 – I took the two-year plan for my senior year – there was a real feeling that young people were going to take over the world. There was even a feeling of empowerment for the youth of Hanover and at John Diefenbaker Secondary School. The senior students at the school had been lobbying for a place where they could hang out in the school when they had spares and other downtime. And low and behold, the next thing we knew the administration at the school announced that a Grade 13 Common Room would be created and it would indeed provide said space for hanging out. We brought in a couple of couches and a record player and a couple of lamps and we were all set.

Problem was that hanging out soon included playing poker, drinking, smoking and doing other untoward stuff which the administration, for some strange reason, didn't seem to expect. I wasn't really a poker player at this point in my life – at least not in the Common Room – but spent endless hours playing Bridge and other games with my fellow students. It was huge fun and sometimes when we'd get some really good cards going, we'd stay late into the night when no one knew we were there. We'd put pillows from the couch under the door so the light from the room wouldn't leak out into the hallway and we'd be quiet for an hour or so after school until everyone had cleared out and then we had the place all to ourselves.

Also during that year, the school staff wanted to do something to lift school spirit at JDSS. You gotta remember that this was the early seventies and there was sort of widespread apathy toward stuff like school clubs and sports and that sort of thing. So, they organized the "House" system. And under the House system, all the students at the school were divided into six "Houses" or sections and each House was given a different colour and the idea was that we'd sort of compete against each other and each try to be the best House. And we'd have these big House meetings to try to ramp us all up into doing spirit type stuff around the school. Of course, it didn't work at all – and one of the reasons it didn't work was because the Houses were all led by senior students like me.

And, one day, there was a big House meeting called for the activity period that was held each day after classes had finished. And, as it turned out, four of the six House Captains – of which I was one – failed to show up for the big meeting. And that was because we were all in the Grade 13 Common Room having huge amounts of great fun. So, when the door to the Common Room swung open and Principal R.A. Crawford burst through the door, we were caught dead to rights. All four of the missing House Captains were in the Common Room and it wasn't a particularly good scene. We were all relieved of our Captaincy and there was a general shakeup of the whole affair. It was okay with me – I didn't want to be a House Captain anyway.....

I Fall in Love Again.....

When I started my supposed final year of high school, I became friends with a girl I'd known for most of my life, but had never really noticed – except for the time she beat me up in Confirmation Class. I quickly fell totally and completely under her spell and she would haunt me for the next two decades. She also showed considerable interest in me and things were going okay.

There was, however, a major problem with our relationship – she had a steady boyfriend – and he was a big tough ox of a guy who liked to beat up people – especially hippies. So every time I was with the girl of my dreams, my life was in considerable danger. The boyfriend knew about me but was told by the girl not to beat me up or she'd dump him. Still, it was a precarious arrangement for a young man of peace like me.

But my infatuation with the girl was such that I couldn't pull myself away from her. I took every chance I had to try to be close to her. We became Bridge partners in the Common Room – I'd walk her home from school, meet her after she finished her parttime job at the town library, and, generally, try to be everywhere she was – and he wasn't. I loved that girl for all she was worth and we spent quite a bit of excellent time together, but I could never persuade her to drop the boyfriend once and for all, so I was pretty much the "other man" in the arrangement. When we finished school, she went off to university and I didn't and that ended it. Still, she haunted my dreams and was part of my life for the next 20 years. I worshipped her and could not get over her. But it was not to be and it never was. In the end, she lived her life and I lived mine. But I've always wondered what could have been.

The Hall of Balls…….

I first started to shoot pool when I started to hang out in Neustadt. You couldn't get into the Hanover Pool Room until you were 16, and it was fairly strictly enforced by the proprietors, Ken and Stogie, the latter named for the rather large stogies he was always puffing….a stogie being a cigar, in case you didn't know. So, by the time I was old enough to get into the Hanover Pool Room, I could already play the game of pool a bit. But it was in Hanover where I honed my skills. Nearly all of the guys I hung out with were part of the pool room gang and we went there pretty well every night after school and again on Saturdays and we played pool, Boston and snooker mostly, until the cows came home. And you've gotta understand that in those days pool rooms were considered to be dens of iniquity, and not a single woman in town would be caught dead in the place. And it's true that the air was always blue and thick with smoke, and there was plenty of cursing and there might even be a bottle of whiskey in the toilet's water closet. Ah, those were the days when the pool room was totally and completely a male preserve. And we loved that environment and soaked up the ambience at every opportunity. Put simply, I loved the pool room.

And there was a definite hierarchy in the pool room and it was sort of based on age, but it was more based on your level of skill. Even though there were no real rules about it, it was just sort of taken for granted that the better shot you were, the closer to the front of the pool room you played, so the very best players – who were usually the older guys – played on the very front table. And the lousier shot you were, the further back you played, so that when you first started playing, you were usually stuck on the Boston tables at the back, and the better you got the more you moved closer to the front.

And, as soon as you were able, you made your way up to the big snooker tables, and you usually started to play for money. Because in addition to the smoking, swearing and drinking, poolrooms were notorious places for gambling. There was lots of snooker played for cash, and, in fact, there was gambling on every game played, but the biggest deal was card pool. I was in many a raging game of card pool over the years I hung out at the poolroom and some of them were for some serious cash. And the games would go from noon until eight or nine at night, with no break. And we'd eat the crappy sandwiches they had there, or we'd cram ourselves with chips and Joe Louis and all sorts of evil stuff. And we'd drink heavily and smoke lots of drugs and it was just a really good way to pass the time.

To say I loved the pool room and that I miss it to this day would be an understatement. If there was some way to travel back in time to some place in your past, my choice would be for the Hanover Pool Room in all its glory. Oh, to see Ken and Stogie there behind the counter again, shooing the young guys out of the magazine stand's skin books, or warning the guys in the back that they were getting too loud and disorderly – to see the boys like Archie Pow and Bill Pentland and Tom Doersam and the rest of the old guys who were such amazing shots and always played on the front table.....It was one of the finest times in my life and one I have nothing but fond memories for. All that came after and all that came before were okay, but my days in the pool room were the most wonderful of times.

Streetwatchin'........

And back during the pool room days, my buddies and I sort of invented a new sport – and even though we never really gave it a name, in later years, I took to calling it streetwatchin'....because it involved nothing more than sitting on the pool room steps or on the benches that were built into the front of the Bank of Montreal, or perhaps on the steps of another storefront or two, and watching what was happening on the street. And Hanover has always had an extremely busy main street with lots of action and stuff to watch. And we'd sit there for hours on end – and Stogie and Ken tried to keep us off the pool room steps, but usually failed, and Don Neilson, the lawyer, brandished a for real gun at us one day, so exasperated did he become at trying to keep the hippies and other assorted vagrants off his front step. Really, though, it was a wonderful way to pass the time and I learned a lot in those days, just from watching life pass me by on the main street of Hanover, the home of my youth....

Of course, the best time to streetwatch was right after school during the spring and fall. All the girls from high school would be walking home and they'd use the main street and it was great just sitting there and ogling them. In fact, once the girls got tired of being ogled, most of them would cross the street and make their pass by on the opposite side of the street from the pool room, so, eventually, there were very few of them that actually passed up our side of the street. In the winter, when we weren't playing pool, we spent a lot of time standing in the pool room's big storefront-style window, watching life pass by from that vantage point. Anyway, streetwatchin' was an important part of life there for a while, and most of my friends played as well. Today, when I visit the old home town, I never see anyone just sort of hanging out on the main street, and, I suppose, people just don't do that sort of thing anymore. And the merchants and police are likely happy about it. In fact, they've even put up iron grates across the built-in benches at the Bank of Montreal so you actually cannot sit there – so even the old guys in town are discouraged from sitting around chewing on the latest news of the day in a public spot – unless I guess they do it at Tim Horton's or McDonalds....and that seems a shame, but is better for business.

Paul's Grill and Tea Room.......

When I got into my senior years in high school, there was a new hang-out spot that opened to me and my friends…..it was a 1920's-style restaurant, almost across the street from the pool room, called Paul's Grill and Tea Room, and it was owned and operated by an old Chinese guy, Paul Lum, and his wife, whose name seemed to be "Horny" – or at least that's what all the high school kids called her – much to our amusement. Now, the interesting thing about Paul's Grill was that I never knew anybody to actually eat there. Absolutely the only people who frequented Paul's when I was a young guy were high school kids – and the only thing they usually bought was pop and chips. My Dad said people ate there all the time when he was a young guy and that Paul had made the best Western sandwich in town at one time. But, gradually, as Paul and Horny got older, the restaurant just sort of stopped serving food….

And it was rumoured that Paul was extremely rich from playing the stock market. And it was true that every day at four o'clock in the afternoon, a whole restaurant full of noisy high school kids would get totally and completely quiet for about five minutes so Paul could listen to the stock market reports on a radio he'd pull out from under the counter, and once in a while, he brought out fairly giant dividend cheques that he got in the mail. And, in the end, when he finally retired and sold the restaurant, the big story in town was that his kids bought him a seat on the Toronto Stock Exchange – whatever that means – as a retirement gift. No clue whether it was a true story or not but it seemed like a good one at the time and I've kept it in my mind ever since.

Paul's had been built in the 1920's, and it had never been refurbished. It had the giant soda fountain sweeping down the one side of the place, with the expected stools all along it, and there were even soda taps behind the counter, and, I think there was a big mirror back behind, but I'm not sure. The floor was a checkerboard of black and white squares, high-back booths lined the side of the restaurant opposite the counter and there was this excellent jukebox sitting right in the middle of the floor. Indeed, I heard many of the era's big songs on that jukebox before I heard them anywhere else. Then, near the end of the restaurant's life, it seemed Paul lost interest in keeping the jukebox current, so it stayed frozen in time there for a quite a while. Paul's was one of the magic places of my youth, for sure. It was where I hung out when I wasn't shooting pool or streetwatchin'. I will forever miss it and feel sad for today's young people who will never know or enjoy such a place of beauty as an after-school hang-out.

Working at the Queen's.....

When I was in my final year of high school, and just as I was finishing up, I only had one class a day and it was in the afternoon. Glen's Dad was looking for someone to clean the hotel beverage rooms in the mornings. Next thing I knew, I was the janitor at the Queen's Hotel. And this was during a time when I was having a lot of fun in my life and staying out 'til all hours of the night and generally partying my ass off. Job started at 6:00 a.m six days a week. That meant very little sleep some nights, but it was okay with me. I worked about 30 hours a week and received $42 for my troubles and I had sort of a lot of money for a young guy. I wasted pretty well all of it, but had fun doing it.

The job was not really all that pleasant and was one of those examples that people will do just about anything for money.....and the worst part of the job was cleaning the washrooms – holy crap were they a mess after playing host to a bunch of extreme drunks the night before. I usually did them first just to get them over with – and I was still half asleep at that point so it was more tolerable.

But some of the stuff I found in the washrooms was spectacular to say the least. Like one morning I came to work and decided to start in the Men's Room. As soon as I opened the door, I knew there was a problem. The smell in the place was so terribly rank that I couldn't even get into the room without retching. I went and fetched a can of Lysol spray, pulled my T-shirt up over my nose and in I went, spraying the Lysol in front of me as I proceeded. It was bad work. I opened the first stall and everything looked okay. I opened the second stall door and it was like....Aaaaahhhhhhh! Some guy had made a hell of a mess of the place and seemingly tried to stuff his totally messy trousers and undershorts down the toilet. Yikes!

I managed to gingerly fish the clothes out of the toilet, but the damned thing was really plugged up tight. So, I retreated and got the hotel plunger, then back into the washroom with the Lysol and plunger. I went directly to the plugged toilet and started plunging away like a mad fool. All of a sudden, the blockage let loose, and with a huge gurgling sound, the toilet cleared. Wow, that wasn't so bad. Then, suddenly, I heard another gurgling sound over in the direction of the bank of urinals on the other side of the room. I looked over and the whole accursed mess that I had just plunged down the toilets had come pouring back up the urinals.....yikes, indeed! I did what any respectable janitor would do.....I went over and plunged the urinals like a mad fool....and understand that the odour in the place was getting worse and worse, so rank I could only stay in the room for brief periods of time before I'd start gagging and retching.

When I plunged the urinals, the mess again went down with a gurgling noise and I thought maybe the problem was solved. Then, however, there was the now familiar gurgling sound again, this time coming from the toilets. You guessed it. When I plunged the toilets, it came up the urinals – when I plunged the urinals, it came back up the toilets. I was clearly overmatched by the whole situation. Time to call for the hotel's actual maintenance man. He grabbed up some wrenches and said he'd head to the basement to see if he could unplug it from there. The next time I saw him, he was soaking wet, covered in excrement and cursing like an old sailor. But the blockage was cleared.

Anyway, that's how it went during my job at the Queen's. It was good money but it was fraught with danger on a regular basis. Still, I learned another valuable lesson from the experience and that was that people will indeed do almost anything for money. Even I was proof of that.

I go on the straight and narrow

Back near the end of high school, I started feeling guilty about the pace of the partying that had been going on lately. I'd been drinking pretty regularly and I was still puffing away and it was all getting to be a little much. So, I quit doing everything. I decided it was time for a good cleanse and I went totally on the straight and narrow. And it was a tough thing to do in the circles I was travelling in back in that other time. I was completely and totally surrounded by a lot of people who were massive partiers, and it was hard going trying to stay in those circles when you were both straight and sober.

Still, it seemed like a good choice for me at the time. And I was to never drink alcohol again. The drinking age dropped to 18 the summer I was 18, so I can safely say that I've never had a legal drink in a hotel. I remember going to the Queen's the day the age dropped, but I only looked on as my buddies downed draft after draft and got fairly drunk. I went home that night stone cold sober and I hung in there with the drinking. In the years ahead, friends and associates would try pretty well anything to try to get me to take a drink....but I held out.

At the end of this straight and sober stretch, I'd end up in an Ontario Hospital, where they took away my belt and my razor blades, but that's another story....another story, for sure.

The Great Hitchhiking Odyssey.....

So it happened that a couple of days before the actual end of my high school career, I was sitting on the school's back campus contemplating life with my good friend, Jim. And this was 1971 and most young people in the world seemed to be out on the highways and byways of the country. Indeed, for a few years there, tens of thousands of young people started hitching around to see if they could somehow find themselves – whatever that meant. It was sort of the hippie thing to do. So, when Jim suggested we go hitchhiking around the country when school ended in a couple of days, I was completely ready to agree to such a venture.

The first thing Jim and I did was travel to Toronto to get some proper supplies for the trip – and that meant a World War II surplus army poncho – pretty well the neatest piece of gear to be developed in wartime. These ponchos were the perfect accessory for hitchhiking around the country..... if you were caught in a downpour while stranded on the side of the road, you pulled it over your head, sat cross-legged on the ground and spread it out like a great big old tent all around you and you were dry as you might like. So, we grabbed a couple of these at the huge Army/Navy Store on Yonge Street, before taking in Woody Allen's new movie, Bananas, at a downtown cinema – laughed my ass off during that one. Great movie for a couple of buddies getting ready to hit the road. It was very On the Roadish......

We headed out on a bright sunny day at the end of June. I had on a big backpack containing a change of clothes, a few cans of food I'd managed to sneak out of my Mom's cupboards, a can of tobacco, some Export rolling papers and I had two bucks in cash as well. Jim had about the same type of stuff and about the same amount of cash. We headed south toward Toronto and that metropolis. Our first major stop was planned for Ottawa and it took us about two days to get there. We hitchhiked down the 401 which was forbidden, so whenever we saw anything resembling a police car, we dove into the ditch and hid for all we were worth.

We'd planned to spend a couple of days in Ottawa, so we did, spending our time hanging out with the other beautiful people we'd met and panhandling for change in the Sparks Street Mall. Everybody was panhandling everywhere so it was tough to actually get much cash, but occasionally someone would come up with enough for a pack of smokes or something to eat, and after the purchase was made, the product was immediately shared around among everyone within range. Jim and I bought a pack of smokes with our loot once, we each took out a cigarette, passed the pack on and that was the last we saw of it – that's just sort of the way it went back in those days. At night, we slept in a park in the very shadow of the Parliament Buildings. It was a strange and wonderful time to be lying there under the stars at the seat of our democracy with all those other young people. It was probably the closest I'd ever get to being a real hippie. On the road with my buddy.

When we went to move on, we made for the TransCanada Highway, and were going to make our way to Thunder Bay and maybe then out West. The way things went back in those olden days was that you had no real plan – you just made it up as you went along and that's what we did. When we got to the edge of Ottawa and onto the TransCanada, there were literally hundreds of other kids there with the same idea. So, we headed to the end of the line of hitchhikers and waited our turn. It took us about three days to get to the head of the line, to the point where we could actually start hitchhiking, and we'd been sleeping by the side of the road and had nothing to eat. Our objective that day was North Bay and it should have been easily reachable in one day. But there were so many people out hitching and we ended up getting a series of short rides so that after 10 hours on the road, we were only about halfway – standing on the edge of the highway in Deep River as night was falling and the black flies were moving in.

There were likely about 30 of us stuck in Deep River for the night and we were tired and hungry and dirty and, generally, miserable at our plight. But, then, someone spotted a line of vehicles coming from town and heading in our direction up the road. At first, we were a bit worried having seen Easy Rider, but it turned out that the vehicles that were approaching were townspeople coming to do a great kindness. In fact, they picked us all up, and drove us back to their homes in Deep River. Jim and I were picked up by an old guy, a widower, who took us back to his home, let us shower and fed us a huge and wonderful dinner. And every single one of the young people stranded out on the highway received the same treatment.

Then, we were invited to spend the night in his basement before he'd feed us breakfast and take us back out to the highway. We asked him why in the world the townspeople would welcome a bunch of scruffy, dirty, hungry vagrants into their homes – even for a night. "We have kids of our own who are out on the road," he answered, "and we hope others would show them a similar kindness." And the people of Deep River shared their homes with young hitchhikers each and every night for several years….it was an experience that forever made me hopeful about the future of humankind……the only bad part of the experience was that when we slept in the old man's basement, Jim got the actual couch and I got a sort of loveseat thing that was pretty much 'way too short for me, so my legs hung over the end from the knees down. Also, we were sharing the basement with a Hungarian Sheep Dog which was in the throes of heat so we had to be constantly watching our backs. At one point, I was actually longing for my place in the ditch by the side of the highway.

The old man was good to his word and left us on the side of the highway the next morning – but not until he'd fed us bacon and eggs and even given us a couple of bucks each. We made North Bay that day without any trouble and North Bay was a wonderful place to be for a young person back in those days. It was sort of at the crossroads of Canada, with young people going in all directions, east, west, north and south from it….so there were large numbers of kids in the city all the time and they'd taken this huge, old Catholic church that was right in the middle of downtown, and converted it into a 24-hour drop-in centre, where you could usually get something to eat and drink if you were desperate – and most of us were.

Jim and I were content to stay in North Bay for several days – there was lots of action and an endless supply of super interesting people to meet. I remember one night I was sitting in the drop-in centre with maybe ten or twelve other young people – and they were from all across North America, including this one guy who claimed to have been at Woodstock two years earlier. Anyway, there was this really nice young couple who were travelling together, and they were heading for Vancouver and the Woodstock guy was heading for Alaska, but by the first light of dawn the Woodstock guy had convinced the nice young couple that they'd rather travel with him to Alaska than head for the coast. So, we all headed outside and watched while they loaded up his yellow Volkswagen Beetle and drove out of the church's parking lot looking for adventure and trying to find themselves. To tell you the truth, I thought the Woodstock guy was after the girl part of the nice, young couple, but that's the way it was back in those days. You sort of followed the wind.

On the third day in North Bay where we were sort of not sleeping and also eating only sporadically, Jim had a stroke of luck. He found his life partner – or at least a good-looking young lady for a night or two – and the bonus was that she had a bunch of LSD. Now, I took this trip while I was in my straight and narrow phase, and although it was tempting beyond belief, I turned down the chance to get high. And it wasn't just that I was in my straight and narrow phase that made me turn down the drugs – it was also that I knew I couldn't do such a mind altering substance while in such uncertain terrain…..you needed good vibes to survive acid and I couldn't be sure of that these days. Jim thought he'd died and gone to Heaven and he and girl wasted no time filling their heads with some of the LSD. Soon, they drifted off to do their thing.

I hung around North Bay for a couple more days – there was no sign of Jim and I figured he was shacked up with the girl – or maybe he'd even headed out for points unknown, deciding to trade me in for a softer, more pliable travel partner. Finally, though, I couldn't take it anymore. I was tired and hungry and dirty and miserable for sure. The West no longer beckoned to me. What beckoned to me was a hot bath and a nice, soft bed. So, I decided to head homeward after only about two weeks on the road. Not quite in the odyssey category, but still I'd had a great chance to get a taste of life on the road – and that was what really mattered to me.

About ten at night, I made my way to the big crossroads corner in the city – where you could pretty well go in any direction you wanted – and I started south toward home. By five the next morning, I was still tired, hungry, dirty and miserable and I was sitting on a picnic table in front of the Simcoe County Museum in Barrie, without a car in sight for miles. Then, as I looked up the highway I'd already travelled, I could see a small speck of a person plodding along. I wondered who else would be out travelling at this early hour of the morning.. Well, it was Jim. What can I say? It might be one of the biggest coincidences that's ever happened to me. Jim was burned out from a two-day acid trip and some extreme boy/girl stuff – he was also tired, hungry and dirty, but he was less miserable because of the boy/girl stuff.

So, he joined me on the picnic table. And I had in my possession one can remaining from the food I'd swiped from my mother's cupboard two weeks earlier. And it was Habitant Pea Soup. So, we opened up the can of Habitant pea soup, lit a can of Sterno we'd brought for such occasions , tried to heat it up and then eat it. And let me say that there are few things worse to eat than luke-warm pea soup, which is sort of gritty and really, really horrible, so that even refugees from Western civilization like us couldn't swallow it. It was truly bad stuff.

Then, we sat forlornly on the picnic table and waited until there might be some traffic. And so it happened that the first vehicle to come along the road was a van driven by a hippie guy, and we hollered and yelled at him as he drove by, and he stopped and we were rejoicing that we had a ride. When we asked the hippie guy where he was going, he answered that there was a big music festival happening at a place called Rockhill Park just about an hour down the road from where we'd been stranded. Well, how could we say no? So we headed for the Rockhill Music Festival, which was apparently being billed as the Canadian Woodstock. It's funny what twists and turns life takes while you're just sort of wandering around.

We ended up at the front gates to the park a while later, but, of course, we had a huge problem – we had no money and we had no tickets. And as it turned out, there were large numbers of other young people there in a similar predicament, because everybody was out hitchhiking and everybody was broke. The solution to this problem presented itself shortly. Someone suggested that if we all rushed the gate at once, the couple of security guards there couldn't really catch all of us and throw us all back out. So, that's what we did. About 30-40 of us would rush the gate at once and in the mad confusion that followed most of us would get in – Jim and I both made it on the first try.

Once we were inside the festival, we were, of course, still tired, hungry and dirty and even Jim was starting to get miserable as well. We ended up laying in front of the concession shack, where we could at least smell the food, using our backpacks as very lumpy pillows, sort of half asleep, watching a whole bunch of naked hippies swimming in a tiny pond. Finally, after a couple of hours like this, I turned to Jim and said, "Let's go home, man." And we did. We walked back through the gate where we'd just snuck in and started to hitch for home. We each had a hot bath, a good meal, a good night's sleep, then Jim borrowed his mother's car and we came back to Rockhill in style. And that was the hitchhiking trip. I could have never made it to the West Coast – I'm just not made of tough enough stuff. But the hitchhiking trip was my first real venture into the big wide world, and it worked out okay. It was memorable to say the least….

My Time in the Loony Bin……

I've been frightened for most of my life. Life frightens me. It just does. I'm just that kind of guy that is afraid of pretty well everything and life is one of the really big things, so I'm really afraid of it. But when I was 20-years-old, two years into my being straight and sober, I crashed and burned. I ended up in the Ontario Hospital in Kitchener on suicide watch for a while and that was by far the scariest time in my life. I was having what they called "emotional difficulties" of epic proportions, spiced up a bit by panic attacks, massive outbreaks of vomiting, and other equally wonderful symptoms..... For a while, I passed gas that could have brought a bull elephant to its knees... ..I left my job at the Queen's and was nearly housebound. I could not force myself to get back into life. I'd exhausted quite an array of prescription narcotics and nothing seemed to be helping. My parents and the doctors I was seeing didn't know what to try next.

Finally, I'd sunk so low that they imprisoned me in the Ontario Hospital in Kitchener so I could be watched and kept alive. My Dad took me there, me with my one small suitcase, and I remember sitting in a cafeteria-type place where a couple of guys in white coats, who I assumed were shrinks, got us to fill out a lot of paperwork. Because I was of legal age, I signed the admittance forms myself without realizing what a crucial act it would turn out to be. I remember saying my goodbyes to my Dad and feeling really tiny, very vulnerable and completely alone. A nurse walked me to my room where she relieved me of my belt and safety razor – strangely, she didn't look inside my shaving kit and I didn't offer it up, so I ended up with a whole package of Gillette razor blades which would have done the job nicely if that had been my path.

And the Ontario Hospital was a really weird place. I'd read "One Flew Over the Cuckoo's Nest" a couple of years earlier, and that had been a scary book for me. I knew I had mental health issues and it had frightened me then that I might end up in my own cuckoo's nest. And, now, here I was. The ward I was on was pretty well all young people about my age and several of them had bandages on their wrists, attesting to the seriousness of their disorder. I thought that perhaps the whole ward was full of people interested in killing themselves. And I was apparently one of them. It was a very regimented schedule for the bunch of us loonies. They kept us going from morning 'til night. If you weren't playing bingo, you were going bowling at the alley up the street. And if you weren't bowling or bingoing, you were usually in therapy......by yourself or with a bunch of other crazies. And that was pretty well the scariest time of a very scary time.

Our evenings were sometimes free, and, so on about the third night I was there, I was out walking around the hallways of the place, sort of on a journey of exploration. And I happened upon a lounge-like room, where a few guys were sitting around a TV set watching the hockey game. Now, I was quite a hockey fan and had been since I first watched "Hockey Night in Canada" with my Dad on a tiny, blurry, flickering TV screen at our house at the lake. So, I sashayed right in, grabbed an empty chair and joined in the watching. And it was quite a bit of fun, watching the game with the other guys – they were nearly all Leaf fans and the Leafs were winning on this particular night, so there was a jovial mood in the TV room.

Then, all of a sudden, in rolls this big nurse-type woman and she makes a big announcement. "I'm sorry gentlemen, but we need this room for bingo tonight. Move along now, I'll be back in a minute to set up." And she leaves. And might I say that this was not the kind of announcement you should make to a bunch of Leaf fans on a night the Leafs are winning. "I'm not moving along," said one of the guys. "I'm staying right here and watching the game," said another. "Where does she expect us to move along to?" added a third. And before you could say, let's barricade the door, that's exactly what the guys had done. The door to the room opened inward, so they started piling furniture in front of it, and before too long had quite a pile built up. "Now, let her play bingo in here," muttered one of the guys, who I suspected were all loony tunes in one way or another – and now I was barricaded in the TV/bingo lounge with the lot of them.

Anyway, we settled back in to watch the hockey game, now sitting on the floor, because all of the chairs were in the pile against the door. The nurse, of course, came back in a couple of minutes and was in for a surprise when she tried to push the door open. "Gentlemen, what have you done. This is not allowed," she said angrily.....But no one moved to unbarricade the door. She tried to persuade us to give up peacefully a couple more times, but when it became clear that we weren't budging, she threatened that she was going to get a doctor and he'd get us out of there. "Could you keep it down – we're trying to hear the game," hollered one of the mad Leaf fans. I was thinking this was exactly what happened to the guys in the Cuckoo's Nest book when they wanted to watch the baseball game. Wow! I half expected the nurse had gone to turn on the fog machine and soon we'd all be floating in a dreamlike fog just like in the book.

Of course, there was no fog and a compromise was reached after a couple of doctors had gotten involved in the incident. We did get to watch the rest of the hockey game and the big nurse set up a couple of tables in the far corner of the room and soon had a very quiet bingo game going. Leafs won and the crazy guys and I were happy as larks. I made it back to my bed in one piece and get a big smile on my face these days just at the thought of it.

I met this one guy on the ward and he was a fairly troubled soul. Even though he was likely around my age, he'd been into some serious drugs in his short life, and left himself in bad shape. His parents had put him in the hospital to try to cure him of his habitual drug use. He was pretty crazy for sure....the first time we chatted, he told me he thought they were pumping marijuana smoke through the ventilation system and into his room at night. "They're really messin' with my mind," he said. "They say they're makin' me straight, but they're really just f***in' with my mind." He, of course, wanted to know if they were pumping pot smoke into my room at night as well. I could only wish.

Anyway, a few days later, I ran into this unfortunate soul again. He was leaning on the wall in one of the corridors. I went over to say hello. He looked at me with a total emptiness I've never seen before or since. It was like he was somehow soulless. Drool was dripping from the corner of his mouth into a small puddle on the floor. I tried again to greet him, but he just continued to stare at me blankly with no sign of recognition at all. Another patient, who was passing us in the hallway, came toward me. "He's had electro shock," she said. "They've zapped him again. He'll be like this for a couple of days. Then, he'll get better, but he won't remember."

I backed away from him. I felt my heart start to pump faster and my mouth went dry. Holy crap! Electro shock! I had thought that was only in the movies. I put my arm on his as if to try to soothe him somehow. Then, I left him there. And it was true, I saw him a couple of days later and he seemed fine. We greeted each other again but sort of for the first time – if you catch my drift.

And that's what they did to people in the cuckoo's nest when I was in there. You better be good, or they'll zap you for sure.

The group therapy sessions were the scariest part of the whole experience for me. At one of these, you could be singled out for attack by the group, sort of like if you were a wounded animal or such. And I had that good fortune only once, when I was accused of being afraid to look inside myself to see my true fears and demons. And I admitted as much right from the start and that really seemed to piss off the rest of the group. In the whole psychiatric thing what they want is for you to fight and resist and pretend you're the sanest person on the planet. If you admit right off the bat that you're a complete and total loony – McMurphy's bull goose loony – it really pisses them off. So, that was the angle I played.

There is, however, a potential problem with playing the part of the bull goose loony, and admitting to the group that you have some seriously big bats in your belfry. And that is that your personal shrink starts to think in terms of more radical treatments than playing bingo or going bowling – or even group therapy. And it was after one of the group sessions where I should have kept my mouth shut but instead got into this tangle with a girl who was indeed very messed up and had some real issues. I got a message from the nurse that I was to report to my doctor's office first thing the next morning. I remember thinking this was odd because I had a regular appointment with him the day after. Oh well, I thought, here we go again. This guy had actually asked me if I was breastfed the first time we'd met. Holy crap! What was he thinking? Why would I know something like that?

Anyway, when he mentioned the possibility of giving me a shock treatment – that maybe I could be zapped back to normal – my huge human brain immediately started thinking that this had gone far enough. I wasn't nearly as crazy as most of the other people I'd met in the hospital – even the doctors and rest of the staff. Maybe I wasn't crazy at all. Maybe it was everybody else who was crazy. Gotta get out of this place really fast. No time to lose. They were threatening to zap me – I had to run.

And it was at this point that I remembered the effect pot had on me. Up until the big straight and narrow experiment, I'd been using it to level me out – to relax me and make it possible for me to live a somewhat more normal life. I never got sick when I played in a band if I puffed a little pot before the gig. Also, at this point, it became important that I'd signed my own admission forms – because I'd signed myself in, rather than have a doctor do it, I could seemingly check out at will. When I found this out, I immediately phoned one of my buddies. "Come get me," I told him, "and bring some pot." He did, and the rest is, as they say, history.

And that ended my time in the cuckoo's nest. It changed me forever. It convinced me that everybody's a little crazy, and it also scared the crap out of me and left me knowing that I could never go back to a place like the hospital. And whatever else I've done in life, I've managed that.

I Go Farming…..

Shortly after I got out of the hospital, I fell in with a great group of guys, who were all intent on moving out of their parents' homes and living on their own. Of course, "on their own", really meant with a bunch of other guys who were perhaps interested in doing a little partying. And it happened that one of the boys had chanced on an old farmhouse a few miles outside of Hanover, and, actually sort of close to the police village of Neustadt and another small village, Ayton. It was a great little house with a huge old farm kitchen, reliable heat and running water, so we rented it. And I still remember that there were seven guys in on the house and rent was seventy bucks a month, so it cost each of us about ten dollars a month to live at the place.

It was, of course, party central. Instead of a kitchen table, one of the guys brought a ping pong table. And the next thing you knew, we had a whole bunch of ping pong paddles and were inventing new ways to play table tennis. At most of the parties we held, tons of people would come – all people our age looking for a place to party – and, sooner or later, a giant game of eight-person table tennis would break out…where you'd hit the ball and then run toward the other end of the table, until you had all eight people, running madly around the table, trying to keep the ball in play. It was madness and mayhem, for sure.

Remembering back to the Good Friday party.....

It was a gorgeous Good Friday one year when we were renting the farm. Me and one of my buddies decided it would be a good day to put the stereo speakers in the front windows of the house, get high and stretch out on the front lawn to watch the farmers and their families as they headed for church. And so we carried out that plan. Well, unbeknown to us, three of the other boys were planning their own Good Friday event and it involved bringing three young ladies out to the farm for a BBQ, and, hopefully, some serious nooky.....So, they were none too happy to see us stretched out on the lawn when they arrived. Oh well, we thought, we'll just keep to ourselves and try not to bother them.

Problem was that they started to bother us. We had some good drugs that day, and they had none, so they started to sneak around the house to have the odd puff. Before long, their party was sort of starting to merge with ours. Even the girls were interested in the odd puff, it seemed. Then, another carload of folks rolled in, and then another carload and soon there were a fairly large number of people hanging out, and most of them were in the front yard with us. This put serious pressure on our pot supply and we soon ran out – which normally would have been a disaster, but, just as we were passing the last joint around, someone arrived who had more. And that's the way it went for the whole day and into the night – just when we thought we'd exhausted the last possible supply of pot, in would drive someone else to keep the party going. By the time it was suppertime, there was another obvious problem. There was no food, except what the couples had brought earlier. And it was like the story of the loaves and fishes that night....feeding the five thousand stuff.

Anyway, the party roared into the wee hours of the next morning and was one of the better ones I've ever attended – and it just sort of happened and that's the way things were back in those days. There always seemed to be party, and if one didn't readily present itself, you made one up and everything was good. By the end of the Good Friday party, I somehow ended up with one of the girls who'd come with another guy earlier. He passed out before me, so I got the girl. I vaguely remember being in the back seat of somebody's car driving this girl home at an ungodly hour of the morning. To this day, I don't remember her name and I have no idea where we took her – or who got us there, but it was an adventure just the same....

By noon the next day, there were only the original two of us who'd started the day before's party and we were starving as we rattled around the now empty house. All there was to eat was a jar of peanut butter, and all we could find to eat it with was a fork. Still, it was perhaps the best peanut butter I'd ever tasted – that's how hungry we were.

One of the things we did as a group back in the farm days was watch Saturday night hockey. All seven of us were Maple Leaf fans and it was excellent fun to watch games with a bunch of other fanatic fans, all cheering for the same team. And while we watched, we'd usually turn down the sound on the TV and pump up the stereo – two favourite albums in those days were Uriah Heep's Demons and Wizards and Jethro Tull's Thick as a Brick., and one or both would hit the turntable every Saturday night. Leafs had a really bad team in those days, much like they usually do, so we had to have something else to do besides just watch the game. I remember, one night we were late settling in for the game and we were all pretty high and we got the stereo going and started to watch. And, holy crap, the Leafs scored about four goals in a row and seemed to be totally dominating the play. Then, we realized the game was at intermission and we'd been watching a replay of the only Leaf goal – they were losing 4-1.....but that's the way it was back in those days.

Like one winter's night, after the game, and after we'd listened to a few more tunes and it was about midnight, and someone suggested we head for the Queen's or the Hanover Inn. There was a general consensus, and so six of us piled into this old white Meteor that belonged to one of the boys – three in the front and three in the back – and we were off. We got as far as the Ayton Road – not too far at all – and when our driver applied the brakes at the actual Ayton Road, the car didn't stop and we cruised right on through. Yikes! The car had no brakes! Now, for most people, the trip would be over at that point. They'd have retreated back to the farm and called it a night. But that wouldn't do for us. We needed to get to the hotel, and there were few things that could discourage the boys from making at least last call at one of the local pubs. The lack of brakes wasn't one of them.

But we needed a strategy, and after serious consideration, it was decided that in order to get the car to stop when we needed it to, we'd get going as slow as we could as we approached a stop sign or other impediment, then at a crucial moment, the driver would give the signal and the outside three guys would jump out of the car, and put their shoulders into stopping it, while the driver applied the emergency brake. That should get us stopped, we thought. So, we were carrying on, perhaps a little more cautiously than before, but things were going okay. Then, we were approaching the first required stop, so everybody got ready to carry out the strategy we'd discussed. I wasn't worried because I was in the middle in the front.

So, we approached the stop sign, the car gradually starting to slow down. Then, at just the right moment, the driver gave the signal for the outside guys to jump out. Problem was that only one of them actually tried to jump out to stop the car, while the other guys had apparently realized that the plan was utter foolishness and decided against participating without generally communicating this with everyone. The result was that the car failed to stop and the one guy who'd tried to carry out the plan was nearly run over and killed. Still, the driver did engage the emergency brake and the car did finally stop. Wow! From then on, we kept going, but even more cautiously than before. So, we eventually made it back to Hanover, but as we were approaching the town, we were starting to wonder how we were going to survive the rest of the trip in a brakeless car. "It's okay," said one of the boys. "Just pull into my place and we'll walk the rest of the way." And it was true that he lived partway around the curve on the way into town. We could head for his driveway.

It was winter and there were high snowbanks along the edges of the road, so the driveways were like gaps in a failing set of teeth, and we'd have to manoeuvre into one halfway around a curve. In order to get into Hanover from the direction we were coming, we'd have to climb a big hill – the same hill that had confronted me some years earlier in Glen's old car – then we'd hit the curve and it was a gradual downhill slope all the way around and all the way into town. We climbed Roland's Hill okay and started around the curve. And, of course, as the car rolled around the curve, it got going faster and faster and faster and we had no way to slow it down. The result was that by the time we reached our buddy's driveway, there was no way the driver was going to hit the gap. He cranked the wheel for all he was worth, but he cranked it just a little too soon, so that he missed the entrance to the driveway, and hit the snowbank on the side of the road going 'way too fast. The car went airborne and came down with a tremendous thud, throwing up a huge amount of powdery snow as it did, right in the middle of my friend's front yard, half buried in the white stuff. It was in so deep we couldn't get the doors open when we tried. Once the snow had settled, we all looked up at the house and there was our friend's father standing in the big picture window with his hands on his hips. He just shook his head and walked away. And that's the way it was back in that other time. When brakes weren't really an issue.

Finally, our time at the farm ended. The guy who owned the place had decided to tear down the old house and build a place for his retirement there. When he came around to see us and give us the news, he told us we could have one last party and to do as much damage as possible to the house – he wasn't planning to salvage anything – he was trashing the whole place so we might as well start the work. Don't remember much about that final party, but do remember one of my buddies ripping the toilet clean out of the floor and tossing it out an upstairs window at one point. I guess we tore that place up real good at the end.

My life was starting to move ever more quickly at this point. Most of the guys I'd gone to school with were off at university, while others, like my friend Glen, now had fulltime jobs and were starting families. Things had not gone well for Glen at school and he'd eventually quit to go on the road with a band as its sound and light man. When that ended, he worked at the Queen's for a while behind the bar and I thought he'd end up taking over the place from his Dad. But he wasn't happy there and finally quit. About this time, he met a girl, fell in love and got married. Her father worked for the railroad and that's where Glen ended up at this point in his life.

It was about this time, just as my first farm was ending, that it was time for me to get out my old Kent bass guitar again. Fortune came calling and it was time to take up the life of a musician once more. I'd still been playing and jamming off and on, but hadn't played regularly for a couple of years. Now, the time seemed right….

Life in the Band......the Second Farm.....

So, about this time, right after I moved back home, a guy I knew from my past approached me about playing in a band with him – he was the drummer. I went out to his place for a jam, carrying the old Kent bass in a garbage bag. And it was in his crowded basement that I'd meet the most awesome guitar player I've ever met or played with. We also became friends for life and stayed in touch no matter what life threw at us. He could play any style of guitar imaginable – he was just so incredibly good that over the next number of years, I'd often marvel that he kept me around to play bass for him. But I was really glad that he did because he put together some simply great bands that I was made part of. But this is the story of the first band I played in with him.

We started to practice together, and within a couple of weeks had decided we wanted to be rock stars, and nothing short of that would satisfy us. And we knew some older guys – musicians – and they were getting pretty successful and their formula had been to rent an old farmhouse, live like church mice for a few years, all the while and through all the deprivation, practicing like music maniacs, thinking about nothing else but their music. And we thought if it was good enough for them, why not us? So, almost immediately, we started searching for an old, dilapidated farmhouse to rent so we could start practicing in earnest. And in a relatively short time we'd located one, with a landlord named Gerald, and a real serious garbage problem caused by the previous tenants. We rented it all the same, and then depended on Gerald to clean up the garbage, which, of course, he never did.

We gathered up a few furnishings from friends and family and almost before we could say, "We're gonna be rock stars", we'd set up house out at the old, dilapidated farmhouse, where you were on a party line with seven other people on the telephone, and the sole source of heat in winter was a great, big, old wood furnace with huge ducts and pipes snaked like giant tentacles in every direction in the basement. We didn't really consider either of these factors when we rented the house, but both would become important in due course – the telephone when one of the guys we rented a room to ended up being a minor league drug dealer – and the furnace as soon as the cold weather set in.

And it was November when we rented the house so it was almost immediately cold weather. It was then we first thought about the heat situation. After all, we were musicians and we had instruments that needed heat – let alone us…..in order to keep the huge furnace going, we obviously needed wood. So, this first time, we did the respectable thing – we bought a load of wood from some guy with a bushlot. It was huge pieces of the stuff, and you couldn't just throw it into the furnace and hope that it would burn – you had to somehow get it into smaller pieces that you could light first. Of course, we had no axe because that would have made it easy. So, we took the biggest piece of wood and set it aside. Then, we'd lean the smaller pieces against the wall in the basement and hurl the really, big piece at them, hoping in the process to smash them to bits we could get into the furnace and manage to light. It was harrowing and hard and messy work, but we took turns doing it and we got the home fire burning.

As I was saying earlier, one of the guys who rented a room off us was a minor league drug dealer – nothing too extreme, just a little pot and hash to keep him in spending money. We also had a cat named Leonard at the farm because we reasoned that in an old farmhouse there could be mice. Well, of course, there were mice but Leonard proved to be a failure at this particular aspect of being a cat and couldn't catch a mouse for trying. Until the minor league drug dealer guy hid about a pound of pot in the wood pile in the basement. And the mice decided to have some greens with their cheese. So, they ate the pot, and it instantly blew their tiny brains out and they started to do very weird things. Like one night, we were sitting eating dinner, and, all of a sudden, this very wobbly mouse staggered right down the middle of the table. The mice lost all fear when they were high. And Leonard could finally catch them. And catch them he did, and he left their little heads all over the place as trophies and it was really pretty gross now that I think back on it.

And, well, the pot was pretty well ruined and got all mixed in with wood stuff and mouse crap, so the minor league drug dealer guy gave up on it. And, as it turned out, the guitar player and I were left stranded at the house the next afternoon and we were bored and had nothing to smoke. So, we took the contaminated pile of pot and tried to dig the worst of the mouse shit and wood stuff out of it, then we rolled what was left into about 20 medium-sized joints – which we then smoked. And we didn't really get high, but we both sort of got headaches and had to lay down for a while. Still, we might be the only guys anywhere who've actually smoked mouse shit and lived to tell about it.

Wood became a constant problem. We knew where to get it but we absolutely never had any money – not because the band wasn't playing – in fact, we were fairly busy. But we were spending all of our money on smoke-able drugs and music gear – both of which we could never get enough of in those days. It seemed like the coldest winter since '06, and we were constantly trying to keep the old house warm. We brought in about five electric space heaters for the practice room and we got one of those brown oil stoves for the kitchen, so at least there were a couple of sort of warm rooms in the house. But in the rest of the place, we mainly just froze our asses off. Very occasionally, we did manage to get some real wood and that was welcome, but it just wasn't adequate.

One night, it was particularly cold outside, a huge storm was blowing, and we were sitting in the living room, trying to watch the Leaf game without freezing to death. We had our winter coats and gloves on and the blankets from our beds, but we were still mighty cold. You could see our breath crystalize right before your eyes. Suddenly, the guitar player leapt to his feet and exclaimed, "I've got to have some heat. I'm going to die without some heat!" The rest of us asked him where he was going to get heat at nine o'clock on Saturday night in the middle of a snow storm. He didn't seem to care – he was going to get some heat.

So, we climbed into the band van in the middle of the storm and headed out on the backroads around the farm looking for heat. Surprising thing was that we found some. Now, we're not normally vandals and we weren't the kind of guys to cause much trouble, but on this occasion, you sort of have to close your eyes and excuse us. Through the storm, we spotted our heat – it was in the shape of a cedar rail fence that had been erected in front of a bush – why in the world would you ever need a rail fence in front of a bush? Right? So, we proceeded to disassemble a section of the fence and cram it into the back of the van, until the whole thing was stuffed full to the roof. It was too long, too, so we couldn't get the doors closed and it hung out the back. Then, we headed back for the farm.

We threw the cedar rails into the basement, and then headed down to use the giant log to break them up. Of course, the log smashed the cedar to complete smithereens and we were left with all sorts of small, medium and bigger pieces. We jammed a whole bunch of it into the big, old furnace, along with some newspaper, and, before you could say, "I've gotta have some heat", it was about 95 degrees in the house and we were shedding clothes at quite a rate. Yea, it was like being in the Bahamas that night. Totally warm and wonderful. And so we basked in the glow for the rest of the night, heading for bed about 4:00 a.m. Of course, when we woke up the next morning, you could again see your breath when you stuck your head out from under the covers, and there was thick frost on the inside of the windows. Then, we laid in bed, each one of us trying to convince one of the others to get his ass out of bed and start the furnace. That was a usual discussion, held most mornings.

The band was good, but not really what we wanted. We were on a constant hunt for a good vocalist – the guitar player was doing his best but even he realized he was no lead singer – and, hopefully, a keyboard player as well. In the meantime, while we were waiting on other personnel, we morphed into a country band because that was sort of where the money was up in our area......lots of country bars, not so many for rock bands. We knew we were sort of whorin' ourselves out, but, hey, it is what it is. And we were, I think, an awesome country band. We had, of course, a phenomenal guitarist, who could play any country song ever written superbly – including some serious guitar pickin' stuff like Chet Atkins and that type of thing. And you can say what you like about country music fans – they know and appreciate good music when they hear it. We looked a little off for a country band, with the long hair and scruffy sort of hippie look, but that made them love us even more when we did a tune like Okie from Muskogee. Anyway, I think we were a really good country trio. And that's the way we made our money.....

The End of the Kent Bass......

So, sometime during the giggin' we were doing, we were playing at the Hillcrest Hotel in Durham on a Friday night and it was last call. We were doing another country classic and I was standing up close to the front of the stage. All of a sudden, my guitar strap let loose, I failed to catch the guitar, and it fell straight down, missing the edge of the stage and crashing onto the dance floor that was in front of the stage. Yikes! The old Kent bass, which had served me so well, was totally destroyed – annihilated by the fall. Two of the tuning pegs were broken right off and there was considerable other damage as well. It was a disaster. I couldn't even finish the night....

The band sat around forlornly after the gig, sort of crying in our beer. We were booked to play the Hillcrest the following night as well, and, now, I had no guitar. What to do? Well, in those days of my youth, almost anything seemed possible, so when someone suggested that we leave right that moment for Toronto to go bass guitar shopping at Long and McQuade's the next morning, no one thought twice.....so, about six of us piled into the band van and we were off to the big city. Sleep? We'd worry about that later....much later.....don't remember too much about the trip, other than stopping in Brampton at three in the morning for Chinese food.

We hit TO really early in the morning – long before the music store opened – so we headed off onto the back streets of downtown Toronto to try find somewhere off the beaten track where we could perhaps catch a little sleep. And we did find such a place, where there seemed to be no traffic, in a quiet residential neighbourhood, and we parked the van under a big tree to try to sleep. Don't know if you've ever tried to sleep in a van with five other guys who are coming down from being drunk and high – you'd have thought they'd had enough to drink or smoke and that they might just pass out. But such was not the case, and in fact there was nothing but bitching about how uncomfortable it was trying to sleep in a van on a backstreet in Toronto. So, by the time the sun was up, and we were thinking of heading at least in the direction of Long and McQuades, there had been absolutely no sleep for any of us. We were at the store at 8:00 a.m., the moment they opened.

And it was true that I'd been thinking of retiring the old Kent bass for a while now, knowing you couldn't really be a rock star on a fifty-dollar guitar that you carried around in a garbage bag. My favourite bass player at the time was Chris Squire from the prog rock band, Yes – who were also one of my favourite bands. He almost always played a black Rickenbacker bass guitar, so that's what I had my sights on. Now, the magic moment had arrived and I was truly excited that I might actually get such a bass guitar and have it on stage at the Hillcrest in Durham that night. Wow!

Well, not a single Rickenbacker in stock, black or otherwise. Yikes! Supreme disappointment. They'd have a new order in next week. What good would that do? I absolutely had to have a guitar today – I absolutely had to. The sales guy shoved another guitar into my hands. "Try this," he said. "It's a Fender Precision – they're only going to make this for one year – with the swamp ash body and Maple neck. Give it a try." I took the guitar from him, but was extremely disappointed and didn't really care what guitar he'd shoved at me. I half-heartedly played a few bass lines on the Fender. "It'll be fine." That's what I told him. But I really didn't care, so I bought the guitar. Our guitar player also bought a couple of guitars and we bought a bunch more stuff….of course, we had no money, so we charged the whole kit and caboodle. They took our photo and asked for a list of our gigs for the next six months. That's what it took to buy a pile of music gear back in the old days….. and I'm pretty sure we paid the whole damned works off at some point – after refinancing about 12 times.

Anyway, then it was back into the van and heading for farm. As soon as we got there, I thought I should try the new guitar out, so it wouldn't be completely strange to me for the night's gig. I stood up and slung the guitar strap over my shoulder, and got the Fender in place. And it was only then that I realized the guitar strap cut across the neck right at the 12th fret – meaning because I was left-handed and played the guitar upsidedown, I couldn't get to part of the neck – a major problem. We had to fix it like pronto, so I could play it that night, so we moved the strap holder just in behind the neck of the guitar, near the truss rod – no small feat when all you have is a screwdriver and you're dealing with Swamp Ash. I can still remember my buddy sort of standing with all his weight on the screwdriver, trying desperately to get the necessary screw-nail into the wood. But he managed it and we got the guitar sort of fixed. I didn't know then that I was messing with a bass guitar that would one day be worth thousands of dollars and be highly coveted by any bass player who knew his stuff.

The Great Mescaline Escapade......

I really hadn't done any chemical drugs for several years when the Great Mescaline Escapade happened. You'll remember that one of the guys we'd rented a room to in the farmhouse was a sort of minor league drug dealer – he gambled for part of his income and sold soft drugs for the other part. He absolutely always dealt in pot and hash and never in any of the other more serious drugs. Well, back in the old days, there would occasionally be a stretch when there would be absolutely no pot. It was desperate times when that happened. I had, of course, quit drinking, and given up chemical drugs, so when there was no smoke around, there was no buzz for me. And one time the pot was running out, so the minor drug dealer guy took a trip to the city to replenish his supplies. He was gone for most of the day and half the night and when he finally did arrive back at the farm, there was bad news – no smoke to be had anywhere. However – and it turned out to be a big however – he had managed to score a bunch of organic mescaline.

And the party sort of started right at that moment as the boys decided they should "test" the product. I went to bed. I told myself I had zero interest in "testing" the product. When I got up the next morning, the party was still going on – the boys wired to the nines, reeling around, laughing at anything and everything. And the word spread quickly that there were new drugs at the farm and the people started to arrive. By the end of the first day, there was a houseful for sure, and people were getting wasted. I saw some of the folks just taking a soup spoon and dipping it into the giant plastic bag of the stuff and snorting the whole damned thing. It was chaos and mayhem of the highest order – music blaring, people everywhere in various states of disre-pair – total debauchery.

I held out for two days. I stayed mostly in my room – straight and sober as I could be. Finally, though, I couldn't take it. I told myself I'd just ingest a small amount of the drugs so I could "test" it as well. And so began the Great Mescaline Escapade – about two weeks of circus-like activities that raged day and night and from which there was no escape. I don't remember sleeping at all, but I must have – at least a bit. I remember getting our faces painted up with day glow paint and going to a hockey game in Durham – I remember going to the Hanover Inn and somehow stealing a whole set of a table and chairs right out the front door of the place – I remember raging this way and that, reeling sort of out of control through the countryside and just having an unbelievable amount of what seemed like fun at the time.

It was winter when the Great Mescaline Escapade happened. And the thing I remember the best was my walk back through the fields with one of the other guys in the band – there was a good blanket of snow on the ground and the moon was out full and it was just as beautiful and peaceful as it could be. We walked, he and I, and we talked about life and where we wanted to go and where we might end up in the great adventure. We seemed to walk away from the farmhouse for a really long time, and, finally, decided to head back. For me, it was one of those times in my life that I hoped would never end. During that walk, I was somehow at peace with the world and with myself – high as a kite on mescaline, but feeling very content with my life and with who I was…..

As we got closer to the house, there was suddenly a most tantalizing aroma – we stopped for a moment and sniffed about like dogs on a hunt. And there was no denying it – it smelled like somebody was cooking. So, when we got back, a bunch of us sat down at the kitchen table – which was actually a Conservation Authority picnic table we'd borrowed – and we ate a full course chicken dinner cooked up by the minor league drug dealer guy. It was about three in the morning when we enjoyed this feast, but I must say that it was one of the best meals I've ever eaten – truly delicious.

Anyway, it finally ended – we basically consumed the entire supply of organic mescaline, the minor league drug dealer guy went back to the city and this time came back with some smoke and life got back to normal. Whew! It was a tough go there for a while. But it pretty well cured me of doing chemical drugs again. I had 'way too much fun doing that stuff. No more of that…. except for this one time….but that' s another story…..another story, for sure.

I Leave the Band……

We never did find a singer or a keyboard player for the band. We were a great, little country trio, but that's not what we wanted to do. Finally, we'd kind of worn out our welcome at the farm, and there was talk of looking for a new place and trying to make a start fresh. I made the move with the other guys, but I left the band a couple of months later. I borrowed some money off my Dad and paid off my part of the music gear debt, and I moved back home. I was so physically and emotionally exhausted, that I sat in my parents' living room in a big easy chair watching game shows and soaps. Man, I was really and truly burned out. Time to recover and find a real job so I could pay off my Dad and get on with my life. It was hard on me, the time in the band, but it taught me a lot about life and about myself. I'm really glad I did it….gave the band thing a shot. I'd keep on playing for most of the next 50 years, but never again would I make a serious attempt at being a real musician. I didn't think I was good enough…..I'd be a writer, for sure. I'd try to write great literature and just have fun with the music. The die was cast. My life was underway……

I Meet My First Wife…….

About this time, when I was sort of wandering in the wilderness, I met my first wife. She had moved to Hanover from the city to escape a bad relationship, and with her was a tiny young person. I met her through Glen and his wife, and somehow, despite the fact I'm really bad dealing with women, the relationship stuck. We became a thing and I started crashing over at her place as often as I could. I guess I sort of fell in love with both the mother and child, and the next thing I knew there was talk of a wedding. I just sort of got swept along in it. Many of my friends were getting married back in that time, and it just sort of seemed like the thing to do. Plus I really liked the girl and enjoyed having the little guy around, so it really did seem like the thing to do. It would still be a couple of years before I actually tied the knot but that was clearly the path I was on.

I'm a Working Stiff.......

After the band I needed work – real work – so I could get my Dad paid back for helping me buy my way out of the band. Plus, I had a girl now and needed cash to wine and dine her. The first real job I got after the band – and I got this job with Glen, who was, for some reason, not working on the railway right at that moment – was working at the plastics factory in Hanover. It was a smallish type factory where they built plastic-moulded furniture parts for plastic furniture – which was kind of ironic when you consider I'd spent my life trying to avoid working in one of the town's furniture factories, and now I was working in a factory that made fake furniture. A real nightmare for sure, but I was still living at home at the time and Dad would have evicted me if I failed to take a job when it was offered. So, it was off to work in the plastics factory with Glen. The only redeeming feature of the job was that it was supposed to be temporary – only three weeks duration.

So, Glen and I reported for work on a bright, sunny Monday morning and we were rarin' to go – not.....anyway, they put us to work building these mould-type things where the job was sort of like they get babies to do, where they got us to pile these bunch of different shaped pieces together into some-thing that looked like a dining room table leg, which they then coated with plastic and attached to the bottom of what I supposed would be a plastic table – although I'm not sure I've ever seen one of these actual tables. Problem was there was no way I could seem to pile up the pieces in the right order. And we had to staple them together into the dining room table leg, and I could never get them stapled together in the right order – so I was constantly having to try to take them back apart and start over – I wasn't really all that produc-tive at this particular job.....

Glen got bored with it really fast and quickly found a way to amuse him-self. The factory was basically a big steel shed and we were working over on this one side of the building stapling together the fake dining room table legs, then beside us were about three really long tables of women who were assem-bling some type of widget and working merrily away. Well, all of a sudden, and with no actual warning, Glen pointed his big staple gun toward the ceiling and fired a volley of staples straight up and into it, then quickly looked back to his work. And, of course, the staples went up, then came showering down on the women who were working merrily away. The women sort of brushed them aside and looked like they were being bothered by a swarm of bugs…..Glen slyly smiled and winked at me. And this occupied our apparently small minds for quite a while that day.

Glen quit one day shortly after we'd started – he didn't last long. He came into work one morning really dragging his ass after a hard night's drinking. He went outside to his car to "get something" at the morning coffee break and just didn't come back. He'd had enough. It kind of pissed me off that he left me there to cope on my own. I was not keen on this arrangement but when you need money you'll do almost anything – as I'd already learned in my young life.

I had a series of mundane and boring tasks assigned to me over the three weeks in the factory. At most of these jobs, I caused chaos and ruin for the people I worked with so that eventually they got me to do things mostly by myself. I sanded the seams off the giant fake dining room table legs once they were coated with plastic, until I toppled several skids of legs and destroyed most of them in the process. They put me on what I think is called a "radial arm saw" for a while. I was cutting the ends off those ornamental things they put in the tops of bed posts – a sort of decorative touch, I guess, but pretty useless otherwise. Anyway, when I was cutting the ends off these things, some of them would bind in the saw and go shooting off across the factory at near light speed. I'd have to duck and they'd shoot right over my shoulder, so the rest of the workers learned to keep their distance from my work station.

As the three weeks passed and I started to get near the end, I was extremely happy that things were winding down and I assumed the people who ran the factory were equally glad my time working for them was pretty well over. I mean, I had proven that I could screw up nearly every task they had given me, and had perhaps set a new record for the diversity of jobs performed in a three-week temporary job. In any case, it was finally the third Friday and the job was ending that afternoon. Just as I was getting my stuff and getting ready to reclaim my freedom, one of the owners of the factory approached me. "Well, you're all finished today," he said. I replied that I was and thanked him for keeping me on. "We were wondering if you'd like to stay on. We think you could do a good job for us." I just about fainted clean away. And it was then that I learned that the bar is not actually all that high to work some places. Still, I knew I couldn't keep working there for fear someone might die if I did, so for the only time in my working career, I lied and told him I already had another job to go to. I was really sorry, but I was going to have to move on. He offered me a raise, but I still moved on.

And what I moved on to was barn painting. And if the Ontario Hospital is the scariest place I've ever been in my life, then barn painting is the scariest job I've ever had in my life. There's absolutely no doubt about that. My wife-to-be's brother-in-law was a barnpainter guy, and when he heard I was out of work after my adventure in the plastics factory, he suggested I also become a barnpainter guy. I remember thinking, oh, what the heck....I can handle a paint brush as well as the next guy. So, I did indeed become a barnpainter type guy, and it was the scariest couple of months I'd spend in my life. I went to bed every night pretty well convinced that I'd die the next day. It turned out that barn painting wasn't exactly the safest of employments – mainly because the only piece of safety equipment used in the business in those days were rubber boots – and that's no lie. So, to tell the truth, the only time even the rubber boots mattered was when you were up in the stratosphere painting the barn roof. Barn roofs are really, really high......they don't look that high from the road when you're cruisin' by, but, take my word for it – they are really, really high. And there's no even ground around a barn to set a ladder, so your ladder is always wobbling around, or sitting precariously on one leg while you're 40 feet in the air.

It was a wild job where they expected you to grab a 40-foot extension ladder straight out from the barn's wall, and balance it, while you moved it down the wall to the next section in need of paint. The only catch was that the ladder had been used for spray painting for several years and there was about a foot of dried paint on the one end of it, making it seriously top heavy. Try balancing that and carrying it over uneven terrain down 10 feet of barn wall. The other two guys on the crew could do this balancing act with apparent ease, but I'm afraid to say that I had absolutely no talent for the job. Every time I tried to move the ladder, I ended up hurling it sort of like Scottish guys in a wild and out of control caber toss event somewhere. It was a disaster every time I tried it. I just could not get the hang of it.

Before I started barn painting, I had no fear of heights that I was aware of. And, for sure, the first couple of weeks I worked with the crew, everything seemed fine. I clambered around up on barn roofs and scaled any ladder they could throw at me. Then, one day, that all changed. I was on the ground working away, doing one thing or another, when my wife-to-be's brother-in-law, my boss, called down to me to bring him something up to the roof. I immediately turned my attention to it, got the required item and danced up the ladder to bring it to him. When I got to the top of the ladder, I climbed up over the eave and onto the roof and delivered it to him. He thanked me, then turned back to his work, with the understanding that I'd now return to what I'd been doing down on the ground. So, I started to walk back down the barn roof to where the ladder was located. The ladder was, of course, stuffed into the eve of the barn. Problem was I wasn't exactly sure where it was. Next thing you know I'm down on my knees on the edge of the roof, looking down at a pile of rocks forty feet below, and feeling around under the eve with my foot, trying desperately to find a rung on the ladder. The fact that I'm sitting here writing is proof that I found the ladder, but when I managed to reach the ground again, my knees were shaking so bad I could barely stand. So, I sat down and smoked about three cigarettes just to steady my nerves. That had been a close one, for sure, and it ended my career as a heights guy. Since that day, I have been totally unable to go more than a couple of steps up even a stepladder.

So, I was pretty much a failure as a factory worker and barn painter and was starting to wonder just where I belonged in life. Meanwhile, my romance was continuing to chug along and there continued to be all indications that wedding bells would eventually ring for me and my wife-to-be. And it was about this time that I got a job on construction. There was this old guy in Hanover named Stan Dawson and he owned several pieces of property on the main street that he was intent on developing. And Stan had no intention of hiring an actual contractor to do what he wanted done. Instead, he would act as contractor himself, hiring whatever help he needed to do the actual work. The first two people he hired were me and a guy named Leo, who I knew a bit because we'd both grown up in town and you sort of knew everybody in town back in those days. And I found out that Leo was a great guy and we became fast friends working for Stan Dawson. He was one of the oddest people I'd ever meet and also perhaps the most sensitive. Like one night, a bunch of us were out touring in Leo's VW bug, and a rabbit darted up out of the ditch and Leo hit it – there was nothing he could have done to avoid it. Suddenly, it was just there and there was nothing to do but hit it.

Leo jammed on the brakes, causing the car to sort of skid to a stop, and he was out of it in a split second and walking back up the road to see what had happened to the rabbit. We all climbed out and followed him. We came upon the poor beast directly, and there was no question that it was completely and totally dead. Leo fell to his knees and started weeping and wailing over it. He was clearly extremely upset at having killed it. And it took some mighty persuading to get him back into the car and only after I'd promised that I'd drive and I'd take him home. Leo had a great deal of trouble coping with life even back in the old days, so it was really no surprise to me that later in his life he was actually certified as crazy and carried around a doctor's letter which listed the many mental illness issues he was dealing with. I always sort of felt sorry for the guy. Under it all, he was a good sort.

And when I first got to know him at Stan Dawson's building project, I liked him right away. He was a gentle sort of guy who wouldn't harm the proverbial fly. And we worked together well. And Stan would hire actual tradespeople, carpenters and bricklayers and plumbers and electricians and people like that, and Leo and I would do all their grunt work for them. It was sort of a fun job and we built a couple of small office buildings on Hanover's main street, one of which is still there to this day, while the other has been obliterated and replaced by an empty lot.

While I was working on the Dawson projects, I had a fortuitous piece of luck. My buddy, whose Dad owned the GM dealership in town and was building a new building for his business, told him that the construction company doing the work needed a few extra hands to do the big cement pour for the floor of the service area. So, being a good and faithful buddy, he phoned me to see if I wanted to earn some extra cash, and I decided on the spot to take a day off from my existing job and help pour cement. I reported for work on the arranged day at six in the morning, I was assigned a ¾ yard cement buggy, and put to work. We poured cement and I pushed that buggy until about two in the afternoon, and the buggy was so heavy, and I was about 140 pounds soaking wet in those days, that I had to back up and take a run at it to get it moving each time after it was filled with fresh cement. And I did that for eight hours straight with no breaks. At the end of it, I was standing there having a cigarette and the project foreman came over. "You're a hell of a worker," he told me. "I wasn't even sure you'd be able to get that buggy moving when I first saw you this morning. If I get an opening for something full time, I'll give you a call." Yowza! Jackpot! A chance for a real job with an actual construction company. Maybe my future life was calling to me and I'd find my place after all.

My Life as a Construction Worker.....

And I did, indeed, get a job with a real construction company – I was hired on as a fulltime labourer with a company called Thomas Construction and I got a hard hat with their name emblazoned across the front of it the morning I started work. Thomas was a medium sized contractor and specialized in building small to medium sized commercial buildings. No real residential work by these guys. And I must tell you that I learned a lot during my time with Thomas. Most of the other guys who worked for the company were older, likely in their forties, when I look back it now. So, they weren't partiers in the least. They'd work all the day, have supper in the hotel dining room, then play cards in their rooms, and go to bed early. It was pretty boring stuff for me, but life had been a little too exciting for me in recent times, so I was ready for a little slowdown myself. We always had a Portuguese crew that travelled with us and they did the cement work and laid bricks, so I guess you'd call them a masonry crew. They were wild drinkers and party animals, stayed up half the night, then walked along block walls 45 feet in the air at seven the next morning like it was nothing. And their lunches really stunk up the trailer where we ate lunch. Good lord, their food stank.

Anyway, what I really learned when I worked for Thomas was that this was yet another thing I wasn't real good at. I was okay at it because I worked my ass off and really tried hard, and my fellow workers could see that and seemed to like me for it. But I was constantly getting hurt in all sorts of minor ways because I usually did the jobs all sort of assbackward. I'm sure it was fairly comical to watch me work. But I kept at things and refused to be defeated and the other guys admired my spirit. It's sort of funny, actually – you see a building and you think it's just sort of been there forever and it's solid and firm and will never fall down. Then, you work on construction for a while, and you end up being amazed that most buildings get built at all, and then you're double amazed that the damned things stay standing. When you think about it, there are a lot of component parts that go into a building, and with each component part there is the potential for a screw-up. So, there are lots of screw-ups.

Like one day I'm working away, minding my own business, and the foreman approaches…..he proceeds to tell me that somehow we've buried the building's water line under eight feet of rocks and dirt, somewhere along the south wall of the building, but we forgot to mark where it was, so now we have no actual idea where it runs under the wall and enters the building. Someone was needed to dig down eight feet starting at one corner of the south wall and then work his way along it until the water line was located. And, apparently, I was the man for the job. And it was a bit of a bugger of a job, to say the least. But I did it nonetheless and in the process acquired more proof that people will do pretty well anything for money……and I made $4.60 an hour when I started at Thomas – huge money back in the olden days. And it was actually pretty good work for a guy like me, because there wasn't all that much I could screw up just digging a hole with a shovel. And over the course of my life, I've discovered that I'm a pretty good ditchdigger in most instances and really don't mind the work.

So, I worked at Thomas for a while and things were going good. I bought my first Volkswagen Beetle to drive back and forth to work and was pretty much rolling in the dough. Things were continuing to be hot and heavy between me and the wife-to-be, and, me, the guy who'd always sworn never to get married or have kids, was closing in on both. And even though I wasn't likely the greatest thing to come along in the construction business, I did okay and the company ended up offering me an apprenticeship to be a carpenter. But calamity struck while I was thinking over whether I should make a life out of building things. I got injured in a fairly serious way. The foreman asked me to get this huge pile of 16 foot 2x12's up onto the roof of the building we were working on and walked away. The roof was at least 20 feet up, so you couldn't just push the wood up onto it and the only way I could think of to do it was by using my hard hat as a slide to get the huge boards at least partway up. Well, that worked for maybe the first 20 pieces of lumber, then my back started to hurt. After a few more, it was really hurting and it was suddenly getting hard to breath. I managed to complete the job, but was labouring pretty good by the time it was finished.

The job foreman spotted me on the way to my car after work and noticed the difficulty I was in. I had been planning on going home to take a hot bath to perhaps soothe my back somewhat. He had other ideas. He sent me straight over to the hospital for X-Rays, and the rest is – as they say – history. I had managed to slip a vertabrae in my back, and I would never work at a manual labouring job again. I was done with that type of work. It was time for a little re-training. It was time for Worker's Compensation.

My Wasted Year.......

So, I was an injured worker for a while – and it was the biggest waste of time in my life, even including the breakdowns I had, because then there was at least a recovery to be undertaken. There was nothing I could do about my back – I did some back exercises on my own but that was about it. My workers' compensation guy was a World War II vet by the name of Paul Morris, who I was fascinated to learn had fought in the actual battle that the movie, "A Bridge Too Far", was based on. In fact, he was, apparently, one the guys who tried to hold the actual bridge. I've always had a keen interest in the second great war, so this sort of impressed me, that here was a guy who'd actually been in the thick of things at a very desperate time in the history of humanity.

Mr. Morris was a wonderful man who really took an interest in my case – he was especially impressed with how widely read I was, and it was true that I was still reading voraciously, pretty well anything I could get my hands on. And Mr. Morris asked me what I was doing working on construction and did I like it when I was so smart. I told him I liked working on construction because I felt it was honest work and if you put your back into it you actually felt like you were accomplishing something. Well, he told me my construction days were over because of the slipped vertebrae so I'd have to find something else to do with my life. Wasn't there anything else I'd ever considered doing back in the days when I was sort of a scholarly guy. I told him I'd once considered being a teacher in some bygone era, but that I'd abandoned the idea because I didn't really want to go to university.

And the reason I didn't want to go to university was because I liked who I was back at that particular time in my life and it was my belief that university would somehow change the fundamental me – that I would become sort of a different person. If you listen to Supertramp's Logical Song which came out a couple of years after the period I'm writing about, you'll get exactly what I was concerned about.....that somehow I would learn to be "logical", "responsible" – that sort of thing, and it truly frightened me to the bottom of my soul that this could happen to me – and it was the big reason I'd not gone off to seek higher education after high school – even though I was accepted at a couple of schools, even with my paltry Grade 13 marks.

But Mr. Morris explained that I simply had to be re-trained – there was no other option for me. So, I'd better decide what I wanted to be re-trained into, and he said teaching would be a good one – he thought he might be able to sell that one to the Board because I had my Grade 13 – most construction workers, injured and otherwise, drop out of high school after a couple of years, because they're not usually cut out for academic work – much like most academic people aren't usually cut out for building or fixing things – although that's a broad generalization, and I'm not sure it's fair to do that. But, anyway, I did go for the teacher option in the end, and it was a good decision, but it was also a frustrating decision – because it took my case just over a year to wind its way through the officialdom that was the Workmen's Compensation Board, because there weren't really workers in those days as much as there were workmen. And, during that time, I wasn't really allowed to do much of anything or it would jeopardize my standing. I wasn't supposed to lift over 30 pounds, nor was I supposed to do anything that involved a lot of lateral motion. There was no quick fix for my problem and if it got worse, it could have led to a spinal fusion operation – and I wasn't too keen on that prospect.

Strangely, though, when I asked one of the doctors if it would be okay if I shot pool, he told me to go for it unless it seemed to be bothering me. And this was good news because it gave me something to do with the stretch of time off while Mr. Morris convinced the Board that I was an ideal candidate to be turned into a teacher. And it is during this period of my life that I was perhaps the most debauched I ever was in my life. For, although things were still hot and heavy with the wife-to-be and I was becoming more attached to her and her young son with every passing day, it was also one of the most free and most irresponsible times in my life. I had oodles of money because Compensation was basically paying me what I made when I worked on construction – without doing anything.

So, I settled into a routine of card pool, poker and horse races every Saturday night – basically, tons and tons of gambling. And I've got to say that I won more than I lost in those days, but I don't know if it had anything to do with whether or not I was a good card player, or whether it was just because I didn't drink and everybody else would get piss-eyed by about three in the morning. I hung around the pool room in those days for hours on end – always looking for a game – and I got pretty good at the fine art of billiards and won quite a bit of money doing it. Also, it was great fun and the wife-to-be I think was actually glad not to have me kicking around the old farmhouse where we were living – because I was pretty well moved in by this time.

And, as it turned out, once Mr. Morris had convinced the Board to pay for three years university – a basic BA – and a year's Teacher's College, there was one last major hurdle to leap over before all would be well. It turned out that the university of my choice – Guelph – would no longer accept my Grade 13 marks. That meant I had to write something called a Mature Student's Exam to get into the school and be re-trained. And the Mature Student's Exam was six hours of gruelling exam writing – three hours on sort of English stuff and three more hours on sort of science and math stuff. I believed that I could do okay on the English part because I was pretty well read – but I was completely terrified at the prospect of having to deal with science and math stuff for three hours. If you remember, my last couple of years in high school had not been stellar ones…..12 in chemistry….23 in physics….36 in math….

Anyway, to make a long story short, I sweated it out until the date of the exam arrived, then I trundled into a classroom- type of place with a whole lot of other "mature" people and took the exam….Because of the ongoing problems with my nerves or stress or emotions or whatever they were calling it at the time, I was sick as a dog the morning I went to Guelph, with my Dad along for moral support – because that's the kind of guy my Dad was…… I was physically sick the whole time right up until I went in to write…..was totally weak and worn out. But I went at that thing with a vengeance, having convinced myself that if I didn't make the grade for some reason, my life was somehow over. And I did it, you know. Even though I'd been out of the formal education system for over five years at this point, I did okay and passed the exam and gained entrance to the university of Guelph. I was going back to school. I was going to be re-trained. I was going to be a teacher. Or not….

I get married and my life changes forever…….

ASSORTED
SHORT
STORIES

ni

The Bike

We were poor when I was a kid. Not real poor like we couldn't afford food and such. But poor just the same, us kids with patches on the knees of our trousers, and sometimes holes in the bottoms of our shoes before the budget afforded new ones. But it was mostly a happy life, what I remember of it. But that could be because people have a memory for the happy things and try to hide the unhappy ones. And no matter how hard a task that becomes as you grow older, because there's plenty of unhappy stuff'll come your way in this life, no matter how hard you try to hide from it, most of us remember our good times and keep strugglin' on.

I had no bike when I was a kid. My Dad couldn't afford to buy me one. But when I was about ten, I had a stroke of good luck, and was able to talk my way into a job as a paper boy -- a considerable accomplishment for a kid with no bike. And so I trudged my route day after day that first summer -- and I remember most the incredible hotness that dripped down my back as I trudged from house to house to house. And I did my collections and my Dad helped me figure what I owed the newspaper company and what I got to keep for my very own self. And I put that money in a jar over the fridge, and, at first, it was a paltry sum, jingling hopelessly against the side of the jar. But, gradually, the jar started to fill, so that by the middle of the summer, it had grown to what seemed a veritable fortune.

Finally, my Dad and I sat together at the kitchen table for the great counting and my Dad produced some brown papers, the kind he used when he counted the church money on Sundays, and we poured that jar of money out onto the table. We separated the different money into its separate piles for its own kind, and, finally, I was able to put a total on my fortune.

"Eight dollars and twenty-four cents," my Dad announced, offering me a wide smile. "You've worked hard and that's what you've earned."

I said nothing but sat wide-eyed, never having been in possession of even a fraction of such a grand sum of money -- never having had more money than the eighty cents I'd won in the fall fair for the zinnias and marigolds my Mom helped me grow from seed.

"What will you ever do with such a fortune?" asked my mother, who'd just come into the room.

I looked up, not really understanding that the question was directed at me; not realizing that the money was really mine, perhaps guessing that it somehow belonged to the family, the way my Dad's money seemed to.

"It's a lot of money," my Dad confirmed. "And it's yours to do with as you please," he added. "You've earned it."

"It's mine to spend?" I asked, somewhat amazed to have discovered this piece of information.

"Yes," my father answered. "It's yours to spend."

"Wow," was the only word that I could manage.

There was a brief silence, as I began to consider my options.

"I have an idea, though," my Dad finally said, breaking into the dream I'd been having. "I've heard that Mr. Stewart up the street has a used bike for sale. He's asking ten dollars for it. I've seen it and that's about right. We'd have to fix it up a bit, add some paint, but it would make your paper route a lot easier. It would be a good investment for you."

"I don't know how to ride a bike," I said.

"You could learn," answered my father. "It's not that hard. All your friends have bikes."

"It looks hard," I answered, unconvinced at the wisdom of making such a purchase.

"You could do it," chimed in my mother.

"I haven't got enough money," I answered, not quite understanding why I was putting up obstacles to getting a bike, when I knew I really wanted one. It did look hard, but I needed a bike to be one of the crowd. Dad had pushed the right button with that one.

"I'll lend you a couple of dollars," my Dad said. "I think you're a good risk."

"What does that mean?" I asked, knowing little of the matters of money.

"It means I'm pretty sure you'll pay me back," my Dad said, smiling warmly and reaching over and tussling my hair.

And so, after supper that night, my Dad and I trundled off up the street to Mr. Stewart's place. Mr. Stewart was an incredibly old guy, who all the neighbour kids steered clear of, mainly, I think, because he looked so very angry all the time.

"Mr. Stewart's son drowned years back down by the big, black railway bridge," my Dad explained, as we walked the few short blocks to our destination. "It was a very sad thing. His wife never got over it and had to be put away for her nerves." He paused. "He's not angry," Dad said. "He's sad."

I'm not sure why my Dad told me that about Mr. Stewart, but when the old man opened the door to see who was calling, I tried to look more closely at him, to see if I could see the sadness in him. A guy I knew from school drowned a couple of summers ago while we were all at the Sunday School picnic and that was a sad affair to be sure. When the door opened, I still thought the old man looked angry, but now that I look back on it, maybe he had reason to be as angry as he liked, having been dealt such an unfair hand in life.

Anyway, we headed out to his garage, off to the side of the house, and Dad helped him swing open the huge wooden doors. And, there, wedged in alongside a car that clearly had not seen the light of day for many a year, was a bicycle, which, by the look of it, had also spent quite some time in the dark, dankness of the garage.

The old man grabbed hold of it and tugged it from its confinement, dragging it out into the driveway.

I took a quick look at it and saw that it was not one of the sleek, slick bicycles my friends were all riding. It was an old-fashioned thing, with a wide, awkward-looking seat and big, balloon-like tires.

"It's a good bike," old Mr. Stewart was saying. "Hardly been used. Was my son's. Ten dollars is a fair price."

"I think you're right, Mr. Stewart," Dad replied. "What do you think, son?"

It wasn't what I wanted -- I wanted a new bike, something I could brag and swagger about -- and this was definitely not it. My Dad could see my hesitation. He pulled me aside.

"It's old, Dad," I said, quietly, not wanting the old man to overhear.

"We can fix it up," Dad answered. "A coat of paint and she'll be good as new. You'll see."

"We could save some more, Dad," I said, sort of pleading with him.

"You need a bike, son," my Dad said. "It'll make your job so much easier. You can always get a better one later."

I stood in silence, knowing I had lost this argument before it had begun. Dad felt I should have a bike -- this bike -- and I would have a bike -- this bike.

So, we took the bike home and prepared to work on it.

And we did work on it. Dad pretty well disassembled the whole thing, and I got to help with the sanding, and we got out a tub of water and tested the tires for leaks. Dad looked at that awkward-looking seat, and said he'd like to get a new one for me, but there just wasn't money right now, so I'd have to make do. It came to me later in life that if you make do, you're usually stuck with the result.

But the more we worked on the bike, the more my excitement level rose, because, even though this wasn't exactly what I wanted, it was still a bike -- and when you're a ten-year-old kid with no bike, a bike is a bike is a bike. So, I waited impatiently for the day when Dad would announce that we'd made her roadworthy. I did all that was asked of me, sanding, then painting, helping to tighten the nuts and bolts, adding a squirt of oil here and there, until the old bike was verily aglow. As my Dad and I stood back to admire her that day she was finally finished, I was beaming with pride, knowing that Dad was the greatest guy in the world to have carried out such a project. And through all of it, I continued to walk my paper route, just waiting for the day when I'd be able to ride the streets with a carrier full of papers and finish my route in a fraction of the time.

But, first, there was learning to ride. As soon as the repairs were complete, my Dad loaded me and the bike into his old clunker of a car and we set off for the other side of town. A short time later, we'd reached our destination

-- the cinder-track road down by the old railroad station. I cringed as I looked at the sharp, knifelike edges of the cinders -- surely this was a bad place to make a beginning as a bike rider. What if I fell? I'd surely be cut to ribbons. I voiced my concern.

"This is where I learned to ride a bike," Dad answered. "On my brother Alf's bike, because we could only afford one bike for the family." I'd often heard the stories of poverty in my Dad's family, how there'd been seven kids and one year they couldn't go to school on the first day because there were no shoes.

"What if I fall?" I asked.

"You don't fall," my Dad said. "That's why we're learning here. You can't fall on a cinder road. When I learned, just the thought of falling on those cinders was enough to keep me up and riding."

"You didn't fall even once?" I asked, wondering how this could be possible.

"Oh, yea, I fell a couple of times, but not too often," Dad answered.

"It must have hurt," I said.

"It did hurt," Dad answered, "but it kept me up and riding."

So, with Dad's help, I climbed aboard the bike. "Remember," he said, "pedal and steer. As long as you keep pedalling, you won't fall over, and as long as you steer, you won't run into anything." Those sounded like wise words of advice.

Dad held onto the bike behind the seat, as I sat on the contraption, my feet on the pedals, a look of grim determination on my face, knowing I must not fall, even once. Finally, Dad started to push me along the cinder-track road, keeping me upright, jogging slowly along, helping me to balance the bike. "Get ready," he warned, starting to puff from his effort. And with that, he gave me a firm push and I was on my own.

I'll never forget that first solo effort on my new, used bike. I swear I could feel the wind in my hair and the freedom of flight even as I struggled to make the pedals turn. I pushed harder and harder, and could feel the bike go faster and faster. It was an odd sensation at first, balancing on that piece of unfamiliar machinery, but it felt good -- oh so good.

"Keep pedalling!" Dad was calling after me. "Remember to steer."

And I was remembering to do both of those things, and I was covering the ground of the cinder-track road -- first, five feet -- then, ten feet -- then, twenty feet -- gaining speed all the time and everything going great.

"Slow her down, son!" I could hear my Dad calling after me from somewhere in the distance. "Stop pedalling and slow down!" I could hear him calling.

But I couldn't stop pedalling. If I stopped pedalling, I'd surely fall over -- I knew that much about riding a bike. Wasn't that what Dad had said. Pedal and steer. Keep on pedalling and steering and what could go wrong.

But it was at that point when I had occasion to look up from my pedalling effort for the first time in a couple of minutes, and it was then that I realized that I had used up nearly the entire cinder-track road. I was out of room and it suddenly occurred to me that there was one thing I didn't know -- and that was how to stop my brand new, used bicycle. Dad had left that part out, likely sure I'd stop in a heap the first couple of times.

And it was at that exact moment that something called panic intruded into my young life. And as I panicked, I also forgot the cardinal rules of bike riding -- keep pedalling and keep steering and nothing could go wrong. So that I immediately forgot to pedal and I threw my hands up in front of my face, crying out in terror, also forgetting to steer, and I crashed into a predictable heap.

So, I sat in a dusty clump, glaring at the fallen bike, my pride hurt far worse than any other part of me. In fact, as I climbed to my feet and inspected the damage, I found that I had sustained only a couple of minor scrapes, courtesy the sharpness of the cinders. It hadn't been as bad as I'd expected. I looked back and saw Dad loping up the road toward me, a wide smile on his face.

"That was great!" he exclaimed, all out of breath.

I beamed back, smiling from ear to ear.

"But you've got to learn to stop," he said. "And you can't stop steering like that."

My smile faded.

"But you did great," he added enthusiastically, tussling my hair.

And, with his help, I climbed back onto the bike and away I went again -- this time even further than before. And I fell a couple more times, and I usually felt most unsteady on my new conveyance, but I kept getting back on and by the end of that time we spent on the cinder-track road, I was feeling a small level of confidence at my accomplishment.

Finally, though, it was time to call an end to the riding lesson and Dad packed me and the bike back into the big, old car and we made for home.

I was treated like a king that night. Mom had made me a special treat and we all ate cookies and drank chocolate milk. It was a grand time indeed.

The riding lesson had taken place on Friday night, so the next day was Saturday, and I was expecting that there was more bike riding in my future. After all, it was Dad's day off.

That's why I was so depressed when the phone rang while we were eating breakfast. It was my father's boss, and he asked if Dad could come in to work for a few hours to try to deal with a problem that had come up. Of course, I knew if there was a problem anywhere in the world, my Dad was the guy to solve it. Still, my heart sank, knowing there'd be no bike riding on this day -- at least for a while.

So, Dad got into his car, and was soon gone to make things right at work. And I was soon out into the garage, and had the bike out in the back yard and was washing it up. I rubbed and scrubbed that thing, until it fairly shone and glistened in the morning sun. It wasn't quite what I'd wanted, but it had become my pride and joy just the same -- that was for sure.

Finally, the bike all spic and span, I walked it around to the front of the house. My mother was just coming back from having a coffee with the next door neighbour.

"Now, don't go on the road with that bike until your father gets home," she cautioned, as she passed on her way into the house.

"No, Mom," I answered dutifully.

But soon after she went inside, a temptation presented itself. A couple of my friends from school, Al and George, came riding up the street on their sleek, slick new-looking bikes.

"Well, well, look who's finally got a bike," George said, as they pulled to a stop in front of my house.

I said nothing, not sure how he meant the statement.

"My, but it's an old-looking thing, though," Al said, disdain in his voice.

"Yea, look at the seat on that thing," George laughed. "It's from before the war."

I could feel my face turn red with embarrassment. They couldn't talk that way about my bike -- the one I'd bought with my own money, and that my Dad had fixed up to look like new. It was my pride and joy. I had to protect it -- I had to protect my Dad.

"It's really fast, though," I said quietly.

"That thing? Fast? You've got to be kidding," laughed George. "I could beat that thing with one hand tied behind my back."

"You could not," I answered, defiance in my voice.

"My sister could beat that old thing," Al mocked. "That thing doesn't even look like a real bike."

"It is too," I answered, angry. "And I could too beat your sister."

Al and George conferred for a moment, keeping their voices quiet, so I couldn't hear what they were saying.

"Meet us at the fairgrounds in an hour," Al said. "I'll get my sister."

"I ain't racing your sister," I answered.

"Afraid you'll get beat?" chided George.

"No," I answered. "I just ain't racing with any girls."

"Fraidy-cat," Al accused.

"Am not," I retorted.

"Then be at the fairgrounds in an hour," George said, a broad grin on his face.

And the two of them pedalled off up the street, leaving me sitting on my front lawn feeling shame-faced and foolish. I wasn't even supposed to leave the property, let alone go to the fairgrounds with my bike. And I knew I couldn't ride well enough to race with anyone -- even a girl. But now, if I failed to show, I'd be the coward of the fourth grade.

And so I had a miserable hour to spend. Should I defy my parents and take my bike out into the world before I was ready, or should I stay put and face the taunting jeers of my so-called friends when they next came upon me? It was a difficult choice, and I buried my head in my hands and gritted my teeth at being faced with such a dilemma at such a tender young age. Life can be hard sometimes.

But the more I thought about it, the more I realized that it wasn't such a difficult decision. I had to go. I was my parents' son, and they professed to love me, so it was unlikely they'd fling me out into the bottomless, blackness of life, just for having disobeyed them. To have to live with an eternity of humiliation at the hands of a band of prepubescent youth seemed the worse fate by far. When I thought the hour was up, I left the yard with nary a look back, walking, and pushing my bike along beside me.

When I reached the corner and was safely out of sight of the house, I ventured to climb onto the bike, seeming to know that if I was to race, I should first make sure I could ride. I was wobbly and unsure of myself as I pushed down on the pedal, propelling the bike slowly forward. Gingerly, I allowed my other foot to leave the ground and to find its spot on the opposite pedal. I pushed hard, and started to move forward. Pedal and steer. I continued to push hard on the pedals, now looking up and beginning also to carry out the second part of the instructions.

And I was amazed -- the bike moved along the street in good order and I could again feel the wind in my hair and the freedom of flight. I was riding, and the harder I pedalled, the faster I went. I smiled broadly at my accomplishment. There was nothing to this and by the time I'd gone a block, I was fairly speeding along. I even managed to avoid an oncoming car, and it came over me that I was now a bike rider. Al's sister should look out. This was indeed a fast bike and I was its equally fast rider.

As I'd expected, Al and George had brought not only Al's sister, but half the fourth grade to the fairgrounds, spreading the word about the proposed great race while riding back through town. But I didn't care. I'd win this day. Of that, I was sure.

"Well, at least you showed up," Al said.

"Let's call this off, Al." I said confidently. "Your sister's no match for me." I looked over to where the tomboyish young girl was standing, her own bike by her side. She seemd to offer me a shy smile. I could feel myself flush.

"We'll see," George answered. "I say she'll beat you by a mile."

"She couldn't beat a dead horse," I answered, cockiness in my voice, avoiding looking toward the girl.

"Let's get on with this," called one of the other kids, come to watch the race of the century.

"Over here, both of you," called George, who dragged his foot across half the town racetrack, creating the apparent starting line.

I lined up beside the girl, arching my leg up and over my bike, getting ready to make a quick start.

"Once around the track. On three," George said.

A hush fell over the crowd of kids, as the moment of truth was at hand.

"One! Two!" George paused, his arm lifted high. "Three!" Down came the arm.

And we were off.

I made an uncertain start, as was perhaps to be expected for a lad who'd only learned his bike riding the previous day. For the first couple of seconds, I was afraid I might fall -- it was a dirt track and harder to get going on than any surface I'd been on before -- including the cinder-track. The girl sped quickly away, obviously an old pro as a bike rider. As I struggled to maintain my balance and strained to push down on the pedals, my eyes were locked on the track in front of me, but I could also see Al's sister pulling speedily away.

"Look, she's got him already!" I heard one kid yell excitedly.

"He looks like he's gonna fall!" cried out another.

But I'd gradually managed to pull myself completely upright, securing my balance and pushing the pedals around and around, faster and faster, and the danger of falling passed, and I started to feel the wind in my hair. Pedal and steer, I thought. And I pedalled with all my might, around and around they went, and I looked ahead, down the track, with a look of incredible ferocity and determination. I could see Al's sister just rounding the track's first turn, glancing back over her shoulder, smiling jubilantly, feeling I'd not be able to surmount her already considerable lead.

But she hadn't counted on having to deal with such a fast bike, or such a fast rider. And, slowly, but surely at first, but then faster and ever faster, I started to make up the ground on her. After all, I was a boy. I was bigger and stronger than she was. And my bike was the best. I grew more and more confident as I started to overtake her. I could hear the rest of the kids yelling excitedly as the two of us rode for all we were worth. The girl's last look back had made her more intent on her task, realizing there was to be a race on this day, afterall.

But she was no match for me, and by the time she'd passed the half pole, I was breathing down her neck. The track was rough at this point, no doubt broken up by the horses that ran over this very ground on the weekly race nights. I was getting bounced about pretty good, but holding my own, as I gradually manouvered my bike out further from the rail, taking up a position to pass the girl -- to claim my rightful victory.

And I pressed harder and harder now that I was upon her. I leaned low over the handlebars, cutting through the wind like a knife, pushing, pushing. I could feel her straining beside me -- could hear her puffing and struggling to get more speed from her bike. I could feel her as I pulled alongside, then started to pass, going ever so slightly out in front. I pressed and I pressed on the pedals. I wouldn't just win the race and beat the girl. I'd win the race and humiliate the girl. I'd show them all. I'd show them good.

And I started to pull away from her, and by the final turn, I was clearly in command of the race, fully three bike lengths out in front. I would win in a walk -- even with such a sad start. I was the great bike racer and no one could beat me. I was champion and would beat all comers.

But it was precisely at that point that things came unglued. I got cocky. There was only a short ways to the finish where I would reign triumphant, and I got cocky. I decided there was nothing to this bike riding thing, that I had it completely mastered, so that perhaps I should do a little showing off. I lifted my hands from the handlebars for a victory wave to my cheering supporters. And at that very moment, the front wheel of my bike hit what must have been the biggest rut in the entire racetrack with a giant thud. It threw me badly off balance, and I grabbed for the bike to try to recover, but there was no hope. The bike veered wildly toward the inside rail and crashed abruptly into one of the white-washed posts. With that, I flew off and landed in a muddy heap in the swampy infield, while the bike sagged directly to the ground.

I lifted my head from its sorry state just in time to see Al's sister pedal furiously by, her victory now assured. My heart sank. It wasn't supposed to end like this. I watched as she cruised across the finish line, lifting her arms high into the air as she celebrated her win. The other kids mobbed her.

I managed to regain my feet and limped back to my bike. Just then, Al and George and few more of the guys came over to where I was inspecting the damage.

"Told you you couldn't beat my little sister," Al sneered.

I looked toward him, but I was beaten, tears in my eyes.

"And get a real bike, would you!" George said, whereupon they all laughed.

And with that, they were off to torment the next loser kid they could find, because that's the way of it when you're a kid -- either you're the one tormenting the loser, or you're the loser -- and on this day, I was clearly the loser.

I had a difficult time of it getting my broken bike back home and there were none who cared to help. The few who'd remained after George and Al and the others had left were standing in a quiet little group, no doubt laughing over their shoulders at me, but doing it in silence, so I gave them a wide berth.

Finally, I came into the yard of our house, and let the remains of my bike settle in a pile on the lawn. It was then that I noticed my Dad sitting on the front verandah watching me.

"That's doesn't look like a very good place to leave that," he said, but there was no sternness in his voice. It was soft and supple as it came to me.

I looked up at him, but said nothing.

"Tough day?" he asked.

"Sort of," I answered, but it was hard to say even that with the considerable lump that was growing in my throat.

"Care to talk about it?" he asked.

And it was then that the tears finally really came, with sobs that shook my ten-year-old body right to its core. He came down off the porch, and put his big arm around me.

"There, there," he said quietly. "We'll talk about it. You'll be all right."

I melted into him, feeling my young body fit snug and secure against him. He started to lead me away; to take me to a place of comfort, but I stopped him. I looked back toward the bike.

"What about my bike?" I asked, my voice halting and unsure.

"I'm afraid I don't have money to fix it right now," he answered. "It might have to wait until you can save a bit of your own money. You might be walking that paper route 'til next spring."

"Yessir," I answered. "But we can fix it?" I asked.

"We fixed it once and we can fix it again," he said. "Don't you worry about that, sport."

"I'm sorry, Dad," I offered.

"I know you are, son," he answered. "But you've got to learn something from this. A bike can always be fixed, but there are things that can't."

"Like what?" I asked.

"Like your Mom's trust in you," he answered. "She trusted you and you let her down. She's been worried sick. I'm very disappointed in you, as well." And I could tell by the tone of his voice that he meant it.

"I'm sorry, Dad," I said.

"I know you are," he answered, "and all's well that ends well. Now, let's go in and see your mother."

And we went into the house. And I'm sure I did learn something that day. It was a hard lesson about winning and losing and not getting too cocky, but it was also a lesson in what was expected of me. And, as odd as it may sound, the memory of me and that first bike and the great race with Al's sister and the way it all ended is mainly a good one. I took a lot of ribbing from the guys for a few days and then it seemed forgotten. And I walked my paper route through the rest of the summer and into the fall and through the winter, until Dad made good on his word and carried out the necessary repairs to my bike just as the warm sun of spring returned. And, again, I felt the wind in my hair and the freedom of flight as I rode. And it was good. Very good.

Once Upon a Time in the Summer

It sounds kind of macabre now that I look back on it, but we used to spend a lot of time hanging around the cemetery when we were kids. There was a bush right beside the cemetery and that was great for playin' in, and right beside the bush was a river and that was great for swimmin' in. So we'd while away the long days of summer at a swimmin' hole that had been created at the river by generations of town kids looking for a place to escape the shimmering heat. It was fun in the sun for us kids in those days. But those were simpler times. Before we grew up and got all serious and filled with awesome responsibility. And I can well remember the summer when it all changed. That was really the summer when I learned a little something about life.

It started innocently enough that spring with my buddy, Josh, and I out scouring the ditches by the cemetery hill, looking for bottles, discarded from passing cars over winter. This was a lucrative profession back when I was a boy, and spring was the best time of all, when it was often possible to gather enough bottles to buy french fries with gravy for the two of us after only a couple hours work.

Anyway, here's Josh and I slugging away in a particularly deep portion of a ditch, when what do my wondering eyes behold, but a stack of magazines, all tied up with string and sitting half submerged in the dank water at the bottom of the ditch. I frogged my way through the reeds and bullrushes, got a soaker for my trouble, but I managed to snag the pile of soggy literature.

"Whatcha got there?" Josh hollered from his vantage point higher up in the ditch.

"Some magazines," I called back, struggling to maintain my balance in the muck.

"What kind? Any good?" he hollered back, and I could hear him starting to clamber down the slope.

"I'm not sure yet," I called. "I'm sort of stuck." And it was true that my running shoe had completely disappeared in the ooze.

"Here, I'll give you a hand," Josh said as he approached, careful where he placed his own feet, so as not to end up in my predicament. He reached out his hand.

I reached back toward him, but I had the magazines in my other hand, and they seemed to pull me more in that direction, so my friend couldn't seem to get the necessary leverage to yank me out of the mud.

"Pass me the magazines," he finally said. "Pass them over."

With great difficulty, I managed to move the magazines from one hand to the other, then extend it out toward Josh. He reached toward me, then made a lunge, grabbing the magazines and falling back onto the ditch bank. The manoeuvre came dangerously close to spilling me entirely into the muck, but I teetered back and forth and finally came to rest still in the upright position. I looked toward Josh, hoping he was ready to pull me out.

There he was, sitting just a short distance away, but making no effort to assist me in my dilemma. He was sitting, wide-eyed, pawing through one of the magazines.

"Get me out of here, Josh," I hollered.

"You've got to see this," he said emphatically. "You won't believe this."

"What?" I asked impatiently. "What's so important about a bunch of magazines?"

"They're filled with bare naked people," my friend said, and it was clear he was incredulous at the discovery.

"What?" I asked.

"They're filled with bare naked people," he repeated. "And you can see everything."

"What do you mean?" I asked with disbelief.

"I mean, they're totally naked. Without a stitch." he answered.

"Comeon," I said. "You never get to see everything. "

"Well, take a look at this," he said, holding aloft the magazine he'd been paging through.

And it was at that point that I completely forgot about my submerged running shoe and I pulled my foot right up and out of it, losing it forever in the bottom of that ditch, just so I could get a look at a bunch of naked people in a magazine.

And it turned out that we'd found a bunch of nudist magazines, about actual nudists, complete with pictures of the required volleyball games and such. And I'll tell you, even though we found those magazines, we really got somebody's money's worth out of them that summer. We lived and breathed for those magazines, with hardly a day passing when we didn't take just a little peek.

Now I don't know if it was those magazines or if it was the age I was at, but I had a heightened interest in things sexual that summer. I know it was the summer of my first boner, which scared the bejeezus out of me, and it was also the summer of one of my life's most embarrassing moments.

We developed a habit of camping out beside the old swimming hole that summer. We'd cart our camping gear and sleeping bags and a few cans of beans through the cemetery and through the bush and down the hill that led to the river -- and we'd set up camp.

And so it happened that on one fine summer's night when the moon was full, we were camped out, and we'd spent the requisite time sitting about the campfire, while the older guys told us tales of their sexual exploits, and we all got about excited as we could considering we were such young and inexperienced men.

Anyway, after the evening had been so occupied, the five of us crammed into one small tent, and prepared for a night of sleep.

It was finally quiet in the tent. Sleep was occurring, when one of the older boys called out my name. I answered.

"Do you know how to do it?" he asked across the darkened space in the tent.

"Do what?" I asked.

"It," he answered.

"What?" I asked again.

"Have sex, of course," he answered.

"Sure," I answered.

"How about telling the rest of us," he said, and by this time every ear in the tent was on us.

"Yea," said one of the other boys. "Tell us all about it."

I was quiet. There was silence in the tent. I could feel myself redden in the darkness.

"Comeon," said the boy who had started it.

"Well......" I started.

"Comeon," was repeated, this time as a chorus.

"Does it have something to do with your bum?" I asked meekly, knowing almost for certain that I was wrong before I said it.

The apparent silliness of my answer nearly brought down the tent, so convulsed in laughter were most of the occupants. I knew I'd never live this down. I'd have to move away and shave my head and become a monk.

But just at that moment, all heck broke loose on the tent. The tiny, canvass structure began to shake and rock back and forth violently and the air outside was filled with hideous and terrifying sounds. All of us inside cried out to God to save us from whatever calamity was happening, my humiliation forgotten, as everyone struggled for the entranceway.

Only when we finally reached the outside and scampered to safety did we realize that we'd been caught in the path of a herd of cows from the neighouring farm. Now, there was a moment to remember.

But I never did live down my answer to the fateful question that had been asked in the tent. It embarrassed me then, and it embarrasses me even now -- even all these years later. It does have something to do with your bum, but that's certainly not the point. And I really didn't know that then.

So there was the magazines and the boner and the tent thing. But then there was this other thing that happened, and I've never told a soul about it until this day, and you'll be the first. And this is really what happened.

One day, it seemed as if all my friends were doing something. It was late in the summer, and we were all bored with most things. I sat for a while on the front porch of my house with my head in my hands, feeling sorry for myself. I'd called about everybody and no one had answered the call. Finally, as a last resort, I thought I'd try to seek out some companionship in person, so I told my mom that I was heading out.

I visited some of the favourite haunts, and finally ended up at the cemetery. I dug the magazines out of their hiding place in a cedar grove, and sat for a while looking at them. I got a boner, but that was normal in those days. But I tired even of that, and decided to go through the bush to the swimming hole.

I was still a kid in those days, and when I was partway through the bush, I decided to play the Indian and see how quietly I could sneak through the undergrowth. I went quietly indeed and finally came upon the swimming hole, where I imagined my enemy lay in wait.

But as I peered out from the edge of the bush, it wasn't my enemy I saw. It was one of the seniors from high school, I recognized her even at a distance from the bugle band. She was laying out sunning herself. Which was all well and good, except that she was totally naked -- just like the girls in the magazines. I could feel myself swallow hard. I got a boner that threatened to pop right out of my pants.

And it was at that precise moment when I inadvertantly chose to quit playing the Indian by stepping on a large branch, which broke with a resounding crack.

"Who's there?" said the young woman, sitting bolt upright and covering herself with a towel.

I said nothing, crouched low to try to avoid detection.

The young woman stood, holding the towel over her. "Who's there?" she repeated. "Please, don't frighten me," she said.

I watched and could tell she was indeed frightened at not knowing who had come upon her.

"Please," she said, some pleading in her voice.

I could take no more and stepped from the brush, standing nervously, eyeing her -- feeling embarrassed.

"Well, hello," she said, and I could hear confidence return to her voice. "Are you alone?"

I nodded in the affirmative, but continued to say nothing.

"Well, quite a little man," she said, and I wasn't sure why, until I followed her gaze in the direction of my stiff, little boner. "How long have you been watching?"

"I just got here," I said, uttering my first words.

Suddenly, she let the towel drop to one side. "And do you like what you see?" she asked.

I nodded, my mouth no doubt hanging open the proverbial country mile.

"Come here, little man," she said, motioning with her finger.

I followed her instruction in that, and it was soon that I was following other instruction, so that I learned my lesson in life on that afternoon in late summer. She taught me the ways of the world, and it was a frightening and wondrous time for me, and I'd had no idea that such strange and unusual things could be accomplished with male and female bodies. I could have died to have stayed in that one afternoon forever and ever.

After it was over, she swore me to secrecy, something not necessary because who would have believed, and bid me leave. I slipped into my pants, my boner finally exhausted and sore between my legs, and made ready to leave.

"Take care, little man," she said, offering me one final kiss.

And I left.

It was years before I had real sex again. It was on my wedding night, and that didn't come nearly close to living up to expectations. And I think that had to do with that one summer, when I got really interested in things sexual. It was a curious period in my life, but was something I'll never forget. It was the summer I learned there was more than fun in the sun. It was quite a time. And that's the god-awful truth.

Fred Encounters Brother Rabbit

T he music was Neil Young, so the decade could have been anything from the sixties to the nineties, but it was definitely not the nineties because that decade is a boring miserable excuse for history and should be stricken from the record. And just as surely it's not the seventies when the money became a factor, nor the eighties when it took complete control. So, that pretty well meant it had to be the sixties, and the only problem with that theory was that if you remembered the sixties, then you surely couldn't have been there -- that was what they said -- whoever they were.

He and Tom were hunting buddies -- had been since the seventh grade when Tom had moved to town from a faraway city. Fred had gotten a BB gun for Christmas that year, a Daisy and a real beauty, but it only figured that Tom would end up with a much more powerful weapon -- a pellet gun. So, they stalked about in the marshes and bushes that surrounded the little town where they lived, shooting some unfortunate small birds, and with the coming of that year's spring, a few even more unfortunate frogs.

And so it went for a couple of years, and they hunted about, not really doing too much damage, not really too serious about the killing thing. But, then, Tom graduated up to a .22 and Fred got the use of the pellet gun and things took on a bit more of a lethal perspective. It continued to be fun, but there was the odd ground hog and the even odder rabbit that fell into the sights of the mighty hunters, and the hapless creatures were deemed to be of no further use and were dispatched without so much as a second thought. What great things these guns are -- that's what the boys thought.

And then came the next level of the deadly and diabolical game -- Tom got a shotgun and Fred ended up with the .22. Now it seemed time for some really big game.

And Fred had felt okay about the hunting thing as long as he'd been carrying nothing mightier than a pellet gun. After all, it was possible to inflict only so much damage with a pellet gun -- there was no gun powder involved. It would stop a sparrow or a frog dead in its tracks -- but there was little chance that anyone, or anything, was actually going to get hurt in a war of pellet guns. Fred thought the world would be a better place if the most powerful weapon ever invented was a pellet gun. But the .22 was another matter. It could really kill something.

One fine winter's morning, the two hunters were making their way along the edge of a cedar bush, crunching through ankle-deep snow, frosty breath swirling about them. Suddenly, without warning, Tom froze, grasping Fred's arm, holding it tight, indicating that all forward motion should cease. The two stood stalk still, statuesque in the cold, winter's air, hardly breathing.

Fred chanced a glance toward his friend and could see Tom was trying to get him to look at something in the direction of the bush. He turned his head slowly, cautiously, not quite sure what to expect. Finally, out of the corner of his eye, he could see the prey -- a pair of white, fluffy ears sticking up above a small snow drift just inside the edge of the treeline.

Fred looked nervously back at Tom. Tom gestured toward the .22. It was an easy shot.

Fred moved slowly to bring the gun to bear on the unfortunate target. The ears remained absolutely motionless, protruding above the drift. It was all he could see, but he aimed just below them, in the middle of the drift, knowing what must surely be attached to the ears. He sighted along the barrel of the gun, looking along its sleek steel and past the tiny cross piece and into the snow.

"Comeon," hissed Tom. "You'll lose him."

Fred's heart was pounding inside his head. He wanted to lose him. He'd never shot anything that might acutally be considered a living, breathing thing -- not like Tom. But he had to play the game. He had to pretend. He squeezed the trigger slowly. Felt the slight recoil. Saw smoke from the barrel.

It all happened in ultra slow motion, so that he felt he might have reached out past the gun and grabbed the bullet and stopped the whole sordid affair even before it happened.

But he didn't. So that blood spattered across the snow and the poor victim was hit and grievously injured with that first shot. And brother rabbit screamed a curdling death scream so its fellow creatures could behold what unfairness had befallen it. Fred had not imagined that a rabbit could cry out at all, let alone with such obvious pain and suffering.

The two hunters crashed through the snow toward the murder scene.

"There it is!" cried Tom. "Finish it!"

The poor rabbit thrashed about, turning the clean whiteness of the snow a dark crimson red with its life's blood. It would die soon enough.

"Kill it!" cried Tom.

Fred sighted the gun on the poor beast. He squeezed the trigger again. Watched as the bullet struck the rabbit and it was no more, except for its broken carcass. He felt a tear trickle down his cheek. But at least the rabbit was quiet.

Tom gathered up the body, and tucked it into the lining of his special hunting parka. "That'll be good for my mother to make stew with," he remarked, kicking about in the blood-red snow.

Fred turned away, not wanting his friend to see tears.

At noon hour, they stopped for lunch. Each of them carried a back pack and had soon emptied the contents out into a clearing in the bush they had been busily scouring for prey. It was hot dogs with all the fixings -- that was all they ever ate on these hunting trips. Tom's mom always packed them everything they'd need, and they'd pull up somewhere and build a fire and cook lunch right out there in the open air where such a meal always tastes best.

But on this day, Fred had some difficulty downing his meal. Once the fire had been coaxed into a roaring blaze, and they had shed their coats and were sitting about in their vests and shirt sleeves, Fred found his gaze returning again and again to his friend's hunting parka -- to where the slain rabbit was contained. And each time he looked in that direction, he felt profound sadness at the part he'd played in the poor victim's demise.

Finally, though, it was time to move on, so they got to their feet and kicked the fire into submission, scattering the coals about in the snow, and stomping on them like crazed fiends.

Once they were sure the site had been secured and that the bush would likely not burn to the ground when they left, they gathered up their guns and were off in pursuit of more ingredients for the stewing pot. Fred had less enthusiasm for the task ahead than he'd had when they'd started the day.

It was mainly quiet between them, the way it should be when you're stalking wild game, but it was an erie silence to Fred's ears, and he felt like he could feel the dead rabbit travelling along with them. The snow crunched under their feet, but it was quiet and uneasy in the woods.

Then, suddenly, as they walked, Tom froze as he had earlier, before the first rabbit incident. Fred felt the hair on the back of his neck stand to attention. He would kill another helpless creature.

He looked cautiously to see what his friend had spotted. He finally saw a small clump of brown fluff just off to the side of the trail they were walking on. He saw Tom gradually start to bring the gun to bear on the unfortunate beast. Then, his friend slowly lowered his weapon and laid it gingerly on the ground, right in the snow. Fred watched as he seemed to gather up all of his energy.

And it was all over in one quick flurry of activity. Tom jumped right on that poor rabbit, grabbed it, but more sort of crashed onto it, so it couldn't escape. Then, he held it tightly, looking back at Fred, a huge grin across his face. Quick as a wink, he had it trapped in the back pouch of his parka -- in the same general location as the rabbit Fred had dispatched earlier in the day. It squirmed and struggled at first, but could go nowhere and soon seemed to settle in -- albeit likely terrified beyond life itself.

"What the hell did you catch it for?" Fred asked, wide-eyed at what had happened.

"I dunno," Tom answered, still grinning triumphantly. "I wasn't sure I could."

"Well, you did," Fred said. "What in the world are you going to do with it?"

"Take it home," Tom answered.

"Home?" Fred exclaimed. "You should let the poor thing go."

"Naw, I'll keep it for a while, then it'll end up in the stew pot," Tom answered. "I just can't believe I caught the damned thing with my bare hands."

"Yea, that was weird," Fred agreed, looking toward the back of his friend's coat and wondering at its cargo -- the dead and the nearly dead. He shivered.

And it was almost time for them to meet Tom's Dad, who was driving them back into town, so they headed for the rendezvous point, and were soon sitting at the country crossroads that had been agreed upon for the meeting.

"Don't mention the rabbit," Tom said, when they saw the old Ford coming up the road.

Fred nodded in agreement.

Now, Tom had the most ideal living accommodations Fred had ever seen for a teenage boy who was interested in exploring some of the unknown and more dubious aspects of life. His parents owned a hotel in town, and the entire family lived above the hotel -- the parents in an apartment at the front of the building, and Tom in a large room that used to be two rooms near the rear of the establishment. It was very much like he had his own place and could come and go as he liked. No curfews for Tom. He was the envy of every kid at school.

So, it was no sweat when it came to smuggling a living, breathing rabbit past the parents and up to Tom's room. The poor creature had been frightened into total silence, so there was no fear that it would give them away. All the boys had to do was keep their mouths shut -- and they were quite able to accomplish that simple task during the drive home and while Tom's Dad parked the car.

Finally, they were up in the room. Tom spread his parka out on the floor -- the dead rabbit had been left in the kitchen and only its lifeblood remained on the coat. He gingerly opened the pouch at the back -- and there was what surely must have been the most bedraggled rabbit in the world. It sat, as still and quiet as it possibly could, no doubt hoping it would soon wake from the bad dream it was having.

"It's scared to death," Fred said.

"I'll get it some food," Tom said. "You keep an eye on it." He got up and headed for the door.

"What do I do if it wants to move?" asked an anxious Fred.

"Just keep an eye on it," said Tom. "I'll just be a minute."

Fred sat on the edge of Tom's bed and watched the rabbit -- and the rabbit seemed to watch him back. It was an unnerving scene. He wondered about the relationship between the rabbit he'd murdered that morning, and the captured one sitting before him on the floor. Perhaps they'd been brothers. Christ, what a stupid way to think -- that's what he thought.

But the rabbit didn't move and Tom was back quickly, having raided a condiment tray in the hotel's dining room, grabbing a great handful of carrot and celery sticks.

"Here, let's try these," Fred's friend said, getting down on his knees and offering the rabbit a carrot stick. "Here, little bunny rabbit. Have some carrot," Tom said in a strange sort of baby talk obviously intended to set his dinner guest at ease.

And, so started the saga of the imprisoned rabbit. The poor thing was really totally out of its element in Tom's hotel room, but the youth kept it fed and watered, and adopted it as a sort of pet. It roamed about the room day and night and seemed to find some comfortable nooks and crannies among the pieces of furniture in which to hide itself away from the commotion that was sometimes about in the place.

Fred thought it was a most unusual arrangement, and a bit unsanitary, as animal droppings started to accumulate in various locations around the room. But he didn't really say much to Tom, thinking that perhaps his friend seemed to find some comfort in having the small beast for company in his usually lonely room. He did suggest picking up after the rabbit, but that was about it.

But there came this one evening when Tom suggested they stay up late and watch a couple of old horror movies on the TV. Fred could sleep on the dilapedated couch in his friend's room. They'd have a grand time. Fred agreed before he really knew what he was doing. He forgot about the captive rabbit.

By the time he remembered the beast -- and he did remember -- it was too late to decline the offer to stay over. He was sitting there halfway through the first horror movie when the tiny creature first made its presence known, and there was suddenly the thought of trying to catch a night's sleep with the four-legged thing free to scurry about the room. He knew that rabbits were supposed to be gentle creatures, but this one had been aggravated beyond all reason over the last little while. Who could tell what might happen in the dead of night?

But Tom distracted him and they were soon immersed in the movie and the third occupant of the room was again forgotten. Finally, the last of the chips had been eaten and the last of the pop drunk, and the credits were running for the last movie. It was time to call it a night.

Fred gathered up Tom's sleeping bag and headed for the couch that sat along one wall. Tom had been laying on his bed to watch the last bit of the movie and was already sawing logs. Fred reached up from the couch and switched off the lamp that had been providing the only light in the room. Soft moonlight entering through partially-open curtains cast a soft glow about the place. Fred fell asleep.

A strange sound awakened him a short time later. He struggled first to open his weary eyes and then to get them to adjust to the lack of light in the room. He strained to see in the direction of the noise -- almost like something was gnawing on something. Then, he saw the rabbit, sitting on the end of the couch, silhouetted in the moonlight, chewing on an old, dried-out carrot.

"Ah, the mighty hunter," said the rabbit as calm as could be. "Sorry to disturb your sleep."

Fred propped himself up on one elbow. For some reason, he didn't seem surprised that the rabbit had spoken, but rather that the creature had chosen this precise moment to utter its words. "Why did you wake me?" he asked.

"I wanted to ask you why you killed my cousin," said the rabbit.

"My friend's mother made a stew out of him," Fred answered.

"Did you eat it?" the rabbit asked.

"No, I don't like rabbit," Fred answered.

There was something of a silence.

"Why do you think you people always have to be killing things?" asked the rabbit, giving its nose a thoughtful twitch or two.

"I'm not sure I've ever really thought about it," answered Fred.

"You know that death is reasonably final," said the rabbit.

"I think I do know that," said Fred.

"What gives you the right to take a life?" asked the rabbit.

"People are the most powerful creatures in the world," Fred answered. "That gives us the right."

"Just because you can kill anything you like, does that mean you actually have to?" asked the rabbit.

"We kill to eat -- to protect ourselves from our enemies," Fred answered.

"You kill for gold, and to take each other's property, and to prove who has more power than the other," said the rabbit. "You killed my cousin, brother rabbit, for no reason whatsoever -- other than to plop in your stew pot to fill your already gorged stomach."

"We are the smartest," answered Fred, feeling slightly put upon by this time.

"Yes, you are the smartest," agreed the rabbit. "You are so smart that you have outwitted even yourselves. You poison the very home you live in. Many of your own kind live in poverty and misery even within plain sight of the golden towers. You fight among yourselves, kill each other and and rape and plunder the sick and the weak. You are surely the smartest of the creatures. And the rest of us who live most of our time in peace and harmony with nature, and who live and die in grace within the great cycle of life, are only the dumb animals." He was finally quiet.

Fred laid in the silence of the room. He could not answer, not because he was only a mere boy confounded by the creature's simple reason, but because there was no reasonable answer to the charges. He knew it even in his boy's mind. He laid his head down on the pillow and wept. He felt profound sadness at the plight of humankind. To have come so far, but to have still come nowhere.

Fred fell into a deep, dreamless sleep. The darkness surrounded him and he was covered in black.

He awoke feeling most refreshed in the morning, early, just as the sun was starting to peek through the room's window. Tom was still in the land of nod, but Fred made no move to disturb him, rising quietly instead, and slipping into his jacket and shoes. The rabbit was waiting for him near the door. He gathered up the furry, little beast and made his way toward the outside. Once there, he walked the few short blocks back to his place, holding the rabbit tight, but not so tight that it might cause discomfort.

Once he got back to his house, he collected up his back sack, gently placing the rabbit inside, and wheeled his bike out of the carport. Then, he made for the country. He took the rabbit home. It was the least he could do.

Fred never hunted again. He knew the error of his ways. He worked for peace and goodness wherever he went. He felt sorry the rest of his life that he'd even killed that one rabbit. He knew that you shouldn't kill something just because you can. It's wrong. In fact, as Fred grew older, he came to know that any killing was wrong. Even the squashing of an unwanted bug is some-how not right in the overall scheme of things. Each living thing has the right to live and die in its own fashion -- in its own time. It makes so much sense, it should be a rule.

Rock 'N' Roll Song

t was a well-worn piece of craftmanship that had served him well back in that other time. But it had sat now for a great many years in the crawl space under the basement stairs, and he'd not bothered with it. To even touch the guitar brought the memories back -- and he didn't want any part of those memories -- those that had devoured him back when he'd been young and before he'd met his good wife and fallen in love and learned to think good and proper thoughts.

Chris had played in a band -- a very good garage band -- back in the sixties, and they'd had a lot of fun and picked up some chicks. But then the end had come and it had seemed to come ever so quickly that there had been no way to escape its onrushing jaws. And death had followed it, and it had been a hard death to take, and he had put the guitar away, and had not had it out since.

And he had settled into an elementary sort of life, giving up his life of music, and becoming an accountant, playing with numbers instead of notes, and he met his wife and she saved him from himself. It had been a hard time for him after Ron had died. He had curled in upon himself and shut out much of the world. He'd gone to classes at the university and studied toward his degree, but his life was barren and desolate, and he allowed no one to intrude. Ron had been his everything back in that other time -- the two of them had met in Sunday School at the age of twelve -- and it wasn't long before they'd formed a pact to share in everything they did.

And that had meant sharing the music. When Ron got a guitar for his thirteenth birthday, it was only natural that the two friends would conspire a way that both could get involved in the music. So, Chris scrounged and saved and soon became the bass player in a local garage band that Ron put together, almost before he could play his own instrument. And much to their surprise, they actually learned to play some songs and were soon playing at house parties, then coffee houses, and, finally, in high school gyms and not only having fun, but getting better and better.

And while Chris struggled with the bass, it was obvious that Ron had been born to play the guitar. He took a few lessons his parents arranged for him, but had soon outdistanced his instructor and seemed to live only to play. He was the natural leader of the band, choosing most of the material and arranging their gigs and handling all the business end of things.

But there were signs early on that not all would be wine and roses. Ron started to crash at school. The more he focussed on the guitar and the band, the less he focussed on school and that area of his life. He seemed to think that he had a part to live; that if he was to be a great and talented man of music, that there was a certain lifestyle that needed to be lived. And that was the beginning of the end for Ron.

It was a special time back then, back when they were all going to be rock 'n' roll stars and set the world on fire. They all chased the dream at the beginning, all thought it was possible. But for most, it was never anything but a dream. And for all but Ron, it eventually became nothing more than the fun and the chicks, but he took it so seriously that it finally killed him.

"I'll tell you, Chris, that new tune we learned is a great one," Ron said one day, as they sat in the uptown hangout after practice.

"You like all the tunes with huge, raunchy guitar solos in them," Chris answered.

"That solo isn't that raunchy -- not the way I play it," Ron countered, defending himself.

"Yea, right," Chris answered.

"I'll tell you, though, have you been watching the news?" Ron asked, enthusiasm in his voice. "The way the younger generation's taking over. Man, it is too cool."

"Yea, groovy, I suppose, eh?" Chris responded sarcastically.

"Hey, the times they are a changin'," Ron said.

"Yea, and I get enough hassle trying to grow my hair a little over my ears," Chris answered.

"We've got to lead the fight," Ron said, a small trace of defiance in his voice.

"I gotta find a summer job," Chris answered.

"The band will be playing by then," his friend answered.

"Well, my Dad will believe it when he sees it," Chris said.

"Chris," Ron started, his voice suddenly all serious like, "we have to show these other sheep the way to go. They are not bright creatures." He paused and gestured to the others in the restaurant. "We have to think for them -- we can do that through the music."

"Pretty heavy stuff for this hicktown," Chris answered.

"It's in this hicktown where we have to work hardest to change attitudes," Ron answered. "My Dad is the biggest racist in town. He hates Commies and thinks we should kill them all. He treats my Mom like a slave. He's a pig, and so are most of the others in this town. They represent the evil empire and it's our job to bring them down."

"What about my Dad?" Chris asked, somewhat alarmed to think his father might also be part of an evil empire.

"Your Dad's kind of cool," Ron answered. "He buys us beer for playing cards. Not all Dads would do that. That's cool. He understands."

"Understands what?" Chris asked, understanding nothing of this himself.

"That the young people are the power," Ron answered. "That we are the power, and that we're going to change it."

"Change what?" Chris asked, continuing his line of questioning.

"The way things work, you lunkhead," Ron said, somewhat exhasperated by the conversation. "The way most people are slaves who have nothing and who are nothing. We're going to make a new way where everyone will count for something -- where there won't be rich and poor and all that dumb junk -- where it'll be more fair."

"It'll never be fair, Ron," Chris said. "Guys like Howie Peterson will always have the great cars and the great chicks because their old men will always own the local movie theatre. We'll struggle away in the band and we'll always be broke, but we might get some great chicks -- you more than me because you're the leader and play the guitar."

"Yea, but the girls always go for the silent, bass player types," Ron chided, reaching across the table and tussling Chris's hair.

"Yea, right, in my dreams," Chris laughed.

"Wet dreams at that," Ron joked back.

But Ron was caught up in the whole thing. He took to writing serious, dark, depressing poetry about the state of world affairs, then putting it to music. And while the songs weren't top forty material, which bothered the other guys in the band, they were well-received by some of the local crowd who wallowed in their pretentious deepness. It was just that time.

But Chris could not see. He could not understand or see as clearly as his friend. Ron was the philosopher who would use his music to spread his ideas and to change the world. Chris was a mediocre bass player who actually did manage to pick up the odd chick.

And the more some adored Ron for his great and wondrous pontificating, and all of his songs about cooperation instead of competition, the more caught up in himself he became. So that when the drugs came, the mind-expanding drugs that would let you see in other dimensions and in new ways, he was ripe for the picking. The first to try them all, then to rave about where he had been and what he had seen. It was funny at first, but it didn't always stay that way. But they couldn't see that at first.

They played a high school reunion one night. They were good. Ron was in rare form. He reached new heights. But a drunk heckled them.

"Why don't you guys get a haircut!" he hollered out between songs.

It got quiet in the gym, almost as if the audience was waiting for an answer. None came.

"God, play some decent music!" cried out the drunk. "You guys sound like shit. We want country. Play something decent!"

It was extremely quiet in the gym, strangely so, for a dance. Ron was the leader. He usually responded to the audience. Chris had no mike -- he couldn't respond. The other guys froze.

"Whatsa matter?" hollered the drunk. "You guys dead, or something!"

There was another moment of awkward silence. Then, suddenly, Ron crashed out the loudest, most distorted sound he could from his guitar. It blasted out into the gym, ricocheting off the barren, brick walls and causing a flash of pain for those who listened. Next, he unslung his guitar, and dropped it right where he stood, so that more ugly, twisted noise reverberated through the gym. Then, he turned and abruptly left the stage, leaving the screaming instrument laying there wailing.

Chris moved quickly to silence the guitar and Chet, the keyboard player, finally seemed to snap back to reality, and announced a short intermission, drawing a chorus of boos from the audience. Bill, the drummer, angrily smashed a cymbal, then threw down his sticks and stormed off.

The scene in the dressing room was not pleasant.

"Christ, what an asshole that guy is," Chet said, clearly upset at what had happened.

"Which asshole would you be talking about?" Bill asked.

"What do you mean by that?" Chris asked, stepping toe to toe with the drummer.

"What's wrong with Ron?" Bill asked, standing back a step. "Christ, he can't just do stuff like that.. We'll never get hired back."

"He's sensitive about his music," Chris answered. "The guy insulted his music."

"Well, the guy's sort of right," Chet interjected.

"And what's that supposed to mean?" Chris asked, turning to face the keyboard player.

"We should be doing more top 40 stuff," Chet answered. "Especially at a gig like this."

"Hey, Ron picks the material," Chris said.

"Well, he ain't doing a great job," said Bill. "Or there wouldn't be scenes like that one."

There was silence in the room.

"Where did he go?" Chris finally asked.

"He's likely outside stuffing a little more dope into him," Bill said, sarcasm in his voice.

"Eat shit," Chris answered, venom in his voice.

He left the room and exited the school, heading around to where Bill's Dad's truck was parked. He found Ron sitting on the running board, a deep scowl on his face.

"The guys are pissed," Chris said.

"Let them be pissed," Ron answered, sullen anger in his words.

"Bad scene," Chris said.

"Yea," Ron answered.

"They want to do more top 40 stuff," Chris said.

"They don't get it," Ron said. "We can't make it playing top 40 stuff. There's got to be a message in the music. It can't just be fluff."

"It's what the audience wants," Chris said.

"The audience doesn't know what it wants, until we give it to them," Ron answered. "They're sheep."

"They're the audience," Chris answered. "They pay the money."

There was quiet.

"All right," Ron finally said.

"All right what?" Chris asked.

"We'll do more top 40 next set," Ron said.

"If they let us back on," Chris said.

"We'll knock 'em dead," the guitar player answered.

"Let's go in and sort things out with the guys," Chris said.

"You go ahead," Ron answered. "I'll be right in."

Chris turned and started to walk, then turned back. He saw Ron try to hide something so he couldn't see. "What are you up to, Ron?" he asked.

"Nothing to worry about," his friend answered, sounding a little anxious and caught-in-the-act.

"You should take it easy when we're playing," Chris advised.

"It makes me play better," Ron answered.

"It also screws up your judgement," Chris said. "I'll see you inside. Think about it."

And it wasn't like the rest of the band were angels. There was beer and there were drugs -- that was just part of the scene -- but it was like Ron believed so strongly in the mind-expanding part and he thought it opened up his consciousness and made him write better songs and play the guitar better. Chris talked to him. Tried to explain that he should take it easy. But Chris knew he was losing his friend -- that Ron was slipping away -- that he believed it was all part of who he was and that he needed the drugs to be part of the scene. So, for some they were recreation, while for others they were life itself, and Ron was one of the latter, and who knows how or why that came to be.

But the band hung together, and so did Ron, so that time passed. Finally, high school ended. For Ron, it meant dropping out just before the end. Chris stayed with it and got his diploma.

It was his graduation night and he'd bought a nickel of reefer for the occasion, and had headed out to the town dam where he sometimes went to reflect. He was surprised to hear something rummaging around in the bushes by the path.

"Christ, hippie, you sure pick the spots," said Ron's voice, as he scrambled up from the brush and onto where Chris was sitting cross-legged.

"I like my solitude," Chris answered. "Thought you'd be out gettin' high tonight. Not interested in what the lowly high schoolers were up to."

"Well, this is a big night for my best buddy," Ron answered. "High school graduate and all that."

"At least it's done," Chris said.

"Well said," answered Ron. He sat beside Chris, and a joint was produced. "This is a special occasion," Ron said quietly. "I've got something better." He produced an aspirin case from his coat and opened it.

"What is it?" asked Chris, trying to peer through the darkness and into the pill box.

"It's a bit of angel dust I won playing pool," Ron said. "How about it, eh? You only live once."

"It's heavy shit, eh?" Chris asked. "I heard it's pretty heavy." There was nervousness in his voice. "You doing a lot of this, Ron?" was the question Chris asked next.

"It feels good, Chris," Ron said. "You can't imagine the freedom it gives me to write."

"But, Ron," Chris answered, "it's awfully hard on the head. It can really screw you up."

"I know what I'm doing," Ron said. "I never lose control. I need the stuff, Chris. Everybody who makes it in the business, uses it. It's just the way. It helps you be creative."

There was a silence. Chris puffed on the joint, not offering it to Ron, feeling it would be a foolish gesture in light of what his friend held in his hand.

"How about it?" Ron asked, offering the pill container. "You up for some fun?"

"Think I'll stick to the reefer," Chris answered.

"Whatever you think," Ron answered, his voice flat and even.

More silence.

"I'm dumping the band," Ron said, interrupting the moment of quiet.

"Why?" asked Chris, also deadpan.

"I'm moving in with some other guys -- you know a couple of them -- and we're going to get serious about the music," Ron answered. "We're getting a farm house. We're going to get good and make it. I've got a boxful of songs just waiting to be played -- there's an important message in them and I've got to get it out. That'll never happen playing top 40 stuff."

"Sounds like you've got plans," Chris remarked.

"We need a bass player," Ron said. "Everything else is in place, and they had their own guy picked out, but I made them wait -- said I had somebody else in mind. You want the job, it's yours."

"Flattering offer," Chris answered. "You think I can cut it?"

"If you put your heart into it," Ron answered. "I'd like to have you along -- just for old times sake."

Chris sat in silence, seeming to mull over the idea in his mind.

"We'll make it, Chris," Ron said. "We're going to help change the world."

Chris remained quiet.

"I love you like a brother," Ron said.

"It's a dream," Chris said. "They'll never let you change things. You just don't understand the way things work. You're my best friend, but you're a dreamer. It can't work the way you want. They won't let you."

"Who the hell are "they"?" asked Ron.

"We never find out," Chris answered.

"What does that mean?" Ron asked.

"All of our lives we talk about "they" -- my Dad talks about them all the time -- but we never really know who "they" are," answered Chris. "It's the guys up there in the stratosphere and they've been there since the beginning of time -- and they used to be stronger and now they're smarter and they've got the power -- not us."

"I don't think you're right," answered Ron. "We can make a difference. I know we can."

"Yea, we can make a difference," Chris agreed. "But they'll twist and distort any difference we make, just like you twist and distort notes on the guitar, until they get us back in line."

"How come you're so damned smart?" asked Ron, putting his hand on his friend's shoulder.

"I'm not so damned smart," answered the friend. "I'm just a realist. I know how things work. You're a musician. You've got your head in the clouds. How can I expect you to understand stuff like this."

There was another moment of quiet.

"I've got to try, you know," Ron said flatly.

"I know," answered Chris.

More quiet.

"You aren't going to come, are you?" Ron more said than asked.

"No," Chris answered.

"Come visit us on the farm?" Ron more asked than said. "Do a little jammin."

"You know I will," Chris answered.

"Got a joint left to share with me?" asked Ron. "Just for old times sake."

And they smoked that joint together, and Ron moved into the farm, and the other bass player took up the job. And Ron's band got to be really, really great and managed to cut a demo record and came ever so close to making it -- but it never could quite seem to get over the hump and out of the bars. And the bars ate Ron alive over that first couple of years they were on the road, and he drank more and more heavily and did more and more drugs. Each time the band went through another rejection, or just missed another record deal, he sank somewhat lower.

Chris worked on construction, but was good to his word and visited the farm fairly often, bringing along his guitar and jamming with Ron and the guys. It was fun at first and he enjoyed his brief forays into such a life. But he could see that as good as the band was getting, it was falling apart, losing its soul, as it lost Ron -- as he disappeared from the surface of life. Finally, Chris drove home late one night from the farm, and put away his guitar, the one he had bought together with Ron all those years before. He put away the guitar and knew it was put away for good.

Some time passed and Chris didn't visit the farm. He heard about the exploits of the band and how there was difficulty with Ron, who was struggling with life and not getting it right. His friend was apparently shacked up most of the time with an alcoholic woman, showing up late for gigs, so drunk and high he couldn't remember which song was being played -- and he'd written them all. Chris tried calling the farm a couple of times, but couldn't catch Ron -- he wanted to talk to him -- see if he could help.

One night, as Chris was just saying good night to his parents, the phone rang. His Dad answered and gestured that it was for him.

"Hello," he said.

"Hi there, buddy," answered Ron's voice.

"How are you?" Chris asked, honest concern in his voice.

"Oh, I'm okay," Ron answered.

There was silence on the line.

"How's life?" asked Ron.

"Great," answered Chris.

"Still workin' on construction?" Ron asked.

"Yup," answered Chris. "It's a living."

More silence.

"You were right, you know," Ron said matter of factly.

"About what?" asked Chris, unsure what his friend was talking about.

"The audience does want fluff," Ron answered. "Actually, we were both right -- they want fluff, but they're sheep, too."

"I don't know, Ron, you guys seem to be doing okay," Chris said. "The last time I heard you, you were sounding great."

"Yea, we sound great all right," said Ron, "but every time we approach a record company or get close to a deal, we get the same old thing -- write us a top 40 piece -- give us something a little more commercial."

"So, why not?" asked Chris.

"I can't write fluff," Ron answered.

"You could write what you wanted," Chris said.

"I don't know," Ron answered.

"What's wrong?" Chris asked. "You sound bummed."

"A couple of the guys are leaving the band," Ron said. "They don't think we're heading in the right direction."

"I'm sorry, Ron," Chris said, but he could feel the disappointment in his friend's voice. "Got any replacements in mind?"

"Likely not," Ron answered. "Likely just going to fold the whole thing up. Give it up." His voice wavered, seemed to lose its composure, as he said the last.

"God, Ron, I'm sorry," Chris said. "After all the work you've put into it."

"The audience wants fluff, Chris," Ron said. "They haven't the balls to face the real stuff."

"Could be you're right," Chris answered. "Your stuff is great."

"From another time," Ron answered.

There was a moment of silence.

"Remember something," Ron said.

"What's that?" asked Chris.

"I never lose control," Ron said, and there was determination in his voice as he spoke the words.

"I know that," Chris said.

"Gotta go," Ron said.

"Let's get together," Chris suggested.

"Soon," Ron agreed.

And the line went dead.

They found Ron at the farm the next day. He was also dead. Overdosed. That's what they said. Overdosed on some very mean drugs. That's what they said. They said he played a pretty good guitar, but that he wouldn't conform -- wouldn't write a top 40 hit. In the end, that's what killed him. They'd all had integrity back in the old days, but only a few kept it for any length of time. For most of them, it was for the fun and the chicks. But there were others who took it more seriously -- and they're dead -- overdosed.

The Great
Car-With-No-Brakes Adventure
and how the boys handled it

The boys were restless. Their favourite hockey team, the Leafs, had lost again. They had watched the game on the prehistoric black and white TV that served as part of their entertainment centre at the dilapidated old farmhouse they were currently calling home. The boys had rented the house with a bunch of other friends back in the summer – all of them looking for a way to get out of their parent's house and into the big, wide party-filled world. And there were ten of them splitting on the rent for the house and it was seventy bucks a month total, so the boys were paying a cool seven dollars each. It was indeed 'way too cool…..

The place was party central. Every kid in the area came calling most weekends, knowing there would be the obligatory party. And parties were an excellent way to grease the gears, so to speak. Despite their reasonably priced living quarters, the boys were, of course, always broke. And the parties brought in much-needed supplies…..when the kids came to party, they brought alcohol, drugs and cigarettes. And those were things that were always in short supply at the farm. The boys were always happy to consume other people's party supplies and felt absolutely good about the arrangement, figuring it was sort of a fair deal…..the boys supplied a place to party…it was the least the kids could do was supply a few simple party favours.

Anyway, on this night, the boys were restless. It was a strange Saturday night that there was no party raging at the farm and that four of them were left alone to cheer on the beloved Leafs. Jay, Sid, Scott and Deli had been friends for years – since public school – and that seemed like years when you were just nineteen. And that's the age they were….nineteen and just finished high school and their parents hot on their heels to continue to higher learning or to get a job – both grim prospects for young men who just wanted to have a little fun and waste a little time. None of the boys could understand exactly why their parents were so anxious to have them take up the same type of boring, meaningless existences that they were apparently stuck in themselves for all eternity.

They had tried playing a little table tennis. The huge farm kitchen was the perfect place for a ping pong table and the table had been home to some stellar action over the last few months. Of course, it didn't always work out when there were more than four of them at home, so they gathered up ten ping pong paddles so everybody had their own. On occasion they would play seven or nine-handed table tennis where the object of the game was to hit the ball then run madly toward the other end of the table. So, they'd all be running madly, chasing each other around the table while trying to keep the ball in play….and, of course, this worked better if you were – as they say – completely blasted out of your shorts. Anyway, tonight, for some reason, the table tennis wasn't cutting it.

It was Deli who suggested they should head for town and last call at the bar. "We should head for town and make last call at the Inn," he'd suggested.

"Christ, I don't know," answered Sid. "It's 12:30 already…..I'm not sure we could make it."

"Twenty minutes tops," said Scott, "but I'm not driving."

"Well, I'm sure as hell not driving," Sid said, echoing Scott's sentiment.

"I've got no gas," Scott said. "I can maybe get to town, but I won't be able to get us back."

"Ah, come on guys," Sid complained. "Goddamned, it's been snowing and it's slippery and I hate driving in that shit. Plus I'm loaded. Let's stay here, smoke a couple more and see what's on the movie."

"Bullshit, Sid!" Deli said raising his voice a bit. "We're wasting time. Let's get rolling. I'm ready." He got to his feet, ready to go.

"Yea, yea, yea….let's go," blurted out Jay who'd been sitting on the end of the couch with his eyes closed, possibly passed out. "Comeon!" he urged the others, getting to his feet…."You only live once…and Sweet Lorraine is in town this week."

"Aaaah!" cried Scott. "I can't bear to see that woman naked again. It'll traumatize me for life. Maybe it already has. On my wedding night, all I'll be able to think about is Sweet Lorraine and I won't be able to get a hard on."

"You'll never get married asshole," Jay answered. "There ain't a respectable chick anywhere'd have you. You better hit on Sweet Lorraine tonight. That's your only hope."

"Asshole," Scott shot back in Jay's direction.

"Let's go," ordered Deli, and again started for the door.

This time, the suggestion worked, and another adventure had begun.

"Has anybody got joints?" Jay asked as they headed toward Sid's old, worn-out white Mercury Meteor.

"I've got a couple," answered Scott, slipping on a patch of ice in the driveway and almost falling. "Christ!" he swore.

Soon , the boys were heading for Hampden, normally a 20-minute drive from the farm. All was going well until they reached the first stop sign on the trip. Their driver, Sid, applied pressure to the brake pedal, and much to his surprise and serious consternation, he found there was no resistance, meaning, of course, that they had no brakes.

Aaaah," cried out Sid. "We've got no brakes!" And as he made the exclamation, they cruised completely through the stop sign and across the county road, where, luckily, there was no other traffic. And they gradually rolled to a stop."

"Wow," said Jay. "That was a little weird, eh?"

"Too weird," agreed Scott.

"Crap," lamented Deli…."I was hoping we'd make it to town…..maybe some chicks."

"Well, horseshit, we're not gonna make it now," said Sid. "We're pretty much beached. I think I can get it back to the farm without us walking."

"Hey, where's that old Hampden High spirit?" Jay asked. "We can still make it….we just need a plan."

"A plan!" said Sid. "We've got no brakes. What type of plan is going to fix that other than taking this piece of shit to Hap Lahn's on Monday morning? And it's likely gonna cost me a fortune….."

"Look," said Jay, "we can still make it to town – we just have to be careful. First, we need to smoke a joint. That would be a good start."

"Jesus, we're gonna die," Scott said. "I'm with Sid on this one. Back to the farm."

"Comeon," Deli answered. "What are you thinkin', Jay?"

"Well," answered Jay. "Scotty get that joint going….here's the plan. Look, we just drive along and when we're getting close to a stop sign or another road, Sid lets the car slow down until we're going really slow…..then, when we get to the actual corner, and we're almost stopped, Sid hollers out, the other three of us jump out and put our shoulders into the car…..Sid throws on the emergency brake…and…presto, we're stopped at the corner. Simple, man."

"Are you nuts?" asked Scott, not sure he could believe what he was hearing. "There are a whole lot of things that are wrong with that plan. Like number one is likely that someone could get killed – and that would be one of us who would be dead."

"Comeon, Scott," said Deli. "It sounds like a sort of a good plan. It's all about the execution. If we work together, we can make it work."

"Geez, I don't know," said Sid, still gripping the steering wheel and thinking about the county road they'd just cruised across and how lucky they'd been that there was nothing coming…."I mean, it could work….under the right conditions."

"Good, Sid, good…that's the spirit," answered Jay. "Let's give it a go…let's try it once and see how it works out."

"I don't believe it," Scott said. "You're all nuts." He passed the joint he'd finally gotten going to Sid.

And, somehow, gradually, Jay's plan started sounding better and better. Of course, they had already missed last call at the Hampden Inn….but that no longer seemed to be the point of the whole exercise. Now, it seemed to be about just making it to town without the benefit of brakes. They had Jay's plan and they were armed and dangerous – that was really all that mattered at this point.

So, they started toward town, and, at first, Sid just more or less inched along the gravel sideroad. They were still passing the joint around so there was that to be considered….and you had to pay attention to the road. Gradually, though, all seemed to be well and they started to move slightly faster…then a little faster than that….and, finally, perhaps a little faster than they should really be going when they had no brakes – begging the question whether they should be going at all.

Finally, they were approaching the first stop sign on the road, so they were reaching the first real chance to try out Jay's plan….Sid lifted his foot off the gas at what he thought was the appropriate time and the car started to gradually slow down as it approached the corner. However, there was really no sure way to judge exactly when was the right time for Sid to start trying to slow the car. There was actually some uncertainty at that point in the overall plan.

"Let us know," instructed Jay. "Let us know when we should jump. Let us know the exact time." He braced himself into the back door of the car and got ready to jerk the door open at the right time. The other boys were doing the same. "Ready on the Emergency Brake."

Closer and closer to the corner they got. The car seemed to be slowing at the right rate…..Sid was a bundle of anticipation, until, finally, he yelled that the others should execute their manoeuver and he yanked the Emergency Brake almost clean out of the car.

And the plan might have worked. Under different conditions. At the last moment, it seemed that Jay, Deli and Sid reconsidered the action of jumping out of a rolling car and declined to carry out such an action. Scott did not reconsider, meaning that he alone threw his door open, jumped out, turned and pushed his shoulder into the body of the car with all his might. And, of course, because he was the only one who carried out such an action, while the car might have stopped with four shoulders pressed into it, it surely wasn't going to stop with only one…and the poor boy was almost dragged under the car and killed – except that the Emergency Brake did stop the car and prevented his almost certain death.

It did knock him clean on his ass, though. "Christ almighty!" he exclaimed, as he got back to his feet and shook the snow off him. "That was good! That was good! I almost die. You assholes….you complete assholes."

"It didn't seem safe, Scotty," said Deli. "What can we say?"

"You guys are assholes," Scott repeated. "Assholes," he added, getting back in the car.

"Now what?" asked Sid.

"Let's go to town," answered Scott. "So I didn't almost die for nothing."

"We've missed last call," said Jay.

"Eh, we can head to Tony's for a burger," said Deli.

"Finally somebody with a decent plan," Scott answered.

And, so, instead of turning around like most sane people would have done, the boys decided to make for the local after-the-hotel-closes burger joint. Scott fired up another joint and the trip was underway.

And it proceeded mostly in an uneventful way, mainly because they didn't really have to pass through any more crucial intersections before they got back to town…..there was the business of getting onto the highway, but they held a meeting of the board and decided to just take their chances and zoom right out onto the main road, hoping not to encounter oncoming traffic in either direction – and that was what actually happened, so that they were either stupidly lucky or luckily stupid.

They made the approach to Hampden at a sort of medium speed, but they were approaching from the south side of town and that meant Roland's Hill was on the horizon. This was an extremely long, steep hill they had to climb at the entrance to town – and after the hill, they had to travel through a long winding S-curve that gradually sloped downhill into town.

"Not sure I can do this," gasped Sid, who was so tense after the drive that he was barely breathing and had his hands clenched tightly on the steering wheel.

"What do you mean?" asked Scott, lunging forward from the back seat and sticking his head between Sid and Deli in the front.

"After we get up the hill, it's all downhill," Sid answered, a tone of minor panic in his voice. "What if I can't get her slowed down? What about Hallman's car lot?"

They were about three quarters of the way up the hill as they discussed the situation.

"Keep her slow, Sid," advised Jay, also sitting forward to join the discussion. "You can do it, man."

"I'm not so sure," Sid answered, just as they cleared the crest of Roland's Hill and started on the downward curving slope. They were holding their collective breath.

"That's it, buddy....you're doing it," Scott said, more loudly than was necessary....

"Holy crap." Sid said, his teeth remaining tightly clenched. "She's really starting to move. I can't slow her down....."

"Hang in there," yelled Deli excitedly.

"I'm not going to make the next curve!" cried out Sid.

"Try for my place!" yelled Scott. "try for my driveway."

And it was true that Scott and his family did live right on the curves leading into the south end of town, so this seemed like an idea that made some sense.

"Quick, Sid!" shouted Jay. "It's right there. Crank the wheel!"

"Aaaaahhhhh!" The boys cried out in unison as Sid cranked the steering wheel and tried desperately to turn the brakeless white Meteor into Scott's Dad's driveway. But it was the dead of winter so that Scott's Dad's driveway was nothing more than a tiny hole in a seemingly endless snowbank . "AAAAAhhhhhhh!!!!" cried out the boys again, as Sid missed the actual driveway and crashed into the snowbank in front of Scott's house at a slightly faster rate of speed than he normally would have liked. And the car sailed, airborne, clean off the ground, up over the snowbank and ended its flight by coming down firmly, but somewhat gently, square in the middle of Scott's parent's front lawn, causing a huge cloud of fresh snow to erupt into the air around it.

"Holy shit," Scott muttered. "Holy shit," he repeated.

Slowly, the snow that had been swirling around the car settled, so they could again see out the front window.

"Wow," said Sid.

"Wow," added Jay....

There was a moment of silence, before Deli uttered some mostly unwelcome words. "Hey, Scott, isn't that your Dad in the window?"

And they all looked out from the beached automobile they were sitting in, and sure enough, there was Scott's Dad standing in the big picture window at the front of the house, hands firmly planted on his hips, with what surely seemed like a look of amused disgust on his face even from this distance.

"Oh, man," said Scott. "This can't be good."

"Don't worry," Sid said to his friend. "I'll explain to your Dad about the brakes. He'll understand. He's a guy."

It turned out they couldn't get out of Sid's car in the usual manner because they were buried up over the rocker panels in the snow and the doors wouldn't open. Finally, they crawled out the windows, congratulated themselves on their latest adventure, waved at Scott's Dad, who motioned at them to get lost – which they did.

They headed over to Tony's – the after-the-hotel-closes burger joint that was within easy walking distance.

"That was unbelievable – the way we cleared that damned snowbank," Jay was saying…."I'll bet you couldn't do that again if you got paid."

"Just incredible skill behind the wheel, buddy," Sid answered.

"What are you talking about," said Scott. "You were scared shitless driving that thing you call a car into town without brakes.

"Hey, hey, we made it," Deli said, as he pulled open the door to Tony's . "Let's put on the feed bag and figure out where we're gonna sleep."

"Don't worry," said Jay, following his friends into the restaurant. "I've got a plan."

"I'm never listening to another one of your plans," said Scott. "I damn near got killed on the backroads of Bentinck Township. I was almost roadkill."

"Yea, anybody who's stupid enough to jump out of a moving car sort of deserves to be roadkill," Sid said.

And that pretty well ended it, except that it was a well told tale for several days at the Hampden Pool Hall…..how Scott was nearly roadkill in the great "car-with-no-brakes" adventure. It did indeed cost Sid a fair percentage of a couple of week's pay to again have brakes on the old Mercury Meteor. But it would be worth it for the sake of future adventures. That was a certainty. Like the "how-did-you-lose-an-ounce-of-black-hash-in-the-goddamned-car-and-now-we-can't-find-it" adventure that followed soon after the "car-with-no-brakes" adventure, but wasn't nearly as much fun because of the situation with the hash. But that's another story.

Once in a Lifetime

t was a clear, cool April night, the kind when you're wishin' that spring was here, and the calendar says it is, but when the season's chill north wind tells you it's not.. He walked back into town, through the quiet darkness of the streets, and into a place that had once meant so much to him. He returned out of the night and out of the dark, places where he had been as no one. He knew each step of this place, as he measured them along the smooth-worn sidewalks of his past. Such was the home of his youth. Such was the home of his youth.

Even as he walked, he felt the waves of memory wash over him, even though it had been some twenty years since he had last come this way. Even as he passed over once familiar and still familiar terrain, and regarded the sights that loomed up out of the blackness, he felt a sense of comfort with both the memories and the place. He knew it well. Yet he knew it not at all.

He walked until he found a coffee shop, not quite all the way into the town, but far enough that he felt the comfort and knew he could rest. He got his coffee and sat in a corner of the place, put his knapsack against the wall, and pulled his tobacco and papers from his jacket pocket. He rolled the cigarette with care, as he always did, performing the oft-repeated action with a ritual deliberateness, studying the finished product for a moment, seeming to weigh the success of the job, before putting it to his lips and lighting it. He had thought he should sit and have a smoke, and perhaps a thought or two, before he continued the walk into town. He was glad he'd found this place. There were people, but only a few, so he could be by himself for a few moments more. He thought he needed that.

Finally, though, he felt it necessary to continue his journey. He had had all of these past two decades to himself, and now it was time for others to return to his life. Since that long ago time when he had left this place behind, thinking he would never return, such had been his feelings in those dark days, when the father and son had parted in anger; bitter, apparently bottom-less anger; the kind that may never beg forgiveness, but which may go on into the forever. Even as he stepped from the coffee shop and shouldered his pack, the thought of it caused a deep and dark pain to rise within him, until it caused him to stand and wait for it to pass. It was hard even after all this time. Such had been the feelings in those dark days.

It had been a time when fathers and sons had fought over nothing, but over everything. Over the length of hair. The choice of friends. The petulant attitude. Over everything, but over nothing. And it had led to the parting, and a mean bitterness toward one another. Not since he had left had he set foot in this place.

But now he'd passed through so much life. And he found that he must return. To lay the past to rest. Before it was too late. A time he felt was coming, even though he could not explain how it was that he knew.

As he continued the walk toward the centre of town, he found that emo-tion continued to wash over him as it had earlier in the form of the memories of the past. Much of the main street hadn't changed, surely many of the names of the stores had, but most of their fronts remained the same, so that the sense of comfort he had felt earlier was reinforced. It was in some ways like he had never left, so strongly did he feel the sameness of the place. Despite the des-tination, he found himself smiling. It was good to be home.

He knew exactly the place where he must go. He walked nearly the entire length of the town's main street, as he headed toward the place where he had spent his life when he'd been young. Although he had no way of knowing for sure, something told him his parents had not moved in all these years. It had been a comfortable, two-storey house they'd lived in, the home they'd bought when they were first married. He thought he knew his father well enough, even having not seen him for all these years, that he felt the old man would always stay in the house, regardless of his financial position, or just about anything else. And his mother would go along with what he said. Because that was the way it always was. It was the way it had been back in those other times, and there would be those who would be unable to leave those times behind, even though the world had, and his father would be one of them.

The house lay just off the main street, and as he approached, he wasn't surprised to see that it was nearly the only residence left on its street, nearly all the other property now being part of one commercial property or another. He wondered how much money his father had been offered for the property, only to turn it down, as much from stubbornness as for any other reason.

Finally, he stood at the end of the sidewalk to the house. He stood feet apart, rocking in his cowboy boots, looking to the side door; the one they had always used to enter and exit the place. He felt tears in his eyes. God, how it felt. What it brought back.

He stood so for a few moments, making no effort to walk the short distance to the door, not really even knowing if his parents still lived in the house, but also knowing that they must, he having been drawn to this place and no other. It was home. His home. And he had come back to it. He shifted under the weight of the pack. Nervousness with the emotion. He breathed deeply, trying to dispel it. Without much apparent success.

Then, it was time.

He headed up the sidewalk to the door. Just before he knocked, even as his hand was poised over the door, he paused, just for a second, and wondered. But only just for a second.

A woman came and peered out of the door's window and into the night. His mother. Changed, but the same.

He held his hand up in a type of abrupt wave, as she seemed to struggle to make him out. Then, a look of recognition flashed across her face, surprise, perhaps even happiness, he thought, and he saw her fingers move to the lock on the door.

"Frank," was the only word she could apparently manage as she threw the door open.

"Momma," he answered, as he stepped inside and put his arms around her.

They just stood, silently, perhaps remembering what it had been like.

Finally, after a few moments of this silent memory, they stepped apart, regarding each other.

"Are you alright?" she asked, her voice hesitant and uncertain.

"Yea, I'm alright," he answered.

There was another silence.

"You heard about your father," she finally said.

"No," he answered, he now filled with her uncertainty. "What about Dad?" he asked.

"He's in the hospital," she answered, her voice filled with hurt and concern. "He's had a heart attack."

He felt the energy drain from him. "Oh, God," were the only words he managed. He stepped forward and embraced her again, holding her close, feeling her against him, closing his eyes and trying to draw some of the pain from out of her and into him.

"When?" he finally asked, pulling away, and swinging his pack to the floor.

She reached behind him to close the door. "Two days ago," she answered. "After supper. We were sitting and watching Jeopardy and all of a sudden he started having trouble breathing."

"How is he?" the son asked.

"He's not great," the mother answered. "The doctor thinks he might pull through if he makes it through tonight and tomorrow."

"Christ," the boy said. "I'm so sorry, Mom."

"I'm just glad you're here," she answered. "I don't know how you knew to come, it must have been my thinking about you, but I'm glad you're here." She leaned over and gave him an abrupt tiny kiss on the cheek. "Come, sit, you must be tired." She offered him a familiar chair at a familiar kitchen table.

He sat.

"Can I get you anything?" she asked. "You're sure you're okay?"

"Yea, Mom, I'm okay," he answered, "and I could use a tea, if you don't mind."

"Heavens no," she replied, as she turned into the kitchen to start preparing it. "I'm just so glad you're home. So glad."

And, as he watched her go about preparing the tea, he also wondered what had brought him back to this place at this particular time. It was an odd thing to have happened. Very odd, indeed. Or so he thought.

Later, in the night, as he lay tucked into the bed he had slept in as a boy by the mother who had tucked him in even in those days, he continued to wonder about such a coincidence. But there was one thing he knew, as he wondered. He was glad he had come to this place. Glad for her. And glad for himself. And perhaps another would also be glad. Or so he hoped.

If there was time for such gladness. If he made it through tonight and tomorrow.

He and his mother had spent a couple of hours talking. Mostly about where he'd been and what he'd done through all his adult life, she not having known him since he'd been but a boy. And he had been many places and done many things with his life, travelling to far off locales and working at whatever presented itself on such occasions. His mother had sat across the kitchen table, appearing to listen intently, but he thought that while she might have listened, she did not hear, her mind being elsewhere, in the stark sterility of the hospital, with the man she had loved since they'd been sweethearts in high school.

And even now as he lay in his bed, and looked out the bedroom window into the reaching finger-like branches of the old maple tree that still lived outside, he found that images of the father also filled his mind. But he found that he remembered the good there had been before the bad; the happy times the family had spent. He remembered laying snug and secure in this bed on a long ago Christmas eve night, filled with nervous excitement at what was to come in the morning, if he could ever bring himself to sleep. He remembered working with his father at his grandmother's house, fixing this or that, as they had often done on the Saturdays of his youth; the old man's patience as he showed the boy how to do this or that. He remembered the two of them skating on the ice-covered river down by the dam, as they had done that one moonlit night when there had been no others around, and there had just been the two of them, and they had talked about men things like hockey and how to get along with a seemingly difficult sister.

There had been good times and they were fond memories. But after had come the bad, as much his fault as the father's; or so he now realized all these years later. The father wanting only what he thought was best for the boy, but the boy unable to see what was best, and really unable to even know what might be best. He remembered the first time he had refused to go to the barbershop with his father. "No son of mine is going to go around looking like a girl," the old man had thundered. The boy had tried to explain. Had tried to tell the father that his generation didn't see things the way the one before had. That things were different now. That the world was changing. But the father had been unable to see -- to understand. Or so the boy had thought.

And although that really hadn't been the beginning of their disagreements, those had started earlier, perhaps when he'd first balked at spending his Saturdays at his grandmother's fixing this or that, or maybe when he'd refused to go to church with the family one Sunday, it seemed the length of his hair became the symbol of the friction between them. He wondered if he had the chance to see the old man, whether the father would notice that his hair was short now, that finally it had been he who had relented and gotten it cut of his own accord. Looking back, it seemed so silly.

Sleep would not come to him, so he climbed out of the snugness of the bed, and slipped into his jeans and jacket. He crept down the stairs, remembering how often he had done so when this had been his home, and silently unlocked the front door and disappeared out onto the porch. Once there, he pulled his papers and tobacco from his jacket pocket and rolled a cigarette. He rolled it carefully between his fingers before putting it to his lips and lighting it.

He sat on the steps to the porch and took a long drag, inhaling deeply, as he looked out across the parking lot of the neighbouring service station to where a restaurant was located. Except for some exterior changes, the restaurant had remained nearly unchanged since he had last sat here and looked toward it. How strange it seemed to be back in this place. To have travelled the world, and to have come back here to where his life had started.

He sat and smoked, soaking up the quiet stillness of the spring night, not really even noticing the coolness. He found himself hoping that his father would be alright and that he would live to see tomorrow. Somewhat to his surprise, he found that he wanted to see the old man again. To see if anything had changed. Or if things had gone beyond change and could not now be undone. Only tomorrow held the answer. He flipped the now-spent cigarette into the driveway and went back into the house hoping for sleep.

And he did sleep, but it was a fitful sort of sleep, the kind where reality mixes with the world of dreams so that sometimes you're not sure which is which. So that he awoke in the morning feeling unrested and rumpled. The clock on the night table said it was only about seven o'clock, but he rolled out of bed anyway, sure he could hear another who was up and about in the house. He slipped into his clothes and headed downstairs.

His mother greeted him as he walked into the kitchen.

"Sleep well?" she asked brightly.

"Not worth a damn," he answered, wondering at how she could always be so bright and alive in the morning, even as she always had been when he'd been young.

"I had trouble too," she said, ignoring his profanity, and the admission seemed to make the brightness dim, so that she suddenly appeared concerned and troubled. But only for an instant.

"You ready for breakfast?" she asked.

"Just some coffee," he answered.

"It'll just be a minute," she said. "I've got a pot on for myself."

And he watched her as she fussed about the kitchen, getting him out a mug and such. It had always been "her" kitchen, even when he'd been a boy. His father had rarely ventured into it, and on the few occasions when he did, she would shoo him from it. Even his sister hadn't seemed to feel entirely comfortable in the place. It was like it was her special place in the house; the place where she felt the most comfortable. He remembered back to when he'd been nearing adulthood, to the time when things with his father had been extremely tense. An evening's entertainment had turned into a night's worth, so that it was early in the morning before he staggered home. It had been about an hour before his father usually got up for work, so he'd assumed no one would be up, and he could creep silently into the house and make his way to his room without the dreaded lecture.

As he'd put his key to the lock, opened the door, and tip-toed into the kitchen, he looked up to see his mother sitting at the kitchen table, hands cupping an early morning coffee.

"You're up early," she'd said.

"Late," he'd answered.

"Frank, what will your father say?" she'd asked, giving him her best scolding look.

"I don't care, Mom. He doesn't care," he'd answered.

"Don't sell him short, son," she'd said. "He cares about you."

He'd not answered, choosing instead to turn away from her as he hung his coat on one of the hooks behind the door.

"You're up awful early," he'd said to her, as he turned back into the kitchen.

"Just having my coffee," she'd answered.

"But Dad won't be up for an hour," he'd remarked.

"I always get up earlier than he does," had been her reply. "I guess it's something I do from when you kids were younger. I used to get up before everybody, just to have some time to think about things before all the commotion started." She'd paused. "I guess you could say it's my quiet time."

He was returned from the memory and back to the present, as she set his coffee in front of him.

"Sorry, if I'm wreckin' your quiet time this morning," he said.

"I'm just glad you're here," she answered.. "It was good to know you were in the house last night. I didn't want to be alone." As she said the last words, tears welled up in her eyes.

He rose to go to her, but she turned away, brushing the tears away with her ever-present apron.

"I'm just a silly, old woman," she said.

"I don't think so," he said ever so softly.

They drank much of their coffee in silence, he seeming not to want to disturb her time, and she seeming to take advantage by disappearing far inside herself.

"What time are you going to the hospital?" he finally asked, as he walked across the kitchen to put the now-empty mug near the sink.

"I'll go about nine," she answered., bringing herself back to the here and now and away from where she might have been as they'd shared the quiet time.

"I'd like to go, but do you think I should?" he asked.

"What do you mean?" she asked in return, her face looking puzzled.

"Well, he's pretty sick by the sound of it, and I wasn't exactly his favourite person when I left," he answered. "I don't want to set off his blood pressure or something."

"Don't be silly," the mother answered. "Of course, you'll come. He'll be glad to see you. It'll do him good," she added, and there was certainty and finality in her voice as she said the last.

So he didn't argue, instead he told her he was going back upstairs to take a shower, and he left her in the kitchen while he did so.

He felt good as he let the too hot water course over him. There had been no shower in the house when he'd been growing up, and he remembered the Saturday night bath ritual, when he and his sister would take the weekly plunge, usually after an argument about the necessity of such an action. Now he couldn't remember the last time he'd had a bath. Usually, when he was on the road, he cleaned himself up as readily as he could depending on what facilities were available, and it seemed he always ended up having showers. He'd had a few baths, but they were rare, and he hadn't had one for a while. Now, as he stood in the makeshift shower his father had pieced together in an old house not built for one, he remembered back to those bath nights, and he remembered how he'd used to like to lay deep in the water, with it just under the bottom of his nose, and watch the steam as it misted and curled off the surface.

But he also remembered his father's concern that too much hot water would be used in each bath, and it was like his Dad was outside the bathroom door even in the present as he showered, listening to the sound of the shower, timing him to make sure he used only the required amount. So he was quick about his business and the memory of the Saturday night baths was a brief one.

Finally, he sat on the front porch, with his morning cigarette, waiting for his mother to announce that it was time to go. She'd again offered something to eat after he'd finished in the shower, but he had again declined, following his habit of usually not eating in the morning.

When it was time, they climbed into his parents' car, and headed for the hospital.

There was little conversation as they drove, she seeming to be caught up in her own thoughts as she had been earlier, while he was also with his, wondering what he would find when they arrived at their destination. It had been a long time. A very long time. Perhaps too long. Perhaps too short.

His father was in the ICU and few visitors were allowed, so they had to stop at a nursing station. The nurse told them he had come through the night fine, but that they could only see him one at a time.

"You go ahead," the son said, as they stood outside the room. "You should maybe warn him I'm here. He should want to see me."

To his surprise, she didn't argue. "I suppose you're right," she said instead. "But I wish we could go in together."

"It's better this way," the son answered. "He should be prepared. It might come as a shock"

"He'll want to see you," she said, and she took her son's hand and gave it a firm, little squeeze, at the same time giving him a soft, sincere kiss on the cheek.

"I hope so," the boy answered . "I really do hope so." And he really felt like he did.

So, he waited. In the small lounge down the hall from the room. And he looked out from the hospital window down the road to where the town cemetery was located; the one where the last two generations of his family were buried. He had found it odd when the town's new hospital had been built and a site had been chosen so close to the cemetery. He and his friends had joked that it wouldn't exactly inspire confidence in those in hospital. He smiled even now as the thought crossed his mind.

But even as he smiled he found himself remembering back to his grandparents. His mother had told him last night that his father's mother was still alive, but all his other grandparents had died when he'd been very young. He could only remember his grandfather on his father's side and even he had died when Frank had been just five. And now that he thought about it, that had been the only real brush with the death of someone close he had experienced in all his life, and he remembered nothing about it, except the drive to his aunt's place in the country following the funeral. Death had always seemed like something far away; a place for others, but not him. While he'd been away, he had wondered once in a while about death, and whether those he had been close to may have perished, but that was hard for him to imagine because he remembered them all being so very young and so very much alive. He'd seen some death in other parts of the world, but it hadn't concerned him.

Even a while back when he'd been in the bus crash in the mountains, and the guy beside him had hit his head and been killed, it had seemed like nothing in particular. He had felt nothing even when he helped carry the body out of the bus, or even when those around wept and talked of the man's family. He had just felt a numbness; the same type of numbness he had carried with him on the road for all these years. And it had stayed with him for some considerable time after, until the one night just a short time ago when he had seemed to see the man's blood-covered face in his dreams, and he had also seen a vision of his mother weeping, seemingly for the stranger who had died on the bus. But perhaps not.

"Frank," he heard his mother's voice say, interrupting his thoughts and returning him to the present. He turned to see her standing over by the doorway to the room.

"How is he?" Frank asked, as he walked toward her.

"He seems better," she answered. "He seems to have more energy."

"That's good," the son said.

There was a slight pause in the room.

"And he wants to see you," she said, answering a question she knew was on his mind.

Frank said nothing at first, but he felt relief flow through him.

"You're sure he's up to it," he finally said, but it was then that he wondered whether perhaps it was he who might not be ready.

"Yes," she said. "He wants to see you," she repeated.

Still, just for a moment, he continued to stand by the window, now looking away from her, out of the window and again toward the cemetery.

"Come, Frank, everything will be fine," his mother said, seeming to be able to sense his discomfort at finally being confronted with a time he had been putting off for all these past twenty years.

He smiled to acknowledge her comment.

"I know," he said softly. "I know," he repeated just as quietly.

And he left the room and walked the short distance to another room where his father lay.

The room was bathed in a semi darkness as he pushed the door open, there being no window, no way for the bright airiness of the outside to intrude into the apparent gloom of the place. He could see the outline of a figure, apparently his father, in a bed at the other end of the room, and he could see the various monitors and other devices that stood by the bed, and he could hear the humming sound they made. He let the door close silently behind him and stood statuesque just inside, seeming to look for a sign that he should approach, while not even knowing if there was another consciousness in the room. Not really knowing what to expect.

He ventured forward a couple of half steps.

"Dad," he softly called.

There was a stirring from the bed.

"Frank," he heard his name called, but it didn't sound like his father, for this voice was filled with weakness and unsureness, not the strength and stubbornness of the man he had known in his youth.

He walked closer, until he could see the man in the bed. His father smiled ever so slightly. He was surprised to receive such a welcome.

"It's good to see you," Frank said, struggling to find the words.

The old man in the bed nodded his head just the tiniest bit but enough to show that he apparently agreed.

"How are you, Frankie?" the father asked, his voice straining and hoarse.

"I'm good, Dad," the boy answered. "How are you?"

"I've been better," the father answered. "I'm so damned tired I can hardly hold my eyes open."

"You rest, Dad," he answered. "I can leave."

"No," protested the father. "I want to talk to you."

"It can wait 'til you're well," he said.

"No. Stay," was the reply.

There was silence in the room, as the son waited, and the father paused, seeming to try to collect what remained of his shattered strength.

"It's over, Frank," he started. "I was a fool. I know that now."

"Dad," interrupted the boy.....

But the father wouldn't let him continue.

"Listen, Frank," he said, and there was conviction in the quietness of his voice. "I know we're both to blame. That's what you're going to say. But you were a kid. I could have afforded to have been more understanding."

"Dad, I was a jerk," interrupted the son.

"No more than I was," answered the father. "I caused your mother a lot of hurt," he continued. "She's the one I hurt by being a stubborn idiot. I thought you should be just like me and I couldn't understand why you weren't. So, I drove you away."

"Naw, I left, Dad," he answered. "It shouldn't have been important how long my hair was and I shouldn't have stayed out 'til all hours, and I should have got a job. Just like you said." He paused. "I haven't amounted to much, Dad."

"I can't be the judge of that," answered the father. "You're the only one who can say how your life's turned out. But I just feel that I really let you down."

The son stood in quiet, not quite knowing what to say.

"If you're surprised, you should be," the father said. "Up until a couple of days ago, I was just as angry at you as the day you left. But this thing has made me think. There's no second chances, boy. This is it."

"I think I know that too," answered the son. "I'm not sure why, but I think I know that too," and for some reason he suddenly saw the man who had been sitting beside him when the bus had crashed, after they'd carried him to the side of the road, and he lay there in death. He felt tears in his eyes.

"You're a good, boy, Frankie," the old man said. "Your mother needs you. And if I get out of here, I'll need you too."

"You'll get out, Pop," the boy said. "You're too tough to just lay there and die," and he punctuated the last remark with a smile, and reached out and took his father's hand.

The father also smiled. "I'm glad you're home, boy," he said through the smile. "Your mother tells me you've been travelling. I'd like to hear."

"When you get out, Pop," he said, softly squeezing the hand.

Again the father smiled.

"Forgive me?" he asked.

"Only if you forgive me," he answered, and he leaned over and hugged the old man.

They were both silent when he stood back up. The father's eyes were closed, his face strained with fatigue.

"I'm going to go now," the boy said.

The father re-opened his eyes, just a little and looked at him. He made an effort to nod his head.

"I'll see you later, Dad," the son said.

And this time it was the father who gave the son's hand a soft, little squeeze, and it was the son who smiled.

And he released his grip on the old man's hand, and turned and walked to the door. And just as he pulled it open, he turned and again regarded the figure laying in stillness on the bed, and he again heard the hum of the monitors and other devices. It was good, he thought. Things would be fine. He knew they would. He just knew.

He hugged him mother when he walked up to her in the lounge.

"He'll be fine," he said to her as he put his arms around her, and again he felt tears starting to fill his eyes. "He's going to be fine," he said, repeating his feelings.

"I know he is," she answered. "I know."

And he was fine, but it took him a long time to recover from the effects of the heart attack. But they worked at it together, helping him with his exercises and walking, and all sharing in the diet the doctor put him on.

And he had a chance to tell his parents, and his sister who he also became re-acquainted with, about all his travels and the rest of his life, and the house was again filled with laughter, as they shared this story or that one, as it had once been filled with laughter when they had all been younger.

And he found a job in the town, not much of a job, just cleaning offices at night, but he was resolved to stay for a while, and to get to know his parents again, and to share in their lives. And when his father was better, they went fishing together, and watched baseball games on the TV, and even once they went to the city to see a live hockey game once that season arrived. And it was good. It was very good. And he felt a belonging. Something he had not felt for many years.

And he didn't know how long he would stay, not knowing when a wanderlust, built up over the years on the road, might come again. But, for the moment, it was good to be home. It was good to remember and to be a part of the memories once again.

You only live once, he often found himself thinking. You only get one chance. Make the most of it.

A Sense of Death

She was a withered old crone of a woman. Gone were the days of fresh beauty, and, indeed, even the days of stately elegance. She was approaching her ninetieth year, yet even at that ripe old age, she continued to tend to her own house, and was, by all accounts, a most independent person. But thoughts of her impending doom, for surely it must be impending, were with her constantly -- not that she feared it, but just that she knew it was coming, almost as if she sensed it. She had heard her grandmother, in another faraway time, tell her mother that she hadn't much longer to spend upon this earth -- that she knew her time was coming -- and, indeed, it had been only a few short months later when they'd laid that old woman to rest. It was like she could sense it. The coming of death.

And she had been revered in her lifetime for her cooking and baking, and even during the Christmas season recently past, she'd baked more than her fair share of special cookies and cakes to dispense to others in her community. And she'd received more than her fair share of praise and compliments, not only for the fine results of her labours, but also just for carrying out such a task at her extreme age. But even while she'd been doing her Christmas baking, she'd been reminded that her days in the kitchen were coming to an end. Once she forgot to add sugar to a batch of cookies and once she forgot to turn off the oven before falling asleep on the chesterfield in the middle of the afternoon -- and that could have been a dangerous turn of events, if only her daughter, Jane, hadn't dropped over a short time after she'd nodded off.

And even now, as she sat in an easy chair in the living room, thumbing through a lady's magazine, scanning the pages for a handy household hint or perhaps a soon-to-be-favourite recipe, she felt worry. She wondered what she could do with a lifetime of recipes as she neared the end of her days. That was what troubled her most -- that her beloved recipes would somehow not be passed along to someone who would know the loving and caring they possessed -- because those were the most important ingredients any of her recipes contained -- the loving and caring she poured into them.

And the reason she worried was because she couldn't see anyone in her immediate family who might qualify for such an important duty as was the shepherding of the family recipes. She presumed that Jane, her only daughter, should be the one to receive them. But she was a woman nearing seventy herself, and she seemed to have no interest in kitchenly things. Jane had never done much baking and cooking over the years, and now that her own child was long since grown, she and her husband, Ed, seemed to be eating out every second night. And last Christmas, she'd bought a Christmas cake. Can you imagine? the old woman thought -- buying a Christmas cake and not using Gram Dunlop's tried and true recipe. It was a serious indiscretion indeed. That's what the old woman had thought.

So it really was a problem. She had a granddaughter, Jane's girl, Alice, but there had been family difficulties. The girl, although she'd be over forty and hardly a girl anymore, had been living away for the past many years and the old woman wasn't surprised that Jane spoke little of her . There was a past the old woman knew of -- and she cringed to think those dark thoughts. It was a sorrowful past, indeed. So that even when word had reached them that Alice was married and had had a child, there was no rejoicing and not even a card sent. It had hurt the old woman to know she had a great grandchild, but to not know that same child. But she never argued with Jane -- that wasn't her way. So, her family was lost to her.

And her mind returned to the recipes. And it seemed the recipes she'd so long ago promised her own mother that she would protect and cherish now seemed to be in a most precarious position.

It was a knock on her door that brought her back to her senses. It took her a couple of minutes to struggle up and out of the chair, and by that time Jane was already into the house and bustling about the place.

"Really, mother, were you having a nap?" her female offspring asked, not actually expecting an answer.

"No," answered the old woman," just collecting my thoughts."

"Well, you seem to be doing a lot of that these days," Jane answered.

"I think I've earned the right," she answered back, perhaps a little more sharply than was necessary.

"No one's saying you haven't," Jane replied.

There was a moment of quiet as Jane bustled over to the kitchen counter and barged through the pile of mail that was sitting there. "I've got some news," she said, hardly turning back toward her mother as she spoke the words.

"Really, dear, good news?" the mother asked.

"Your great granddaughter is coming for a visit," Jane answered. "Alice's daughter. She's out on her own now and she wants to come for a visit -- to get to know us -- that's what she said on the phone."

The old woman was silent, wondering what her reaction should be, but not really sure, so giving none.

"She's sent you some cards, Mom," the daughter offered. "But she's never been here. She was born after Alice moved out west almost twenty-five years ago."

"Oh, I don't think I know her," the old woman said, a little unsure of herself, continuing to think even of her granddaughter and how long it had been since she had seen her.

"No, Mom, you really don't know her," Jane answered. "Neither do I. But she's coming and expects to stay for a week. I guess she'll stay with us, but I could put her up here for a couple of nights because we're supposed to be going away. We just weren't expecting to have company." Her voice was chopped and sharp, betraying those same emotions.

"She might stay here?" the old woman asked, hoping she'd heard right.

"Well, for a couple of nights," Jane answered. "Is that okay, Mom?"

"Oh, that would be fine," the old woman answered, and she knew it would be -- it would be very fine to have some company in the house, even if it was someone she was a little unsure about.

And the very next day she set about cleaning out the extra room, the one that had belonged to Jane all those years ago when that sharp-tongued woman had been a tender child. She tumbled the sheets from the bed down the laundry shoot, then chased them down the two flights of stairs to the basement to wash them. And she dusted about and got out the little hand-held vacuum cleaner she used now that she couldn't handle the big upright anymore. Soon, she had the room all tidied up and ready to receive a guest.

Much to Jane's chagrin, the young woman arrived on a Sunday, two days earlier than had been expected. And she could hardly be asked to cook a meal for such a multitude as that one extra mouth constituted, especially when the arrival was so unannounced, so she persuaded Ed to take them out for Sunday dinner -- and wouldn't it be nice if they invited Mother along so she could meet her great granddaughter. So, they did.

The old woman was ready twenty minutes early, as was her custom to always be ready a little early, and was sitting in a chair by the door waiting for her son-in-law's big, blue car to pull up out in front of the house. When it did, she was quickly outside and down the walk.

A fresh-looking, attractive younger woman she didn't recognize bounded out of the car to meet her.

"Great grandma!" the young woman exclaimed, gathering the old woman up in her arms for a big hug.

The old woman said nothing, but was somewhat overwhelmed.

"Great grandma," the young woman repeated. "I'm Mary, your great granddaughter."

The old woman stepped back from her and gave a long look up and down, then smiled and leaned forward, giving her a light kiss on the cheek. "Welcome, child," she said.

And they climbed back into the car, paying attention to Ed's clearing of his throat as a sign of impatience, and were off to the restaurant. They rode mainly in quiet, but the young woman did ask after her great grandmother's health and offered her a warm, pleasing smile, which the old woman found that she returned.

It was a pleasant enough dinner, the food was good, and the company was okay, but Jane, the grandmother, peppered her granddaughter with a seemingly endless string of questions in an apparent attempt to discover everything about the young woman on this initial meeting.

After the meal had been consumed, and the tip had been paid, Ed had gone to get the car and Jane was in the washroom. The great grandmother and the young woman stood alone just inside the front door.

"Don't pay your grandmother no never mind," the old woman said, breaking the silence that stood on guard between them.

"I don't think she likes me," answered Mary, the great grandchild.

"She doesn't like anybody," the old woman commented. "She's been a bitter woman for a very long time. It's what drove your mother away."

"What made her like that?" the young woman asked.

"There's a reason to it," the great grandmother answered. "She wasn't always like this. She was a beautiful, kind child."

"What could have made her so miserable," the young woman asked again. "I wish you could tell me. I want to try to understand why Mom hates her so."

Just then Jane appeared, heading in their direction.

"Come stay with me later in the week," the old woman advised quietly. "Your grandmother wants you to anyway."

"I will," answered the young woman, speaking in a hushed tone under her breath.

And Jane, that formidable battleaxe rejoined them, and Ed arrived with the car.

It was just the next day when the great granddaughter first came calling.

"Grandma had to go to the church," she said. "I asked if she'd drop me here."

"Yes, she's a busy woman, that Jane," the old woman said, as she welcomed her great granddaughter into her house. "I was hoping you'd come and stay," she added.

"Oh, I'm coming on Thursday and Friday," Mary answered. "If that's okay."

"That would be fine, dear," she answered. "But what will we do for two whole days together? There's not much around here for a young person like you."

"I thought we might bake something," suggested the great granddaughter, offering a sly smile. "If I could talk you into it. Grandma says you don't do much baking anymore."

"No, I don't," the old woman answered. "You can buy most everything you want these days -- no need for all that work -- that's what your Grandmother says."

"I know what Grandma says," Mary answered, "but Mother has talked to me about you and your cookies ever since I was a little girl. I told myself years ago that if I ever worked up the courage to come back here that I'd just have to have some of your cookies."

"You don't say -- your Mother still talks about me," the old woman reflected, remembering the young Alice when she'd been but a girl and before the seemingly lifelong rift between mother and daughter.

"Oh, yes, she's missed you," said the great granddaughter.

"Then, why didn't she call or write?" asked the old woman.

"She told me once that she had to cut herself right off from here," answered the great granddaughter. "That she couldn't have any contact -- that it was the only way."

"You know, it's caused me great heartache, what happened between your mother and grandmother," the old woman said. "I used to try to talk to your grandmother about it, but if I even brought it up, she'd just get quiet on me -- and Ed curses your mother, won't even discuss her. Alice was a rebellious youngster, but it really wasn't her fault -- and she probably doesn't even know the truth of the matter."

"I need to know" said the young woman. "What would cause a mother and daughter to fall so far apart. It's so very sad."

"What's sad is that you haven't had a chance to taste any of my cookies," the old woman replied, obviously attempting to break the somewhat sombre mood that had descended over the two. "And that I haven't invited you in for tea."

And it was true that the entire conversation had been conducted in the front hallway to the house, and they had fallen into it so quickly that the great grandmother hadn't even invited the other inside.

But before long, they were seated in a room that would have once been known as the parlour, and they were sipping on tea, and the old woman had dragged out her large wooden recipe box, the repository of the family recipes, and the young woman was sitting on the floor surrounded by so many of the tastes that had come down through the generations of her family. She seemed in her glory.

"Oh, these are so wonderful," she said. "I couldn't have imagined that there would be such a collection."

"My great grandmother was the first generation to come to this part of the world, and she brought a few recipes from her mother with her," said the old woman. "That was the beginning and it's carried on to me."

"What about grandmother?" Mary asked.

"She has no interest," answered the great grandmother. "She'd rather buy something than go to the trouble of baking it."

"That's a shame," said the young woman. "What will happen to the family tradition?"

"I don't know," answered the old woman, but she was already hoping.

They picked out a few recipes over the next hour or two, while the great granddaughter waited for her grandmother to reclaim her -- recipes they had resolved to try later in the week when the young woman came for her stay.

"Oh, I'm so looking forward to it," Mary said, as she prepared to disappear out the door to the waiting car.

The old woman smiled.

And it seemed as if Thursday might never come, and the old woman saw nothing of her great granddaughter over the next couple of days, and she hoped nothing had come up that might prevent the planned baking spree. She checked her stock of ingredients and took a cab to the grocery market in search of the supplies she thought she might need, arriving home with several bags of selected items.

And, finally, it was Thursday. The old woman was up early and was waiting with anticipation when the phone rang. It was the great granddaughter, calling to see what time she should come. Come as soon as you wish, answered the old woman, and it was true that she wanted the young woman to come extremely soon.

And she did come, about an hour later, carrying her tote bag, so there was no doubt that she was staying over. The great grandmother swept open the door and welcomed her in.

"I've been looking forward to this all week," said the great granddaughter.

The old woman wanted to exclaim, 'Me, too', but managed instead to ask where Jane and Ed were off to.

"Oh, they've likely got a motel booked on the edge of town," replied the young woman. "Anything to get rid of me."

"I'm sure it's not as bad as all that," answered the old woman. "Your Grandmother's likely very glad to have you here for a visit. She's just not good at showing her emotions."

"She seems like a very mean woman," the great granddaughter said.

"Well, you should know the story before you judge her," the old woman said.

"Then, tell me," implored the young woman. "I should know."

"Yes, you should," answered the old woman. "Let's fix a cup of tea and we'll talk before we start the baking."

And with that settled, the two of them went into the kitchen and had soon fixed steaming hot cups of tea. Then, they retired to the parlour.

"I'm not even sure I should be doing this," said the great grandmother. "Perhaps if your grandmother wants you to know, she should tell you."

"Great Grandma, don't shut me out now," pleaded the young woman.

"It won't fix things," said the great grandmother.

"I don't care," said the young woman. "I just want to know what happened."

"Well, it goes back a long way," the great grandmother started; "to when your grandmother was a young woman -- during the war. She fell desparately in love with a young man from town here. He was quite a young man, too. A star athlete and high marks at school and could have had his pick of the girls -- but chose your grandmother above all the rest. Your great granddad and I couldn't have been happier." The old woman paused, and her gaze disappeared into a time past as she seemed to be remembering.

"But it was the war," she continued. "And every young man in town was signing up and going off to fight. I know young people today wouldn't understand, but it was the thing to do back then. There was a job to do and the young men went off to do it -- that's all there was to it."

"You're right," interjected the young woman; "people today wouldn't understand doing something like that."

"It was different back then," said the old woman. "Things seemed more cut and dried." Again, she paused.

"So, what happened, Great Grandma?" asked the great granddaughter.

"Well, it was just a matter of time before Jane's beau signed up to fight," said the old woman. "He joined the air corps. Jane was so proud of him when he came home on leave with his new uniform on. She paraded him all over town and made sure everybody had a good look at the two of them together. And they did make a handsome couple to be sure." There was another moment taken for more quiet reflection.

But the great granddaughter was impatient for the story to continue. "Was he killed?" she asked. "Killed overseas?"

"No, in some ways, that would have been the easier," the old woman answered.

"Then, what?" asked the young woman, sitting forward on the couch, anxious for more of the tale.

"He came home midway through the war," the great grandmother answered. "And he was already a big hero and he'd been on plenty of missions. The whole town came out to see him. Your grandmother was in her glory, and somebody suggested the two of them should get married -- I don't even really know where the idea came from -- but it came nonetheless, and the next thing you know it was arranged and they were married."

"God, I thought Grandpa Ed was Grandma's only husband," the young woman said, obviously surprised at this bit of news.

"Well, that's what your Grandmother would wish," continued the great grandmother. "You see, the happy couple spent a wedding night before he went back to the war." The old woman faltered.

"And what?" asked the great granddaughter. "What happened?"

"There was a seed planted on that one night," the old woman said.

"Grandma was pregnant?" asked the young woman.

"Yes, and she hadn't found out for a week and she got a letter from her young man," the old woman answered. "He apologized for marrying her. Said he got carried away when he was home and didn't really mean it. Said he knew she really didn't want to be tied down. Besides, he'd met a girl near where he was stationed, and he knew she was his true love -- and she'd gotten pregnant -- and he'd promised to marry her as soon as he could get a divorce." The old woman stopped, abruptly, breathless after the words poured out of her. Tears welled up in her eyes. "It's hard to remember," she said.

A silence hung in the air.

"So, grandma told him she was pregnant?" asked the great granddaughter. "She had to tell him."

"No, your grandmother didn't want him from the minute she read his letter," said the old woman. "She surely didn't want him back just because of the baby -- and that was what she thought would happen if she told him."

"You're kidding. She kept it to herself." The great granddaughter seemed to realize the enormity of that situation during that time.

"I knew," answered the old woman, "but not even your great granddad. It was a closely guarded secret until today."

"My mother doesn't know?" asked the great granddaughter.

"No, she thinks Ed is her father -- just as you've always thought," answered the old woman. "Your grandmother hooked onto Ed right away and he just played the part for all these years."

"But then why the bitterness between my mother and grandmother? And why does Ed hate my Mom?" came the questions.

"Remember, your grandmother loved her pilot," the great grandmother started. "It was like she was destroyed by that one lesson in love -- it changed her into a bitter, miserable person, who, it seemed, could love nothing else in life." She hesitated and stifled a gentle tear. "She was my baby, my little girl, all that we had, and she lost her heart and was ruined by that one lesson in love.

"She took it out on your mother," she continued. "Not so much in obvious ways, but you could tell she had a dislike for the child -- like it reminded her -- and when Ed found out your grandmother couldn't love him, he hated it because of that. Your mother had a most unhappy childhood. I tried to help but your grandmother shut me out." There were more tears.

The great granddaughter wept at what had been to have made so much unhappiness. She came to her great grandmother and the two gathered each other up in solemn embrace.

"You're wonderful, great grandmother," said the young woman.

"Oh, child," answered the old woman. "That so much has passed, and I didn't do more."

And they wept all the harder and held each other, and felt sad and sorry for one another, and for the others who'd been part of the story. But, finally, the great grandmother composed herself and gently caressed the young woman who lay with her head upon the old woman's lap.

"Has your mother lived a happy life out where she lives?" asked the great grandmother, her voice soft and quiet.

"I think she has," answered the great granddaughter. "I think she and my Dad are pretty happy together."

"I hope they are," answered the old woman. "I really hope they are, because your mom deserves that."

There was a moment of silence.

"We should work on them," said the young woman.

"What do you mean?" asked the great grandmother.

"We should get them together," said the young woman. "My mom and grandma."

"That may have to be your job," answered the old woman.

"Why's that?" asked the great granddaughter.

"I'm too old to get involved in any of this," answered the great grandmother.

"I need your help," said the great granddaughter. "I can't do it without you."

"I suppose I'll do what I can," answered the old woman, "with the time that's left to me."

"Oh, great grandma, you'll live forever," said the young woman, and this time there was a smile on her face and the tears were swept away. She got up from the couch and reached back and helped the old woman to her feet.

"I don't know about that," said the great grandmother, "but I guess I'll be around long enough to do a little baking, as long as we hurry up and get started." She returned the smile and the two headed for the kitchen.

And they spent the rest of the next two days up to their elbows in flour and other assorted sundry baking products and it was a most pleasant time. And they talked about all manner of things, including what steps might be taken to heal the family rift, but there was a lightness to the conversation and no more of the dark, desolation of that first little while. There was laughter and happiness and it was as if they had been best friends always, and not like they'd not set eyes on each other for less than a week. It was a most joyous time.

And it so happened that the great grandaughter left at the end of the week, having to return to her own life, but not before the two women had sworn a pact to try to lessen the hostility in the world by some two souls. It seemed a tall order, indeed.

But the old woman was good to her word, and soon after the younger one had departed, she took it upon herself to try to make a start in the conversion. She contrived a way to get Jane away from Ed for some length of time, and she spoke to her daughter of many serious things on the supposed pretense that her own life was drawing to a close, and that she must make some effort to save her soul by repenting for her many misgivings. She began with Alice.

And the young woman returned to her home, and had soon managed to arrange a girls' weekend out for she and her mother, so they could discuss some matters of concern to both of them. And because of where the girl had recently been, the mother suspected the nature of the concern.

And it's hard to say whether either of those discussions of serious concern did any good, except to say that a few months later, the old woman died. It came suddenly and only a week after she'd packaged up the family treasure of recipes, and presented it to Jane, saying it was for the great granddaughter, the next time she came. Her death took them all by surprise, excepting perhaps one.

And when they laid her to rest in the family plot, it was the first time the townsfolk, those who came to pay homage to the old woman, had seen the old woman's daughter and granddaughter together in quite some time. But they held and consoled each other while a great granddaughter stood to the side and shed her own tears.

The old woman had said she would do what she could to get the two together. And she had. And it was a sad and happy time.

Forget-Me-Not

I twas true that he had come into the world with nothing, but he had always thought it was not true that he would leave it with nothing. When he came to the end of life's journey, he would carry a lifetime of memories -- that was what he had become aware of as he had reached middle age -- that no matter what should befall him, whether good or bad, he would carry it locked in his memory until he gasped his final breath and the curtain fell on his particular act. But now he was afraid something was happening to him, so that he feared his very memories would be taken from him, stripped away with each passing day, and every morning when he awoke, he felt the grip of fear at what might be forgotten today.

It must have come upon him in the night, this thing that tried to rob him of his memories. It must have come upon him in the night, because if it had come in the daylight, he surely would have been able to see it and to struggle against it, and to vanquish it and to drive it away. But it had come upon him insidiously, with stealth, so he had not even known it was happening......until it seemed to be too late.

It had started with little things. Misplaced keys. A lost wallet, when he had not lost a wallet in his whole life since his father had given him that cowboy wallet for his ninth birthday. But, still, no need for concern. He was sixty-eight and entitled to become a little forgetful -- that's what the doctor said when he first asked him about it.

But then it seemed to get more serious. He went downtown one day to pay a couple of bills. He remembered coming out of the gas office, but then he got confused. He thought his car was parked close, but he walked and walked and just couldn't find it. As he walked streets he had walked for a lifetime, he thought everything looked unfamiliar and there was a surrealness to it. He remembered feeling unsettled, uneasy, but he finally found himself sitting on a bench over by the park. He wasn't sure how he got there. He walked the few blocks back to his car without incident, but the experience scared the hell out of him. He'd never had anything like that happen to him before.

But he didn't tell his wife. He kept it deep inside him, working hard not to let her know that something might be wrong. Instead, he called the doctor in secret, arranged an appointment, and resolved he would say nothing until there was actually something to say. The doctor expressed concern, but told him not to worry -- probably good advice, but stupid advice just the same. He could do nothing but worry. He had always considered himself a fairly normal guy with fairly normal faculties, and, hence, a fairly normal memory, so that he had always forgotten things through his whole life. But, now, each time he committed even the slightest oversight, he was engulfed in waves of panic and anxiety for fear he would again disappear into the hazy confusion of that day when he'd gone to pay the bills.

It was difficult hiding his worry from his wife. She had been his everything for nearly a lifetime, and he had endeavoured to hide nothing from her since that day so long ago when he'd played the groom and she was his bride -- and he had done well at the endeavour, keeping all things between them open and uncovered -- except perhaps for that time he'd planned a surprise fiftieth birthday party for her and a few other similar occasions. So, he kept mostly to himself, puttering in his workshop, re-arranging his tools, re-finishing an old chest of drawers that had been in the garage for at least a decade. His wife didn't bother him, and she was busy because she was convenor of the church bazaar, and it seemed that she did not suspect -- at least for now -- because if it was as he feared, he would not hide it for long.

For the first while after the incident paying the bills, he was almost afraid to go out, and this made life difficult. He was able to go for the tests the doctor ordered, because he got a friend to drive him. After all, he was older, and it was not unusual for him to go see the doctor to seek treatment for one minor ache or another, and it was also not unusual for the doctor to send him for tests of one kind or another. So, he went for various bouts of poking and prodding, and no one was any the wiser.

And, finally, the tests were done, and the doctor's appointment was set to reveal what was to become of him, although he felt already certain of the outcome. And it was during this time when the workshop became a death cell, where he waited to walk his final steps toward execution -- slow, suffering execution while the world watched and pitied him his demise. He could already hear them talking, saying that it was too bad that he was so afflicted, but perhaps adding that he had lived a good life, toiling long and hard and bringing up a good Christian family.

But where had it gone? He sat for hours on end in the shabby, dilapidated easy chair in the corner of his workshop and wondered where it had all gone -- this life that now seemed so very, very short. He had always been a god-fearing, church-going man who was certain his place in the glorious afterlife was assured. But that had been before -- when it had seemed he was immortal and would have no need of an afterlife, glorious or otherwise. Now he struggled with his faith, and as he sat watching the evening news, he could not help but be reminded of the apparent godlessness of his world. He prayed fervently several times a day, kneeling in secret, speaking in hushed tones filled with earnestness, hoping there might be a sign that his faith had not been in vain, but knowing it was unlikely such a sign would come.

And even though he tried to remain firm in that faith, a tiny corner of him wondered if maybe, just maybe, there was nothing but this life. There would be nothing to come after -- nothing but to lay in the ground and rot. And even for all his faith, that he was nothing more than a creature of flesh and blood and that he had no more soul than a beast of the forest. And sometimes as he thought such thoughts, he wept. He didn't want to be swept away into a void of nothingness. He was afraid -- very afraid of that end.

One morning, as he stood in front of the mirror shaving, he was surprised to see the face of another seeming to regard him. It was his grandfather. People had always said when he'd been a boy that he bore an uncanny resemblance to the old man -- but he'd never been able to see it. After all, when he'd been a boy, his grandfather had seemed an ancient wreck of a man who'd likely helped Noah build the Ark. But now, as he looked into the mirror and watched himself shave, he remembered another time when he'd been but a wee boy, and he'd sat on a countertop and watched the old man shave. And as he looked, it was like he was cast back into that faraway time.

"Well, boy, you've done quite a bit of growin' since I last saw you," the old man said, speaking out of the side of his mouth as he continued with his shaving. "What do you think about having your old Granddad come to live with you?"

He didn't answer, but continued to watch as the old man evenly stroked the straight razor across his face.

"Well, I don't know that I'm all that set on it," the grandfather continued. "Since your grandma died, I've been quite happy bein' on my own. I've always been a solitary soul, not too keen for the company of other folk." He paused to get at a difficult place. "I appreciate your dad's offer -- and I suppose he's right and it's for the best -- but I just don't want to be a weight on nobody. No, I hope it's quick when it comes." He shook his head slowly side to side, pausing in his shaving, looking to regard the young boy by his side.

"Your grandma suffered. I held her hand 'til the end, but it was an awful thing she had to go through," he said. He paused again, looking away, clearing his throat. Such was the boy's youthful innocence that he couldn't know, but the old man was overcome by an immense sadness. "God, how she suffered." He disappeared into the memory for a moment.

"Anyway, I guess I'll be here for the duration," the grandfather said after a moment, and he resumed shaving until the task was complete, and then wiped a towel over his face to finish with the remainder of the shaving soap.

When he had finished with that, he turned to face the youngster. "You know," he started, "if I had one piece of advice I could offer you -- they always say us old folks are the wise ones -- I'd tell you to make sure you live life to the fullest because you only get one chance at it. Don't fill your life with regrets. Do your best to help others and make the world a better place." He paused. "And if you do that, and you can look yourself straight in the eye and say that you done your best, then that's about all anybody can ask."

The boy looked up to see the old man, and saw that he was smiling, and looked warm and comfortable and inviting. The old man reached out a gnarled hand, hoary with age, and tousled his grandson's hair. "But when I look in your face, and I see all that hope and promise, I somehow know it's all worthwhile -- all this damned life stuff." He paused. "I done my best. I feel that. I ain't seen the great wide world, and I ain't educated -- all I done was work there in the factory -- but I always tried to make my little corner of the world a little better for your Grandma and the kids after her........and I feel I done that. At least I tried. You should to." And he finished.

The grandfather had gotten out his bottle of blue aftershave, and he splashed it liberally about, then reached out and applied some to the boy's peach-fuzz face, before tweaking his nose, and making him hoot with delight. The old man put an arm around his grandson and gently lowered him from the counter to the floor. "Comeon," he said, "let's rejoin the world." And he took the boy's hand and they walked from the bathroom.

"Are you all right?" asked a woman's voice that intruded into the moment. "Are you okay?"

And the old man was gone, and he saw only himself in the mirror, and was surprised to see his shave was complete, and he turned to regard his wife, who was standing in the doorway to the bathroom, a concerned look on her face.

"Yes," he answered, and he smiled at her. "I'm fine." And it was true that he felt fine in the aftermath of this particular peculiar moment in his life, when his grandfather had come back to him for a few moments -- and had talked to him about life. He felt warm and comfortable, as if some part of the old man had somehow stayed with him.

"You looked kind of funny there," his wife said, and she paused, an expression of uncertainty on her face .

"I'm fine," he answered. "I'll be right down. I've just got to clean up a little."

And with that, the wife finally turned and started for the kitchen, seemingly satisfied that nothing serious was amiss.

And as he walked down the stairs toward the breakfast table, he knew that what the old man had been talking about was true -- and he wondered if he had lived up to that advice. He'd always tried to live his life to the fullest, and he didn't feel like he had a lot of regrets -- maybe that he hadn't tried even once to get out of the little town where he'd been born -- to try to find his way in the great, wide world -- to see what he could have made of himself. Instead, he'd stayed behind, while many of his boyhood friends had migrated to the city, and taken a job in the office at the furniture factory, worked there for forty years, and raised his family in the dependable, reliable fashion that he was known for. But he didn't really consider that a regret. Even though he wondered about it every once in a while, it had caused him no grief in life. No, not really a regret.

His son came to visit that weekend, bringing his young family with him, and the old man was just as glad to see the brood because it distracted him from his ominous thoughts regarding the doctor's appointment and what news that might bring. He found himself smiling broadly and he almost forgot his troubles as he watched his son's two small children scramble from the back seat of the car.

And it was a hectic evening they spent, with the children climbing and scampering over everything, while mother and grandmother scampered after them, and the father and son attempted to make small talk over a glass of beer. But, finally, the children were put to bed, the mother and grand-mother were gone to the kitchen to drink coffee and discuss womanly things, so the old man was left alone in the downstairs rec room with his own child -- his firstborn son.

"Dad, Mom's been telling me that you haven't been yourself for the last couple of weeks," the boy started out, almost as soon as they were alone.

"Is that why you're here?" the old man asked, and there was a defensive tone to his voice.

"Sort of," answered the son. "We were planning to come anyway -- were sort of overdue for a visit -- so it was good timing."

There was a moment of silence. The old man regarded the younger version of himself. "I'm fine," he finally said, feeling he might be lying and feeling a twinge of guilt because of it.

"I figured you were," his son answered, "but you know how Mom gets worrying about you."

"Why didn't she just ask me herself?" he asked. "She's never afraid to speak her mind."

"You two always talk about everything," the son said, "and she thought if there was something you were holding back, that it must be serious, and that maybe you might tell me -- because she wanted you to be able to talk to someone about it." There was a pause. The son looked intently into the father's face. "Is there something?"

Another pause, this one more ominous and much longer than the last.

"I don't know," the father finally answered, his voice slow and deliberate, his head hung low and forlorn. "I don't know," he repeated, again very slowly.

"What is it?" the son asked. "What could be so bad?" His voice was serious and filled with concern.

"I'm worried I have Alzheimers," the old man said.

There was a brief pause.

"Christ," said the son. He screwed a fist into the palm of his hand. "Oh, Dad," he said, his voice thick with emotion, and he came forward from his spot on the couch to the old man's chair, and took his father in a short embrace. "How could you hold this back? -- keep this inside of you?" he asked.

"Look, there's really only been one serious incident," the father said, and he proceeded to tell his son about his experience the day he'd been uptown paying bills.

"Man, it's no wonder you're worried," the son said, after he'd finished his tale.

"But I don't want to make too much of it," the father said. "It might just have been a temporary thing -- that's what I'm hoping. After all, I am getting older, and things like this could happen. I've never gotten old before. I probably should have told your mother," he admitted, "but I didn't want to worry her, and now it turns out I've probably worried her more than if I had just been honest with her. Remember what I used to tell you about always being honest and straight with people in your life. I should have followed my own advice."

There was another pause in the room.

"When will they know something?" the son finally asked. "I mean, can they do a test, or something?"

"I've had the tests," the father answered. "I'll know the beginning of the week what's going on."

"Christ, Dad," his son said, repeating his earlier sentiment, while at the same time looking extremely dejected and morose.

It was quiet.

"Are you two all right down there?" called a voice from another part of the house. "You're awfully quiet. Is everything all right?"

"Yea, everything's fine!" the father shouted back. "Any coffee left?" he hollered.

"Sure!" came the reply.

"We'll be up in a minute!" he shouted.

There was more quiet. The son sat quietly, his head hanging disconsolate, his gaze directed at the floor.

"It's all right," the father said to him, reaching out and putting a gentle hand on the boy's knee. "Who knows what the future holds? It might be nothing."

The son looked up to regard him.

The father smiled, reached up and tousled his son's hair, the way he might have back many years ago when the son was but a tiny boy held on his lap.

The younger man attempted a smile.

"Let's go upstairs," the old man said. "I've got something I've got to talk over with your mother -- and you guys might as well be part of it -- it could affect all of us."

He started to get up, but the boy reached forward and stopped him. "What will you do if you've got it?" his son asked.

"I guess I'll get my life in order," the father answered.

"That simple," the boy said.

"There are some things in life you can't control," the old man answered. "You've just got to make the best of what you're given. I'm not so sure I haven't done all right with the time I've had. I'm not sure I have any regrets." And even as he spoke the words, he surprised himself, because he wasn't so sure he'd known the answer to the boy's question even five minutes earlier, or even a split second earlier -- it seemed the answer just popped into his head and it seemed the most natural thing to say.

"That's good, Dad," the boy said; "that you can look at it like that."

"Don't get me wrong," the father said. "I don't want this to happen, but if it does, I've got to try to be ready."

This time, it was the son who smiled. "I'll help all I can -- I'll do anything," he said.

"Let's go upstairs to the kitchen," the old man said. "I've really botched this up with your mother, and I've got to set things straight. That woman is my whole life."

"Whatever happens, Dad, I'm with you," the boy said.

"I know," answered the father.

And the two of them went up to the kitchen, where the women had just brewed a fresh pot of coffee. And they spent a long night there, and there was considerable heart-wrenching dialogue spilled on that night and great concern was expressed, but by first light of morning, the four of them had resolved to see it through for what was best, and there was actually a contentment to the resolve. They sat for that last half hour, hands held, in silence, peace and calm filling their hearts.

But then it was time for the children to arise, because that is the way with young children, that they like to rise early in the morning, perhaps fearful that they might miss some aspect of the new day.

The old man sat, drained of all emotion, and watched as the youngsters ate their breakfasts. He smiled, as he watched the mess they made.

"Dad," his son said to him during the clean-up. "You should get some sleep."

"I'm fine," the father answered. "I'll have a nap later if it catches up to me."

And he did go up to lay on the bed a short time later. But he felt restless, and was soon up again. He was tired, but couldn't sleep, his mind alive from the conversations of the previous night. He walked the length of the bedroom, paced, and then caught sight of himself in the mirror over his wife's dresser. 'I need a shave,' he thought. And he walked the short distance to the bathroom.

As he was lathering his face, using the shaving mug his son had given him as a Christmas gift one time many years ago, he heard a noise by the door. He paused in his lathering, and turned to see what might be afoot. A small grandson stood just outside the door, peering in through the crack the door was open. He was quiet, thumb wedged into his mouth, stoic expression on his face, as if he might be considering some important and far reaching matter. The grandfather offered a smile, but there was no reaction. The old man thought for a moment.

"Would you like to come in and watch me shave?" he finally asked, uncertain what the response would be.

The small boy eyed him suspiciously.

"Come on in, if you want," the grandfather said, making his voice sound as inviting as possible.

At this, the youngster finally broke into a slight smile.

The old man reached over and swung the door open. "Come on," he said, and he reached out and took the lad by the shoulder as he came into the room. "Why don't you sit up here?" he suggested, and he hoisted his grandson up onto the top of the vanity. The young boy broke into a broad grin at this latest development, indicating his apparent pleasure.

And the old man shaved, drawing the straight razor evenly up and down his now craggy features, scraping away another layer of flesh until there might be no more. And the young boy watched, perhaps storing up a memory for another time in his life when he might stand in similar fashion, before a bathroom mirror, and as grandfather.

"Well, boy, what have you and your Dad been up to lately," the old man started, speaking out of the side of his mouth as he continued with his shaving.

And the two were as one, even for that brief time. And it was somehow like the circle was complete.

The tests came back negative. The doctor couldn't really explain what had happened to him that day when he'd been lost in a hazy confusion after paying his bills, but said maybe he'd had a bout of low blood sugar or some other such thing. They'd keep an eye on that. And as far as the rest of the stuff went, he had to realize that he was sixty-eight and entitled to become a little forgetful -- just like the doctor had said when he first asked him about it.

Still, that experience somehow changed him. He became more aware of everything surrounding him, and tried to take nothing for granted. He endeavoured to make his little corner of the world somehow better. And, from time to time, he forgot things. But it didn't make him cower with fear. He knew that was life and he was doing the best he could.

I Get Cursed and Find My Heart

'm the kind of guy who can sit on a street corner for hours on end just watchin' humanity crawl by -- because that's what humanity does best -- crawl. I don't work. Why would I want to support a corrupt capitalist system that has fostered so much hatred and evil in this fine world? I live off the refuse of society. It's the way I like it. I don't feel like I'm a real drain on the system -- no more so than one of those great big megacorporations that gobble up the government hand-outs faster than you can put shit through a horn.

So, I watch the silly people crawling by, leaving trails of slime as they go. They have no heart. They couldn't support a capitalist society if they did. The two just don't go together -- capitalism and having a heart. It's like oil and water. I think I got a heart. But sometimes I'm not even really sure about that. Maybe I'm like the Tin Man guy in that Oz movie -- still looking for my heart and having a heck of a time finding it.

One day, I'm sittin' in my regular spot, down by the big, old church, under the only tree for blocks, and I see an ancient haglike woman coming up the street pushing a shopping cart before her. As she comes closer, she seems headed in my direction, a disconcerting development for a watcher such as me, to have one of the watched burst from the scene and into my reality. I don't want contact. It leads to complications, and I don't need no complications in my meagre life. All I want to do is go about my business, live my life and die. I don't want contact. Not if I can avoid it.

"Hey," said the old hag, "you're in my place."

I said nothing, cowered away, tried to ignore her. But she jabbed her boney finger into me and insisted I was in her spot under the tree. I knew she was mistaken -- this was my place and had been for all of the past two summers since old Bob passed away right before my eyes and right on this very spot. And he told me with his dyin' words that I should take the spot and make it mine because I was good at heart. Old Bob could sense stuff like that, like whether you were good or evil, or had a poor disposition -- it was his gift in life -- that's what he used to say.

"You're in my place," hissed the old hag. "You better move on if you know what's good for you."

"I think this is my place," I finally managed to protest. "I've been sitting here all along."

"Well, you better clear out," she warned, "because this is my place now. I need shade. I have to watch out for the ozone. That's what my specialist says."

"Old Bob gave me this place," I insisted. "I can't just give it to you. Where would I go?"

"You can go down there on the corner," she said, pointing down the street to the busy intersection. "It's better down there anyway. It's better for panhandling."

"I don't panhandle," I said.

"Well, aren't we the royal sir," she said, sarcasm in her voice.

"I just watch the people," I said.

"Well, the watchin's better down on the corner," she said, trying to push the shopping cart up onto the spot I was occupying.

I resisted her efforts and in the struggle the shopping cart went for a tumble spilling its contents onto the street.

The old woman cried out as the cart went crashing over, and her life's belongings spilled onto the asphalt. "I curse you," she cried. "I've got powers," she warned, looking at me menacingly. "I curse you that whatever you most detest and hate about life shall come to fill your miserable existence and poison your very soul. I curse you with all the powers I possess." She pointed at me in deliberate fashion. "With all the powers I possess," she repeated.

And she gathered up her stuff and packed it back into the shopping cart, and made her way off up the street, turning back several times to shoot me looks of apparent black death, but on the last occasion, offering me a strange sort of smile, then breaking into hysterical laughter. It unsettled me.

But, finally, she was gone. And my place was secure. I almost smiled with satisfaction, but remembered that it was somehow wrong to be happy when you're on the bottom of life.

I found that the exchange with the old woman had seemed to tire me, so that a short time later, I decided to return to my night time haunt, which was down in a city ravine. I'd constructed myself a small shelter from scraps of wood and such many years past, and no one, not even police, had ever bothered me about it. Even though, high above, some of the finest homes in the city sat on the edge of the ravine. I was away down in the bottom of hell and no one seemed to give a damned from their place up in heaven. Which was fine with me. I don't normally want to see a soul. So I don't.

But that afternoon, as I clambered down the steep slope to my humble abode, something caught my eye. I paused in my descent and looked more closely into some bushes beside me and was surprised to find a running shoe -- a brand new running shoe, the kind that the trendy kids like to wear. I searched further and came out with the other one. Very strange, I thought, as I stood holding the shoes.

I looked about to see if there was anyone accompanying the shoes. There seemed to be no one. I chanced to notice my own bedraggled, beaten boots. I sized up the running shoes. You just never know when good fortune is going to smile on you. So, I carried those trendy, new running shoes back down to my hovel and figured that no one would ever be the wiser.

And the next morning, when I came up out of the ravine and headed back for my spot to watch, I was wearing those new shoes and was most glad about it. They fit absolutely perfectly, as if I'd gone in and been fitted for them.

And, so, I walked along the busy city streets with my new shoes. I headed back for my spot down by the church, but, as I approached from across the street, I could see that someone else was already under the tree. The old hag. I should have gone right over there and confronted that useless, old woman, but I didn't. For some reason, I kept to my own side of the street and just walked straight on by and headed further downtown. For some reason, I quit without even a hint of a fight.

The new shoes had a good spring to them -- I felt like I was floating on air -- and I kept looking down to check them out -- to make sure I wasn't just a few inches off the sidewalk. Then, one time, when I looked down, there was something stuck to the bottom of my left shoe. I paused in my walking, and reached down to remove it. It was a lottery ticket. I studied it for a moment. It appeared it hadn't been checked to see whether it was a winner or loser. Although my experience with these things was limited, I suspected you scratched such tickets to discover if they had value.

I was standing in the middle of the sidewalk, transfixed by the ticket, but not able to quite figure things out, when a voice intruded.

"Hey, man, you got a winner?" it asked.

I looked to see a snotty-nosed kid standing astride a beat-up bicycle.

"The ticket? Is it a winner?" the kid asked, repeating his question.

"I'm not sure," I answered truthfully. "I just got it and haven't had time to check." This time I sort of lied.

"You scratch it, eh?" the kid commented. "My mom buys them all the time. She even wins sometimes."

"Well, maybe I'll scratch it later," I said, starting to put the ticket in my pocket.

"No, how can you wait?" insisted the kid. "What if it's a winner?"

"I haven't had one of these before," I said. "I need time to figure it out."

"Ah, comeon!" barked the kid. "I'll help you. It's easy."

I stood hesitantly, unsure.

"Comeon, man," the kid pressed.

"Well.....okay," I finally agreed.

"Great! Let's have a look!" he exclaimed. "This is great."

I offered him the ticket, and he grabbed it away, peering closely at it, studying it as I had a few moments earlier. "Here," he finally said, "you scratch these things here," he pointed to one area of the ticket, "and if you get three matches, then you scratch here to see what your prize is." He moved his finger to another area of the ticket . He offered it back to me.

"Do you want to scratch it?" I asked, feeling a little surge of excitement for the first time since finding the ticket.

"You want me to scratch it? Wow," he said.

"You might be lucky," I said, knowing that I wasn't.

So, the kid produced a pen knife from the pocket of his jacket, and we both watched closely, as he scratched the first area of the ticket ever so slowly and deliberately.

"Look at that," he finally said, a sound of honest amazement in his voice. "Three of a kind."

"What does that mean?" I asked, my own level of excitement rising somewhat.

"It means we've won something," the kid said.

"What?" I asked.

"We've got to scratch here to find out," he answered, pointing to a small gray area of the ticket. "Maybe you should scratch," he said, starting to offer it back to me again.

"No, you keep it," I said. "You're doing really well so far. Go ahead, scratch it."

"Keep your fingers crossed," advised the kid. And he brought his pen knife to bear on the unscratched area.

"Oh, my God," said the kid, having completed the scratching. "Oh, my God," he repeated.

"What is it?" I cried. "What did we win?"

The kid threw his bike down to the sidewalk, and started dancing about in a most jubilant fashion. Then, he suddenly stopped, and grabbed me.

"What have we won?" I asked again.

"Fifty thousand dollars!" exclaimed the kid.

And my life changed at that moment. Not dramatically. Not at first.

I gave the kid a thousand dollars as his share and he was about as happy as I've seen a kid in these modern times, because his mom was on her own and they had a most difficult struggle. He raced right out to buy her a token of his affection, knowing how hard she worked to make a home for him.

I gave up the hovel in the ravine, deciding that perhaps I'd earned a comfortable bed after all these years of bumming it. I found a small, inexpensive rooming house close to downtown, and took up accommodation there, paying my entire first year's lodging in advance, much to the surprise and delight of the woman who ran the place.

Then, I approached the man who ran one of the downtown missions and asked for his advice on what to do with the remainder of my fortune. He took me to a kind of bank, I guess, because they took most of the money and said they'd invest it for me, but that I could get it back if I needed it -- not all at once, but a little bit at a time. I liked the guy from the bank. He seemed like a nice enough young fellow. He seemed very happy to get my money.

So, I settled in to enjoy my newfound wealth. There were several months of comfortableness in my life; something that had not been there for a long, long time; perhaps since I'd moved from my parents' home all those years ago.

One day, though, as I was fixing myself a cup of tea and piece of toast for my breakfast, there was a knock at the door. I was somewhat surprised, not accustomed to having callers, but went to answer the summons.

When I opened the door, I was completely surprised to see the young man from the bank standing there, an awkward look on his face. I welcomed him into my room and we were soon sitting across from one another at the table in the tiny kitchenette.

"I don't know how to tell you this," he started.

I feared the worst -- the money gone -- back to the street.

"I can't explain it," he started again, but it was obvious he was having difficulty.

"Is something wrong?" I asked. "Is there a problem?"

"You tell me," he said, and he got up from his chair, and adjusted his tie before continuing.

I swallowed.

"I invested your money just like I said I would," he said. "You remember. I told you I could earn you a tidy little bit of cash on your investments and keep you living modestly for some time. Remember?"

I nodded.

"Well, I invested the money -- in medium risk investments -- just like I would for any client," he continued. "Well, I always put a little of each portfolio into some high risk stuff -- I mean, why not? So, I did the same with yours." He paused.

"So, you lost the money," I offered, perhaps trying to spare him an admission of failure.

"No," he stated flatly. "The stock has exploded off the map. And when it started, I saw it, and dumped more of your money into it. And it just kept on exploding. I sold yesterday at the close. You're rich." He smiled nervously like a kid caught doing something he perhaps shouldn't.

"What do you mean, I'm rich?" I asked, indeed confused to have acquired such knowledge.

"You've got millions," the young man beamed. "Millions." And he could no longer contain himself, and he laughed and danced about the place as if possessed by the raptures. "Millions," he repeated over and over.

I sat in silence -- stunned beyond belief. "I'm rich," I mumbled as if in the deepest of drug-induced stupors.

But the young man grabbed me and pulled me out of my chair and we danced about the room like madmen, so that I was taken up with the hysteria that had overwhelmed him. "I'm rich!" I cried with all my might. And I couldn't have imagined that I could have been happier.

Any my life did change dramatically at that moment.

And it wasn't long before I'd married the woman who ran the rooming house, because she came to me one time in the night -- just after I got rich -- with a bottle of wine and played the newlywed game with me. I hadn't had a woman for a very long time, and it was embarrassing to be with her at first, but she was patient and seemed to sense that it would be worth it in the long run. She loved me good and I married her for it and promised to care for her in sickness and in health and in good times and in bad.

But it seemed she wasn't happy with my mere millions, and wanted even more, so that she insisted that we set up a company and get about the business of exploiting the poor, unwashed masses for the greater good of the few. So, I found myself getting up and out of bed in my new larger-than-life house each morning, challenging even the early bird for the worm, showering the night's sleep away, and riding into the city to my office where I made huge and large decisions about the disposition of wealth in many far corners of the globe.

And all seemed well with my new life for the longest time -- we decided we should have children -- so she produced a couple, fully-grown, from a previous marriage -- and everything was hunky-dory. I went about all of the high-finance and continued to make more and more money. It was easy once you got the hang of it.

So, one day, we're sitting around the kidney-shaped swimming pool, and the kids are taking a dip, after playing a few matches on the nearby tennis courts. The young guy from the bank -- the guy who started it all -- is over for lunch, and we're all laughing merrily away, sharing a few tales of the rich and famous and who's sleeping with who and that sort of thing.

Suddenly, there's a commotion over on the other side of the property.

"Dirty rich scum!" I hear a voice cry out. "I wasn't hurting no one. Leave me be."

I looked over and one of my security people had a rather scruffy-looking fellow by the arm and was leading him across the grounds. For some reason, I stopped laughing, got to my feet and headed across to where the security officer had the scruffy fellow contained.

"I'm sorry, sir," said the security officer. "I was trying to get him out of here without bothering you."

"What's the problem?" I asked.

"He's been living down in the ravine -- in a shack down there," the officer said. "You're developing that area for elusive condos. We've chased him out more than once, but he keeps coming back."

"It's my home," the scruffy fellow offered somewhat defiantly, before quickly cowering.

"I'm sorry, sir," interrupted the security officer. "I'll get rid of him." He started to push the bum in the intended direction.

And just in that moment, I saw my life flash before my eyes. "Wait," I said.

"Sir?" asked the security officer.

"Wait," I said. "Take him to the kitchen and give him something to eat. Then, find him somewhere else to live."

"Sir?" the security guard repeated.

"You heard me," I said flatly.

The bum smiled. "Thank-you very much," he said. "But I'd rather just go back to the ravine."

"Why?" I asked.

"Because I don't really want to be part of your system," he said.

"Why not?" I asked. "It's okay to be comfortable."

"You don't even know what your money does," said the bum. "How many underdeveloped countries it exploits, how much of the environment it pollutes, and how many people die in the name of it. You have no idea."

I said nothing, but regarded the bum. "I don't think what you're saying is true," I finally offered. "My companies make the products that society needs."

"Needs?" the bum mocked. "Take a look at the products in your stores. It's a pile of crap. You make the products that you brainwash people into thinking they need. What society needs and what society wants are two different things."

I was taken aback. I recognized his attitude. I had seen it before.

"Take him back to the ravine," I told the security officer. "Take him back where he belongs."

"Yes, sir," the officer answered.

And I went back to rejoin the festive group. And the partying began anew.

But, later that night, long after the rest of the household had retired for the night, I was up and about and checking on the activities of my many and various companies, exploring and examining the numerous and diverse tentacles that stretched out in all directions from my office building in the city.

Early that very morning, I went out of the larger-than-life house, and made my way to the downtown of the city, where I came upon a church, and just down the street, a lonely tree. It was there that I saw the old hag.

She laughed uproariously to see me come. "What's the matter, oh high and mighty one?" she said, between peels of derisive laughter.

"You cursed me," I said. "And it has all come true -- that I have come to live the life that I most detested -- as you said."

"What did you expect?" she cackled. "You're part of the system you once hated so much."

"How did it happen?" I asked.

"It happens when you're not looking," she said.

"How?" I asked.

"It just sort of happens," she said. "You get a little comfortable, and you want to be more comfortable. Then, you want to be more comfortable and more comfortable yet. Once you get in, you can't get out. It's the way of the world."

"I can't believe it can happen so easily," I said.

"It's called greed," she said.

"Lift the curse," I said. "I've learned my lesson."

"Tell others," she said.

"I will," I promised.

"I can't lift the curse," she said. "You are who you've become. But you can live a better life if you really do know the truth."

"I think I know," I said.

"I hope you do," she answered.

There was a moment of silence between us, and just for a second, I saw not the old hag, but a beautiful, young princess, soft and radiant in the warm, morning sun.

"Go out and teach," she said.

"I will," I answered.

And I did indeed go out into the world to try to make my change with it. I set a new policy for my company that all would do business in a kind and charitable manner and that no peoples should be exploited, nor any environment be polluted. And it was a bold and venturesome course for a captain of industry such as I, but I would attempt to make my mark. And, hopefully, to do what I could. I'm trying to make the two go together - capitalism and having a heart. I know it's like oil and water. But I think I got a heart, and I'm going to prove it to the people at the bottom -- 'cause I been there -- where they are. I can't just sit anymore and watch it go by. I gotta try to make a difference. Because I think there might be a chance.

When I Laugh in the Night

I was a meek and mild guy when I was younger. I did all the usual rebellious sort of stuff, but I really wasn't into it, and it made me more than a little bit nervous. But I was most nervous around girls. So, while I played the part I had sort of fallen into back there in high school, it wasn't something I felt real comfortable with. I was constantly struggling with my identity -- as I guess most teenagers have to do -- but it seemed I had a more desparate fight than most.

I was fifteen when I visited my first psychiatrist. Where I came from, if you saw a shrink, you were crazy. It was about that simple. My own family doctor tried to assure me I wasn't crazy, but I was reserving judgement, not really convinced that I might not be totally nuts, given the wide assortment of health-related disorders I'd been subjected to over my first few years of adolescence. I was so afflicted that whenever I got into a tight spot, I could be overwhelmed by an anxiety and panic that made my life a very hell on earth. So that even going to school was a nightmare and most social events could not be handled. It was a bleak and miserable existence that brought me to see the shrink.

"Hello, how are you?" asked the huge, well-dressed man.

But I said nothing. I'd heard about these guys.

"Are you comfortable?" he asked. "Can I get you anything?"

I declined to answer. I watched him. What would he do? How would he try to twist and turn me?

"This will be a long hour," he said. "But perhaps this is what you need."

I wondered at this, but continued to be silent.

"Still, there isn't much I can do, if you won't talk to me," he said.

And it was quiet for the remainder of the appointment time.

"You'll have to decide if you want to come back," he said at the end of it.

I decided not to, but I've seen others of his kind over the years. They're all the same. They try to trick you into saying something that matters, and you try to hide your deep dark secrets from them as much as you can. It's kind of like a game. Just leave it to say that I had my problems when I was a young guy. It wasn't too good for my self esteem to think that I might somehow be less than normal. That kind of thinking really beats up on a teenager.

But the worst were girls. I became terrified of them early on and when trapped into a close-up, personal exchange with one, I very nearly came apart at the seams on every occasion. I could not interact with them in any kind of serious way. They were my great grief as a young guy because I wanted to feel and touch one of them in the worst way -- a big part of me wanted to know a girl, but another part wouldn't let me get close enough to even consider it. So, I steered well clear of the girls during most of my high school days.

Then, in my last year, just as I was about to clear that part of my life, a new girl came to the school. Mary Carmichael. She almost ran over me in the hallway on the first day of school, running, late for class. Her books went flying every which way. I helped her gather them up.

"Oh, I'm the new girl," she said to me in a matter-of-fact sort of way. "But you've probably guessed."

I didn't answer, came face to face with her, and was totally unsure of what to say.

"Say, you must know where 128 is," she more said than asked.

"I'm on my way," I answered, and it was true that I was.

"English?" she asked.

"Afraid so," I answered.

"We're going to be late," she said.

"It's the first day," I said. "They'll likely forgive us."

"Mind if I walk with you?" she asked.

"If you like," I said, and we set off.

Now, it would be fair to say that my heart was beating at about the speed of sound during this exchange. My palms were a mess and I got the queasy feeling in my stomach. But I sweated it out. I didn't run away. I walked down the hall with her, feeling light-headed and dizzy all the way, but not really caring for perhaps the first time in my young life.

We arrived at the class and were suitably admonished for our lateness and shown to our seats -- which happened to be directly side by side so that we could have held hands if we'd wanted.

And from that moment on, I was obsessed with the new girl. It turned out that English was the only class we shared, but I watched for her throughout the school each and every day, wanting even to just catch a glimpse of her.

She was indeed a rare beauty and much sought out by the other guys at the school as well. I never really approached her -- never really had the confidence to say boo to any member of the opposite sex for any real serious reason. So, as the year progressed, she went through a series of boyfriends and treated me as merely a friend who shared her English class. I coveted her from afar and she barely knew who I was.

And it never ceased to amaze me, the string of lunkheads she chose for her social enjoyment. It was like she was being passed from loser to loser in a steady progression to see who could cause her the most grief. So, she finally ended up with the king loser of them all, a guy who'd be lucky to make it out of high school, and was intent on setting the record as the idiot who could consume the largest amount of alcohol in the shortest amount of time before getting nasty and miserable and beating somebody up, or throwing up all over. He was a total jerk. But she clung to him like a fly to flypaper.

One Saturday night in the dead of winter, the three of us, me and the girl and the lunkhead, ended up at the same party -- along with quite a number of other miscreants and would-be delinquents. Well, the lunkhead proceeded to do what he did best -- drink copious quantities of alcoholic elixer until he could barely stand. I'd sat in a corner of the room and watched him become more and more abusive to the other party goers.

Then, the girl got bumped by a guy trying to squeeze through a too small space in the crowd and he spilled some of his drink on her. The lunkhead roared and bellowed and came to his feet, causing a couple of other people to be put off balance and to career into still other people, until a suitable fracas had been initiated.

When the dust had settled, the lunkhead had the unfortunate fellow who'd spilled the drink by the throat and was threatening to rip the kid's head off. The girl came pleading between them, begging for the young man's life. Then, with an unpredictable rush of fury, the lunkhead cast the young man aside and turned toward the girl.

"Never," he said far too loudly, "tell me what to do." His hand was raised over her, violence seeming unavoidable.

The entire party was quiet. Nobody moved. It was a tense and awkward moment. The girl had a look of fear on her face. The lunkhead appeared ready to strike.

"Or what!" I cried, also much louder than was necessary. I sprang from my seat in the corner of the room and came out front and centre. I came to rest very close to him, my hands in front of me, ready for something, but not exactly sure what.

"Who the hell are you?" sneered the lunkhead.

"Your worst nightmare," I answered, realizing it was a stupid thing to say, but not able to think of anything else.

"You look more like a pimple on my ass," my adversary replied. "I think I'll squeeze you."

"Leave him alone, Mitch!" cried out the girl, coming between me and the lunkhead just in the nick of time.

As soon as she spoke, it seemed to break the spell that had come over the place when the altercation had begun, and other people jostled into the scene, ending the confrontation. Mitch snarled once more in my direction, but somebody jammed a beer in his hand and he quickly lost interest in me. I gradually worked my way out of the action, eternally grateful for having lived through such a situation.

"Thanks," I heard the girl's voice say. I let out a sigh, but said nothing. She took my hand and gave it a quick little squeeze. "Meet me down by the park after the party," she whispered, and I could feel her move away.

I stayed at the party for a while, because I'd have looked like I'd lost the war of nerves if I'd left too soon after my run-in with Mitch. But as soon as I felt there'd been suitable strutting and puffing done, I made a quiet exit from the place and had soon disappeared down into the park to wait. I had no idea how long I might be there, but I was content that she would come, so I was content to wait for some considerable length of time.

I decided to wait in the band shell, because it was high ground and I could see the comings and goings of the park, and also because it offered some shelter from winter's blast. I wanted to be able to see her if she came. I was nervous and anxious, but filled with excited anticipation. This was the first time I'd waited at such a rendezvous. I had no idea what to expect.

It was a long, cold wait so that I had almost given her up. I wanted her to come so bad, but had learned through even my brief life that I rarely got what I really wanted and usually ended up having to deal with second-best. And so it was that I failed to see her when she first entered the park, but rather caught sight of her when she was nearly at the band shell.

"How are you?" I called out when she was still at a reasonable distance, not wanting to frighten her.

"My hero," she said.

I jumped down from the band shell, choosing not to use the steps, my own little act of machismo. "I wasn't sure you'd come," I said, as I landed unsteadily.

"I wanted to see you -- to thank you for coming to my rescue," she answered.

"Why do you keep going around with such idiots?" I more said than asked. "You'll end up getting seriously hurt one of these times."

She shrugged her shoulders.

"You know they're idiots," I said. "I can tell you're a smart girl."

We walked for a moment in silence. She took my hand, which caused a ripple of excitement to pass through me -- I had not walked hand in hand with a girl in my life. What should I be doing? I walked. Waited.

"I'm not sure why I do what I do sometimes," she finally answered, as they arrived at the edge of the river that normally flowed through the park, now a frozen highway through a snowy country. "Anyway, those guys aren't bad guys -- they have another side."

"I'd like to see it," I answered. "They drink gallons of beer and fight everything that moves -- they're just not nice people. Why hang with them?"

"And what makes you so special?" she asked. We stood, looking out over the frozen river.

"Oh, I'm not so special," I answered. "But I can see outside of here. I can imagine what there might be outside of here."

"I can't wait to get out of this hick town," she said defiantly. "All small towns seem pretty much the same -- boringsville. I want more out of my life than just this old place."

"Well, you sure don't act like it by hanging out with morons," I answered. "Those guys aren't going anywhere except the factory."

"And what's wrong with the factory?" she asked.

"If you'd lived here all your life like I have, you wouldn't even be asking a question like that," I answered. "When I used to walk to public school, I'd have to go along the main street, right past the Big Shop, and I'd look in through those windows -- with the wire mesh on them -- and I'd think those guys looked like caged animals in there." I paused for effect. "Anyway, maybe there's nothing wrong with working in the factory, but you should surely get out of town and see a bit of something before you just settle in for it."

I could feel her shiver from the cold. "We should walk," I said. "It's cold."

And we did walk, along the edge of the river, some of it tough going in the snow. She almost lost her balance on a couple of occasions, but used me to right herself. I could feel her against me when she stumbled and could smell her as she swept by me. When she looked up at me, her cheeks were rosey and radiant and her breath whisped about her head in angelic fashion. My heart pounded in my ears, to be even so close to one such as her.

"Why did you want to meet me?" I finally managed to blurt out after a few moments of silence -- it was the question I'd wanted to ask since she'd come.

"I'm not sure," she said. "You intrigue me. You're always so quiet."

"I'm not much different than most other guys," I said.

"I think you are," she answered. "Most others would have tried something by now. You just walk along holding my hand."

"I don't want to lose what I already have," I answered.

"What do you mean?" she asked.

"If I make a play for you, you might tell me to get lost and dump me," I answered. "I'd rather hold your hand than have you tell me to get lost."

"But if you made a play for me, I might offer you a kiss," she said, and she stepped in front of me and kissed me full on the lips.

She caught me totally by surprise. I stood, dumbfounded. Then, she let go of my hand, reached down for a handful of snow which she promptly sprayed in my face, then she bolted out across the park with a peel of laughter.

I took out after her and caught her directly. I pretended to be the big, macho tough guy and threw her on her back in the snow, then sat down on her, before grabbing up a big handful of snow which I applied liberally to her face. We both laughed uproariously, until I finally collapsed on my side into the snow and let her up.

She charged back at me and I reached toward her, my arms encircling her, and we fell into an entangled heap. I dared to kiss her and she let me. We lay close together in the snow for a few moments, kissing, fondling each other gently, even through our winter clothes.

Finally, we parted and got to our feet. There were a couple minutes of embarrassed silence.

"Let's make snow angels!" she suddenly cried out, with all the glee of a small child. And there we were, the two of us, nearly graduated from high school, and we were flat on our backs making snow angels in the town park. It was perhaps one of the only moments in my life when I was really, truly happy -- when I felt like the other guys must have felt, and when I really, truly didn't care what anybody thought. I thought I was in love.

Then, we stopped for a moment, breathless. "That's what I like about you," she called out.

"What's that?" I questioned.

"I don't know anybody else who'd make snow angels with me," she said, laughing. "Those other guys have no sense of humour."

"But they have cars and money and stuff like that," I answered, and I got serious all of a sudden -- the fun seemed to leave the moment.

She also stopped short and looked over at me.

"It's not what it's about," I said. "But that's why you're meeting me in the town park in the middle of the night."

"I like you," she said.

"But you like Mitch, too," I answered.

"Mitch needs me," she answered. "He's had a tough life -- things haven't always gone his way."

"Tell me about it," I said. "His old man owns the biggest car dealership in town, he's the captain and star of every sports team at school, and he gets all the chicks. Sounds like he's having it pretty tough all right."

"You just don't understand," she said.

"You're right," I answered, and I lay down my head with a thud on the frozen ground.

"I can still like you," she said.

"But just not in public," I added.

"We can be friends," she said.

"After tonight, Mitch'll rip my head off at the first chance he gets," I answered.

"Not if I tell him not to," she said.

"Great," I answered, some sarcasm in the word, seeming to finally realize that the love of my life just wanted to be friends.

"I should get going," she suddenly said. "My parents don't know I'm out."

"It's late," I said. "I'll walk you home." I wanted to add that I was sure no one would see us at this late hour, but thought that might be too much of a strain on our newfound friendship.

And I did walk her home -- at least to the end of her block -- and I watched her from there to make sure she made it okay the rest of the way. You can say one thing about me -- I'm dependable as the day is long. I just can't get the girls.

Well, some of the girls. I have been married three times. I'd have given it up after the first one, but my therapist says I've got to keep trying to find some true happiness in life. Yes, I did indeed go back into therapy, and what do you know if it didn't end up sort of being the thing to do all these years later. What do you think about that? Maybe I wasn't as crazy as I thought.

And the wife I've got now keeps saying that I do a lot of talking in my sleep, mostly unintelligible garbage and that I do a whole lot of laughing as well. I have no idea why I laugh in my sleep, but I like to think that maybe it's because me and Mary are back in the town park making snow angels and laughing like the dickens. Wouldn't that be nice if that's what it was? It would just be the nicest thing. I loved that girl.